Manxiety

A Collection of Disturbing Stories

Daemon Manx

Last Waltz Publishing

"Our anxiety does not empty tomorrow of its sorrows, but only empties today of its strengths." —— **C. H. Spurgeon**

MANXIETY: A COLLECTION OF DISTURBING STORIES

"For Scarlett Johansson. You're a great girl, but I am seeing someone. I think we should just be friends."

Introduction

The stories in this book were inspired by real-life events. Some are loose interpretations of my nightmares and experiences, and others are dark memoirs. All were designed to evoke emotion. Longing, fear, remorse, desperation, and of course, anxiety, are a few of the horrors we all face and the ones from which there is often no escape. These stories were written during the most difficult periods in my life. Addiction, incarceration, and depression are the demons of which I speak. Creating this compilation became the tool I used to overcome these demons. This is the product of that struggle. This is Manxiety.

One

THE BOY IN THE CENTER OF THE ROAD

A boy lies in the center of a road he cannot recognize. He is bruised and he is broken. Every nerve is electrified and rings with a sense of raw exposure as if the topmost layers of his skin have been stripped away and discarded like an orange rind. He tries to raise his head, and sirens scream from somewhere within. A sea of faces blur before him. He tries to speak, but the world turns liquid; it swims in an unreachable flow of waves and motion. He tries to hold on to consciousness, but his exhaustion is more than physical; it is all-encompassing.

"M-mom," he utters weakly before succumbing to unconsciousness.

"I didn't see him," a frantic woman cries. "He just came out of nowhere! I-I didn't have time to stop!" Her voice is shrill and panicked as she tries to explain the incident to the police officer. "Oh, God, I didn't see him! Is he going to be all right? Tell me he's going to be all right!"

Trying to calm the woman, the officer says the paramedics are doing everything they can for the injured boy. He leads her away from the growing crowd moments before the child's parents arrive.

The boy's leg is broken and twisted at an impossible angle underneath him. His thigh has grown to the size of an overinflated basketball, but the head wound concerns the paramedics the most. It appears he was thrown from the bicycle when the car hit him and impacted the street with his skull. Tiny pieces of gravel have taken occupancy in the boy's exposed flesh; his face and arms are red and raw and look as angry as a nest of hornets. A nauseating indentation screams in the center of his forehead; it resembles the cola can he crushed and threw in the trash less than a half-hour ago. His mother had served meatloaf while his father had sat in silence. Just another Wednesday evening in the suburbs of Middle America.

“Can I go over to Avery’s house after dinner?” asked the boy. “Just for a little while.”

“Oh, I don’t know.” His mother looked at him and then quickly glanced at her husband for a response.

There was none. The man instead focused on the latest national crisis being sensationalized in the *Daily News*. He mindlessly maneuvered a forkful of meatloaf into his trap like a program stuck in an endless loop. His fork navigated the trajectory from plate to mouth effortlessly and efficiently.

“What about your homework?” she asked.

“Finished,” answered the boy through a mouthful of mashed potatoes.

“Don’t talk with your mouth full,” his mother scolded in an attempt to show a little spine, especially in front of her husband. Everyone knew she would ultimately agree to her son’s request. He was her only child and the love of her life. She would do anything for him.

“Sorry, Mom,” he said, wiping his mouth with a paper napkin. “I finished it already.” Then he preemptively added, “I cleaned my room before dinner.”

“Well…” She hesitated to see if her husband had anything to contribute.

He didn’t.

“I want you home before dark,” she continued, “and you’re only going to Avery’s. I don’t want you traipsing off to parts unknown.”

He tried to hide a smile. “Just to Avery’s and home before dark, I promise.” He inhaled the last of his dinner and waited impatiently to be excused.

“Go ahead,” she said.

The boy sprang from his chair and carried his plate to the sink. He turned, started to leave the room, and then doubled back to hug and kiss his mother. “I love you, Mom.”

“I love you, honey.”

“See ya later, Dad,” he said as he left the kitchen.

“Um-hmmm,” the meatloaf machine answered, continuing to execute the program to the letter.

The paramedics hover over him while he tries to focus on any single image. He has no idea how long he has been lying there. The world has been reduced to shapes and shadows. The agonizing thrum of an angry bell fills his sinuses, echoing in his teeth as if some deranged lunatic has assumed control of his internal alarm system.

Why is this happening to me?

The din gives way to an even more unnerving sensation. For a moment, he is acutely aware of the space just between his eyes. He moans when he feels something drawn from the center of his head, thick, wet, and excruciating.

Dear God, help me.

The boy's swollen brain can't comprehend what is happening to him internally. He imagines a large spool of knotted wire coiled in his head. Someone has found the loose end of the cord exiting his skull from the center of his forehead, just between his eyes. The line is slowly, purposefully pulled millimeter by millimeter through his brain's soft tissue. It is not easy; there is tremendous resistance. With the cord's removal comes a paralyzing reverberance that cancels out all other sounds.

He cannot label or even recognize this sound; it's like the noise of wet fingers clutching a balloon inflated past its limit. As they grasp the taut plastic, they create a gnawing, maddening sound, like rats chewing on Styrofoam. The gnawing increases in volume and intensity and consumes him. The world is liquid once again. He bobs like a cork in and out of lucid nightmares.

Thrust into the memory of last year's class trip to Mt. Berkshire with the ski club, he relives the events as if they are happening now. His mother kisses him and slips a five-dollar bill into his coat pocket. *I love you, baby. Have fun.* She's always there for him. The atmosphere inside the bus is electric and feels the same as it had on that day. The anticipation of thirty-five fourth graders ready to get their first crack at the bunny slope fills the vehicle with canned heat. It's quickly replaced by the vivid mental image of his skis, their slick undersides preparing to propel him for the first time. The gentle incline of the bunny slope looms before him. The memory is titanically disproportionate. Excitement. Adrenaline. Elation. Suddenly, he's in motion, rocketing forward like a clown on a roller coaster.

Faster, he glides down the ever-steepening terrain. His legs are frozen in place, and his skis hold tightly to the mountain. For a lifetime, the world is grey. Then the blanket of snow that rushes before him disappears. The mountain, the trail, and his body are gone. All are static, electric white noise as if he's stuck between channels on a TV. He has somehow wandered from the safety of his memory to find himself again in the madness of the dream.

A loud snap originates from within his head. He is smacked in the face by something scratchy that smells like disinfectant.

His skis leave the safety of the bunny trail and are now streaking through the woods. The incline is so severe, and his speed so intense, he nearly falls as he sails within inches of several hulking trees. Narrowly avoiding disaster, the branches of a large pine slap him in the face. Needles drag across his skin like the claws of a cat thrown into a bathtub.

Faster, he's flung down a slope that continues to drop out from under him. Fir trees miraculously jump out of his path at the last second, though their outstretched branches repeatedly assault him. Pines and hemlocks react to his presence, scratching and striking.

He should have been knocked off his skis with the slap of the first bough, but somehow, he remains upright. Then he realizes his legs aren't bearing the weight of his body. He is suspended like a bobber on a line. *Dear God*, he thinks, *it's the cord!*

Initially, the sensation of the cord suggested it was coiled inside his head and pulled from within. The reality is much worse. The thread runs through him, entering his forehead at a point just between his eyes and exiting the back of his skull. One end of the cord attaches to a stationary anchor at the top of the mountain; the other end fastens to an immovable object at the base of the slope. He is propelled along the line like a gondola.

The faster he moves down the mountain, the harder the branches assault him. All the while, the rats continue to gnaw at the Styrofoam inside his head. Rubbing plastic, waxy and wet, consuming and overpowering.

I'm dying, he thinks as he surrenders to the rats.

∞

"No, not my baby!" screams his mother as she rushes to him.

A large policeman prevents her from knocking over the paramedics frantically trying to save her boy. She looks haggard and crazed; her hair is a mess, and her eyes are deep red. She has been crying since she first heard the screech of tires from two blocks away. Instinctively she knew something had happened to her baby. A sour knot in her stomach took her breath like an arctic blast and spread like a frost throughout her body.

She was clearing the table when she heard the horrible sound of screaming rubber on pavement followed by a dull, sickening thud. She dropped what she was holding, and the platter shattered against the tabletop along with the scavenged remains of the meatloaf. Her husband looked up from his *Daily News*. A shared look of horror, fear, and denial weighed between them for what felt like years. Instant understanding accompanied that look. *Our boy!*

∞

Avery had firecrackers—three packs of blackjacks from one of the older boys in school. They planned to light them off in the woods after dinner. The boy darted out of his driveway on the Mongoose his parents gave him last Christmas. It was silver with knobby black tires and soft black handgrips and flew like a zephyr. Gravel spit from the back tire as he took to the asphalt of Midland Avenue. Legs pumping, heart racing, he built up speed with a sole focus—firecrackers. He had to get to Avery's fast, or his friend might start setting them off without him. He peddled hard against the light evening breeze; he imagined it slowing his every move, like cinder blocks strapped to his back. He pumped feverishly as the small dirt bike jerked clumsily to the left and the right.

Both tires left the ground for several seconds when he jumped the curb and turned onto Jackson Avenue. He maneuvered the sidewalk like a pro racer, clearing the gradual berm of each driveway, avoiding fire hydrants and telephone poles like a seasoned vet. He crossed Cedar Street and poured on the gas.

"Don't you start without me, Avery," he chanted under his breath like a divine mantra. "Don't you start without me!"

He saw the large spruce lumbering before him. At this point, he would change directions, crossing Jackson Avenue and cutting through a small subdivision called The Village. A loose patch of gravel caught under his front tire, causing it to weave slightly to the right. He quickly jerked the handlebars to compensate but nearly lost control. He narrowly managed to avoid wiping out and missed his turn as the giant spruce sailed past him. His heart jumped, fearing he wouldn't make it to Avery's in time. He swerved the Mongoose; the tires left the sidewalk and entered the street.

He jerks and is half aware of motion, weight, and mass. Something is extremely close. It is grey, possibly; he isn't sure. But it's moving fast and nearly on top of him. He doesn't register what happens next and likely never will.

Fear, all-consuming fear, blinds him. For one fleeting second, he is there, sensing, feeling, and aware. Then he is gone. Darkness and disorientation filter through the void. He's adrift in the rinse cycle of nothingness. All that is left is sound—the gnawing of the rats.

His father holds his mother. Both watch the paramedics check their son's pupils and listen to his heart. The men ask him questions, but neither he nor his parents understand what they are saying. The volume of the words is either too loud or too quiet to discern; it's impossible to tell which one. The men secure the boy's neck and head. Then they strap him to a tortuous wooden plank before transferring him to the back of the ambulance.

"You can both ride with me," someone says. One of the officers has approached the boy's parents and offered to drive them to the hospital. "There isn't enough room for you to ride in the ambulance, but you can come with me. We can be there in five minutes."

The flashing lights of the ambulance and police cruiser dissolve into a dark amber bath as an indifferent August sun sets in the west. Stunned neighbors and shocked observers watch the emergency vehicles speed away. The blare of the sirens is arrested by the hush of a most unnatural quiet.

The world is in flux. Faces swim in and out of focus, and the smell of alcohol is overwhelming. The boy's mother and father are there. Somehow, they look different, smaller, broken, and much older. They talk to him. Some he can understand, but most of it is muffled, waxy, and so very thin. His mother tries to smile and hold his hand. She says, "I love you, baby. It's going to be all right."

He hears the words "I love you too" and sees his father standing there, looking grave and shattered.

Another voice causes his parents to smile. It's his own, though he has no idea what he's said.

"Hey, kiddo," says his dad. "The guy in the next bed has a fishhook stuck in his nose." He nervously attempts to lighten the mood.

The boy wants to turn and see the man with the hook in his nose, and he struggles to do so. The effort is exhausting; he can't find the strength to move a single muscle. He believes he must have smiled because his father offers a weak one.

Another face hovers over him. The man's features meld into view, and he begins to speak. The wavering figure nods and speaks, but the boy has no idea what he has said. The man could be Chinese or even Japanese, but it's impossible to tell as his features blur in the blinding light of the emergency room. The man, who must be a doctor, says something to his parents. Most of the conveyance is lost, but several words make it through the mist. Words like concussion and femur seem as though they should mean something. The boy struggles to cross the bridge, but something blocks his path. Something prevents him from getting back to the place where words hold meaning.

Thoughts confuse him; he has never felt like this and doesn't know how he got here. He pictures the grey flash of a charging Elephant or Rhino for one moment. Then the image is gone. There is pressure—not pain—but tremendous pressure on his leg. His parent's faces lean over him, trying to keep his attention from the force exerted on his leg.

There is a crunch and then a snap; he feels it in the pit of his stomach. He thinks he's going to be sick, or possibly he already has. There is a shining silver basin in front of him and an acrid taste in his mouth. The last of his strength leaves him as the cord is tugged at once again. Blinding pain pours out from the center of his forehead as the sound of the resistance cripples him.

Running through his brain, in one end and out the other. Tangled and knotted, supporting the weight of his entire body. The cord is pulled, and he falls uncontrollably forever downward.

Styrofoam squeals against wet rubber gloves like raw flesh over-cleansed by industrial-strength detergent. The sound of balloons rubbing together fills him as the cord wrenches from inside his brain.

It is ceaseless. The rats invade his mind and gnaw at the cord. Worst of all, they gnaw at the parts of his brain surrounding the cord. He's exhausted. The pressure in his leg has subsided, only to be replaced by an entirely new sensation. Hot and white and alien.

Something is in my leg, he thinks.

The volume and intensity of the world become that of a three-ring circus in a volcano. The assault of the emergency room's glaring surfaces becomes too bright. The sensation of a foreign object forcing its way inside his body is too intrusive, and the unrelenting gnaw of the rats is unbearable.

"I'm so tired," he says before the grey fades to black.

Finally, there is silence, satisfying, peaceful silence.

For days, maybe longer, he sleeps. It's a restless, bitter sleep infested by the constant dream of the mountain and the hopeless sensation of falling. At times, the intensity of the vision throws him into consciousness. Then there are moments when the teeth-splitting sound of the rats wakes him. Always, he finds himself feverish and soaked in his own sweat. He opens his eyes long enough to see his mother or father sitting beside the bed. He sometimes looks around the room, lost and confused ... until his eyes focus on the leg. It is swollen, purple, and elevated above him in some medieval torture device. Then he sees the steel dart skewered through his leg just below the kneecap. He manages to get a few words out, but they are fuzzy and hard to understand, even for his mother. Most of the time, he wakes only long enough to shake the dream.

And this is his reality for what feels like forever. He enters the dream, propelled like a bullet. Finally, the overload of sensation and sound expels him from the nightmare, and he is spit into the stark light of the hospital room.

There, the women in white attempt to ease his tremors by wiping his face and feeding him ice chips. The fleeting relief of the cold is soothing and momentarily quiets the storm. It is here, in the moments when he opens his eyes, that he always sees them. His parents never leave his side.

A boy lies in a hospital bed in the center of a room he doesn't recognize. His mouth is dry, and his head rages. He opens his eyes and immediately wishes he hadn't. He is weak and exhausted, and there isn't one part of his body that doesn't register pain. Some are worse than others. His leg throbs with its own heartbeat—hot, white, and pulsing. It's suspended about nine inches above the bed, supported by a network of padding and straps. A large steel pin penetrates his knee, and a cable is clamped to the pin with a device oddly resembling a horseshoe. From there, the line reaches a series of pulleys that hang above his bed and connect to the footboard. Large, weighted sandbags hang from the end of the cord to apply the barbaric tension needed for his broken femur to realign correctly. His head is alive with its own individual pulse and a very distinct brand of pain. It is duller than in the leg, thick and constant. It is acute enough that he squints when he first surveys the room.

His father sits beside the bed, half asleep with a magazine spread across his lap. He jumps out of his chair when the boy finally speaks.

"Dad." His voice is thin, and his mouth dry.

The man rushes to his son's bedside and takes his hand.

"It hurts," whispers the boy.

His father smiles and wipes a tear from his cheek. "Yeah, I know, kiddo. You're gonna hurt for a while, but you're gonna be okay."

There's something different about his dad; the boy notices but can't quite place it.

"You really scared the hell out of us, kiddo."

The boy tries to lift his head but only manages to rise an inch from the pillow. He looks to the left and then back at his father.

"Mom went to the cafeteria to get some coffee. She'll be back in a minute or two. She's gonna be so happy to see you up."

"What ... how?" The boy has many questions, but getting the words out is hard.

Knowing how difficult it must be, his father answers: "You got hit by a car, kiddo. You've suffered a concussion and a broken femur."

The boy squints as if the news hurts his head.

"You're gonna have some pretty bad headaches for a while," his dad continues. "But ... you're gonna be okay."

The boy can't remember his father ever speaking so much at one time. But there's something else that's different about him. Then it hits him.

"Your hair!" says the boy. "What happened to your hair?"

His father looks at him, puzzled for a moment. "What about my hair?" he asks.

"It's grey," says the boy. "It's all grey."

His father's hair, which had been dark and youthful when he'd read his paper and ate his meatloaf, has turned almost entirely grey.

"Why's your hair so grey?" asks the boy.

"Well, I was worried about you," he answers.

Lying in bed, looking up at his father and his new head of grey hair, he watches tears roll down the man's face. Seeing his father cry is strange; he can't recall if he ever has.

"I'm thirsty," he manages, squeezing the words through a throat that feels on fire.

His father wheels a tray to the bed and transfers several ice chips from a plastic bucket to a Styrofoam cup. He lifts the cup to his son's lips and is suddenly aware of the look of panic that's crossed the boy's face. "What's wrong?" he asks.

The boy, unsure why the cup's appearance has caused him distress, manages to push it aside. He lets his father lift the cup and eagerly accepts the ice chips. They are refreshing, soothing, and magical. The ice momentarily dulls the pressure in his head. He lets his father feed him more.

The man focuses a tremendous amount of attention on the act. He doesn't want his son to choke by giving him too many at once, but he imagines the child is far beyond thirsty. He allows him a few at a time and then offers a few more once he has finished. The act is methodical and deliberate, far different from the actions the man usually exhibits at the dinner table.

From the doorway to the hospital room, his mother watches. She sees her husband tending to their child, who is finally awake. She stops herself from rushing into the room, if only for a moment. The sight of the man and boy engaged, and bonding causes her heart to swell. The man raises the cup to his son's lips and gently pushes the child's hair back. Something has changed, and profoundly so. She watches it from the doorway. It is so direct and yet so subtle. She prays for her boy and husband, then puts on her bravest face and steps forward.

"Hey, sport," says his father. "Look who's here."

The boy raises his eyes to see his mother entering the room.

Two

RECALCULATING

"Same time tomorrow."

Paul Davis looked down at the woman on the bed.

She stared up at him from a tangle of sheets, her hair messier than the bed itself.

"Is that a question?" she asked.

Paul grabbed his jacket and briefcase. "No, it wasn't. I'll see you the same time tomorrow." He leaned down and kissed her.

"What about your wife?" She inquired.

"Well, you know what they say ... while the cat's away." Paul seized the woman by the back of the head and bit her neck.

"Oh," she moaned, grabbing his belt and starting to unfasten it. "Why don't you stay just a little longer? I can make it worth your while."

"Sorry, baby." He released his grip and pulled away. "As tempting as that sounds, duty calls. Same time tomorrow!" He smirked and took his exit.

Paul opened the driver's side door of his Lexus, deposited his briefcase into the backseat, and smiled. The intoxicating new car smell warmed him like a fuzzy blanket. He loved new things: new cars, new clothes, new toys, but most of all, new women. He and Jan had been meeting for afternoon delight for the past month and a half. Before Jan, it had been Amy. Before Amy, it had been Gail. And before Gail, it had been ... for the life of him, Paul couldn't remember her name. Not that it mattered. There was always another tryst to fill the shoes (or the sheets) of the previous. At the moment, Paul basked in his glory, enjoying the sensory stimuli of his newest toy—a 2023 Lexus LC 500 and its state-of-the-art, integrated Ferdinand Navigation and Communication system. He started the car and checked the time, 12:15 p.m.

"Ferdinand," he said, "directions to 16 Fruitville Road, Sarasota, Florida."

A pleasant male voice with an English accent replied. *"16 Fruitville Road, Sarasota Florida ... Recalculating ... Turn left onto Route Three."*

Paul left the Pelican Point condominium parking lot, turned left onto Route 3, and headed to Dr. Taylor's office. He figured if traffic were light, he would arrive just in time to meet his wife, Susan, for her first scheduled ultrasound. She insisted he be there. *And don't be late!* Her exact words. Paul didn't get it; Susan was only three months pregnant, and there would be plenty of time for him to see the baby once it was born. More than enough. Just another way to mess up his day. He originally planned to see Jan, take care of a few business arrangements, then grab a couple of drinks with his buddy, Ziegler, at the Beach Club on Siesta Key. There were still several new barmaids that hadn't had the pleasure of meeting Paul Davis. And Paul Davis hadn't had the pleasure of pleasuring them. What could he say? He liked new things.

"Ferdinand," he said, "call Ethan Ziegler."

A second later, the sound of a telephone ringing filled the speakers of the Lexus. A man answered on the third ring: "Hello."

"Ethan," Paul greeted, "it's Paul. How's the second luckiest guy in the world doing today?"

"P-Diddle," Ethan Ziegler mused. "I tried to call you. Don't tell me you were with that dancer again?"

"That's yesterday's news, my friend," Paul replied. "I'm on to bigger and better things."

"I hope not too big."

"36-24-36, with an ass you could bounce a quarter off."

"Hahaha." Ethan fed on his friend's vulgarity. "So, where are you? Let's get a few martinis and check out the new talent at the Beach Club."

"No can do, mi amigo. Today is Susan's ultrasound," Paul explained, "and I promised her I'd be there. You know, first picture of the baby and all. I don't get it, but it's a big deal to her. Gonna have to take a rain check."

"Look at you, hombre. You're about to be a dad, and you're scoring more tail than I did in college."

"Well, you know what they say—when you got it, you got it." Paul chuckled heartily. "Besides, you never got that much squeeze anyway."

"Hahaha, you got me there. I'll see you tomorrow at the Beach Club at 2:30. The first round is on me."

"Mmm, better make it three. I'm seeing Jan for lunch. I had to rush her today, so I owe her a good one tomorrow."

"Man, when I grow up, I want to be just like you," Ethan said.

"You couldn't handle being me," Paul gloated. "Tomorrow at three. Ciao." Paul pressed the computer screen on the dash and hung up. He checked himself in the rearview mirror and smirked. He liked what he saw. He liked it very much.

"In three miles, turn right on Bee Ridge Road," Ferdinand informed him. *"Recalculating..."*

Paul visualized his schedule as he continued to drive. After leaving the doctor's office, he needed to head to Barrow Industries in Tampa and then hightail it to Devlin & Son in New Port Richey. Although both appointments were important, he'd reschedule Barrow in a heartbeat to ensure a prompt arrival at Devlin & Son. Max Devlin was Paul's cash cow; he made the majority of his living from the man as the company's stockbroker, hedge fund proprietor, and Max's personal accountant. Paul worked for only a handful of clients, all of whom stood slightly suspect in the eyes of the law, much like Paul himself. He was happy to work for shady clients like Max Devlin and more than happy to cook their books to line his own pockets. New toys and girlfriends didn't come cheap these days. And Paul loved new things.

He raised his hand to scratch his chin and was greeted by an arousing concoction of Jan's perfume, sweat, and sex. He couldn't wait to see her again.

Ferdinand interrupted his train of thought. *"In one mile, turn right on Route 75 ... scumbag."*

Paul jumped in his seat and stared at the computer screen. *"... Recalculating,"* Ferdinand finished.

He dismissed what he thought he had heard and merged, taking the on-ramp to 75.

"Proceed for five miles, then turn right on Vamo Road."

He relaxed in his seat, convinced that his ears had deceived him. Traffic was light on the interstate; he would make it to the doctor's office with time to spare.

"In three miles, turn right on Vamo Road, you two-timing son of a bitch," stated the computer clearly. *"Recalculating..."*

Paul jumped and jerked the wheel, nearly driving off the road. "What the fuck is going on?" he shouted.

"You tell me, Paul," spoke the navigation system, but now it was Susan's voice coming through the speakers. *"You tell me what the fuck is going on."*

His pulse ran like a greyhound. "Susan, is that you?"

He was answered only with silence, and then...

"Heh ... heh ... heh ... Recalculating," the strange static voice mocked Paul from the Lexus's speaker system.

Paul took his foot off the gas and attempted to slow the vehicle. Instead, the tires squealed, and the Lexus accelerated on its own as if fed a dose of nitrous oxide. Panicked, he tried to pull the car over, but the wheel wouldn't respond to his touch. He pumped the brake, but that did nothing either. The car sped up to 75 miles per hour.

"Buckle up, Buttercup ... Recalculating."

Sweat broke out on Paul's forehead as he white-knuckled the wheel and slammed the brake pedal to the floor. But the Lexus wouldn't respond and only rocketed to 87 miles per hour. Nothing Paul tried had any effect on the vehicle. It appeared to be operating autonomously. Further prompted by panic, he beat his fist against the steering wheel to regain control, but it was useless—Ferdinand was driving.

A million scenarios raced through his mind: factory defects, sunspots, practical jokers, hackers, and even corporate espionage. None seemed plausible. Paul punched the nav's display, breaking the skin on his fingers and two knuckles.

"For God's sake, stop!" he screamed.

Blood flowed from his hand and dripped onto the new carpet. His hair, now plastered to his forehead with sweat, gave him the appearance of a lunatic. And then, as if to tip his sanity from its delicate precipice, the mocking laughter emitted from the speakers once again. *"Heh-heh-heh. I wouldn't want to be you right now, Shithead."* It was the distorted voice of a madman.

Paul was thrown like a brick into the steering wheel when the brakes caught, forcing the tires to lock up. His head, and the bridge of his nose, smacked against the fine leather grips of the wheel, and he nearly lost consciousness. Somehow, he remained awake and took back control of the vehicle. He jerked the wheel to the right, and the car responded, narrowly avoiding a collision with an Old Dominion 18-wheeler bearing down on him like a Sherman tank. All four tires of the Lexus seized and caught the hot Florida pavement like a wad of bubble gum on the bottom of a shoe. It skidded to a halt in the breakdown lane of Route 75, where it idled as if nothing had happened. Paul examined himself in the rearview mirror. The face that stared back at him was battered, bloody, and dripping sweat. He looked like a scared little boy who had just pissed off the class bully.

"I told you to buckle up, Shit-stain," Ferdinand chuckled.

Paul struggled to focus, clearly dazed and probably concussed. "Huh," he managed to say through a mouth filling with blood. "Who are you?"

The Rolling Stones erupted from the car's speakers, and Mick Jagger screamed how nice it was to meet him and hoped he might guess his name.

"What the hell is going on?" he cried.

The radio station changed to a smooth jazz channel. *"This one goes out to Paul Davis. It's an oldie but goodie by the late Teddy Jackson. This one's called Hell on Wheels."*

The speakers went silent for a second, then the static voice returned. *"Heh-heh-heh. Lucy, you got some 'splainin' to do,"* Desi Arnaz bellowed through the system, loud enough to cause Paul's ears to ring.

He sat frozen as traffic raced past him. His heart pounded in his chest, and he began to tremble and cry. Paul was certain he had shattered his nose, and when he rechecked himself in the mirror, he noticed he had also broken his front tooth. He didn't like what he saw now.

"Aw, did you get a boo-boo? The ladies are going to love the new look, old bean!" Ferdinand mocked.

"What do you want from me?" he whimpered.

"Aw, does da wittle baby want his bottewl. Heh-heh-heh … Recalculating."

Tears streamed down Paul's cheeks and landed on his suit. He tried to wipe them from the lapel of his jacket but only managed to smear a long streak of blood from his freshly broken fingers down the front of his tailor-made Armani. The jacket was ruined, and Paul was no longer basking.

"Don't sweat it; Tide stick will get it!" Ferdinand chuckled.

"What do you want?" He mumbled through swollen lips and the hole where his front tooth had been.

John Wayne answered in a voice as big as Texas: *"It's time to come clean, Lil pilgrim. If ya wanna dance to the music, ya gotta pay the band … Recalculating."*

Paul grabbed the door handle and pulled just as the lock engaged. He slammed his shoulder against the window to force his escape, but the door wouldn't budge. He pounded against the window but only exacerbated the pain in his broken fingers. Fresh blood prints in the shape of his fists smeared the driver's side windowpane.

"You shouldn't have done that, wabbit," Ferdinand stated in the voice of Elmer J. Fudd. *"What we have here is a failure to communicate."* The voice changed again. *"I'm gonna make you an offer you can't refuse."*

Paul screamed. "This isn't happening!"

"Oh, it's happening, sweetheart!" The navigational system went blank, and Paul was greeted by his own voice over the speaker system. *"Call Max Devlin,"* it said.

The phone dialed Devlin's private number and was picked up on the second ring. "Paul, I didn't expect to hear from you until 3:30," Max greeted him.

Ferdinand replied in Paul's voice. *"Listen here, you bloated sack of shit."*

Paul screamed and desperately tried to disconnect the call. "No! Max, that's not me; it's the car."

Devlin didn't hear Paul as Ferdinand continued. *"You're gonna want to check your books, Max. I've been robbing you blind for the past year, you backwoods hillbilly. Oh yeah, I also slept with your daughter. She wasn't very good either, so I'll send you the bill for my services."*

"Paul!" Max barked. "Are you drunk? What's the meaning of this?"

"The meaning of this, Max, is that while you sat there in your fat-cat office, on your fat, bloated keister, I robbed you blind. It was like taking candy from a baby, too. I emptied that bogus offshore account in the Caymans and deposited it into the

Paul Davis fund. Then I sweet-talked that little troll of a daughter you got and took her out for a test drive. Truthfully, I've been on better rides at the carnival."

"Now, you look here. I can cause you pain you couldn't even imagine. You're finished, Davis. I'll make sure you never work again. If I choose to let you live at all!" Max Devlin screamed into the phone. No one in their right mind would ever think to talk to him like that. He wasn't just threatening Paul; he was making a promise.

Paul had seen what happened to guys that pissed off Max Devlin. Most of them ended up at the bottom of Tampa Bay or found themselves tied to a tree somewhere in the everglades with a few dozen canned hams attached to them. If there was one thing that alligators couldn't resist, it was pork. They loved the stuff. By the time they got done with you, there was nothing left to identify.

"First of all, dumbass, you don't have a sack big enough to do a thing about it. In fact, your little gremlin daughter has a bigger pair than you. If you want me, come and find me. I won't be hard to miss either. I'll be the one spending all your money." The call terminated.

"No!" Paul tried to redial Max, but the keypad wouldn't respond to his touch.

Static flooded the speakers, and Clint Eastwood's voice spoke: *"Go ahead, make my day."*

"What do you want?" Paul sobbed.

The English voice of Ferdinand returned. *"I already told you, old chap. It's time to come clean. You've been a rather naughty boy. In fact, you, sir, are a scoundrel. It's time to repent, you saucy tart!"*

Paul was hit with a brilliant idea. He reached under the steering column and grabbed a handful of wires. He yanked as hard as he could; they broke free from their contacts in the fuse box and ignition. He felt a moment of relief that was instantly squashed. The Lexus continued to idle, and the speakers exploded again. This time it was the tune of an '80s pop song.

"The devil's in my car ... oh, what a feeling ... I got the devil in my car."

The Lexus jumped into drive and screamed back onto Route 75, cutting off several cars. Its speed exceeded fifty-five miles per hour in less than four seconds, and it kept accelerating. Paul grabbed at the wheel but had absolutely no control over the vehicle. Ferdinand manipulated both the car and Paul. The Lexus swerved in and out of traffic as if driven by a madman. The other vehicles on the interstate slammed their brakes as the derelict motorist narrowly missed colliding with them. Their drivers watched the frantic man behind the wheel of the Lexus, ranting and raving as if he had gone insane. Paul had gone insane a long time ago. He had been living in a fantasy world with zero regard for anyone around him. He had become a man with no remorse, compassion, or empathy for anyone other than himself.

"You're despicable," the computer said, using the voice of Daffy Duck.

Paul was flung like a ragdoll while the Lexus, now doing well over seventy, jumped the median and bolted into oncoming traffic. A large Ford truck pulling a horse trailer swerved at the last second, narrowly avoiding a head-on collision with the Lexus.

"Heh-heh-heh." The voice morphed into Clint Eastwood's again. *"Do ya feel lucky? Well, do ya, punk? Recalculating…"*

The Lexus sped up as two large semis loomed into Paul's view. There was no way the car could avoid impact. Sweat soaked his clothes, and blood ran from his mouth, nose, and broken fingers. The Lexus increased its speed to breakneck velocity and bee-lined directly for the massive 18-wheelers. The truck's grill was the last thing Paul saw before he closed his eyes and screamed.

"Alright, you win! I'll do whatever you want!"

He waited for the impact to end his life … but it never happened. He kept his eyes shut for what felt like an eternity. Then he heard the polite man's voice with the English accent: *"Recalculating…"*

A rush of cold air-conditioning, mixed with the intoxicating new car smell, blasted Paul's senses. His body shook as he cried.

Recalculating…

He slowly opened his eyes. The Lexus idled in the parking lot of the Pelican Point condominium complex where Jan lived. He stared at the computer screen; the clock read 12:15 p.m. He looked at his hands to find his fingers intact and then checked his face in the rearview. He was sweating and shaking, but not a hair was out of place. There was no blood in his mouth, his nose was unbroken, and his lips were fine; even the tooth that had been knocked out was present. Other than a bit of stress-related perspiration, there was no sign of recent trauma.

Ferdinand spoke, *"Your move, Paul."*

Paul let out a deep, exhausted sigh and sat for a long moment contemplating who he was, what was important to him, and his own mortality. Then Paul Davis thought of his unborn child and made a decision. "Ferdinand, call Susan."

The phone began to ring, and Susan answered: "Hi, honey. Don't tell me you're at the doctor's office already.

"Susan," Paul wiped away the tears before they could fall onto his suit. "I've got something to tell you."

Afterword

Imagine, if you will, the following text read aloud in the voice of Twilight Zone's creator and host, the legendary Mr. Rod Serling. Under the right setting and proper mood lighting, that should do the trick.

As mankind races at breakneck speed to achieve the latest and greatest advances in the technological world, he inputs the culmination of his existence into the ghost we so proudly refer to as the machine. The quest for instant information has given man his much-needed edge to succeed in the modern world. But has he lost something in the process? We upload our pictures to Instagram and share our lives on Facebook in a most cavalier fashion; our history and language have been minimized to a file on Wikipedia. Our children can't tell us the capital of the state they live in without consulting SIRI.

And that's what we call progress.

Because, just like Paul Davis, we love new things. We want that new toy. We must have the latest iPhone. And we can't live without the new Lexus 500, with its state-of-the-art Ferdinand Navigation and Communication system. With technology at our fingertips, our lives have become minimized to a three-by-five LCD screen. But do we want our lives minimized? Is the evolution of mankind marked by advances in technology? Do we need Ferdinand to justify our relevance in society?

The children of the modern world can't remember their grandmother's phone number. They are incapable of placing a handwritten letter in the mailbox. But they can jailbreak a Firestick, beat the high score at Wordle, and find the answers to their history final at punkmyprofessor.com. As life becomes more impersonal and our technologies become more advanced, we are oblivious to the fusion of the two and what is lost in the process. Our lives are available for all to see at the click of a mouse. In fact, there's so much of us inside our computers that soon there will be no separation at all. Is technology making our lives simpler, or is it making us simple? Who is the one receiving the information, and who is the one in the driver's seat? Perhaps the only other question left to ask is this:

"Who is the one being programmed?"

Recalculating...

<u>Three</u>

5:56 PM

D on Reed stared up at the cold fluorescent light fixture above his bed. The steady rhythm of the machines monitoring his vitals proved strangely hypnotic. He had been diagnosed with Non-Small Cell Carcinoma, which had attacked his lungs and lymphatic system with a vengeance. Don's liver, however, would give out long before the cancer did the trick. And despite a life-long battle with John Barleycorn, Don's true nemesis remained his own demons. He was drowning in an ocean of regret.

"Can I get you anything, Mr. Reed?" Nurse Caldwell poked her head into Room 116.

Don waved her off and turned toward the window. A late afternoon storm had kicked up and begun to assault the hospital's exterior with an endless barrage of indiscriminate rain. At times it attacked the glass so aggressively it appeared to Don as if it were coming for him.

"Well, just buzz me if you need me," she said, leaving him to his isolation.

Don's mind crept back to the night his world ended. For a brief moment, he had everything he could wish for; then it was all gone as if it never existed.

It had been so dark, and the rain had been relentless. The storm had followed and become part of him. Like a passenger, it latched onto his soul and blanketed his heart with a memory he would never allow himself to shake. It didn't matter how much he drank; it failed to numb the pain. No amount of liquor could silence the rain. Still, for one fleeting instant, he had it all. For that brief moment in time, he had been happy.

∞

Kim Jefferies had dark brown hair and chestnut-colored eyes that penetrated Don's soul. She sat next to him in homeroom and across from him in science lab. After several months of struggling to muster the courage, Don finally asked her to go out with him. On a Tuesday, they drank milkshakes and ate French fries at Flip's Diner. By Friday, they were 'head over heels' and well on their way to being 'in love.' Don walked Kim home from school every day, and on one exceptionally perfect afternoon, they kissed for the first time beneath the sycamore in her front yard. He could still remember the smell of her shampoo, the feel of the fresh fallen leaves, and the way they crunched beneath their feet as they held each other close. She had worn lip gloss that day.

What flavor had it been? he wondered.

Don was startled from his daydream and lifted from the veil of semi-consciousness when something brushed against his hand.

"It was strawberry," replied a woman's voice.

Don opened his eyes and gasped. *I must be dreaming*, he told himself, looking up at the vision that stood before him.

Kim bent down and kissed his cheek. "It was strawberry-flavored, and it was October beneath the sycamore."

"How ... how can this be?" he asked.

"Don't worry about that," she said. "Remember the dance?"

It had been Senior Prom 1985. Don remembered the wash of red and green and the flash of strobe lights waltzing off the gymnasium floor. There was music, a melody so close and familiar yet so far away. He struggled to recall but could not remember the tune for the life of him. Don pushed himself to the threshold of tears but still could not grasp the melody. *What had been the song?*

Kim leaned closer and pressed her lips against his ear. Then, in the sweetest, most angelic voice, she sang, "Forever, I am yours, eternally."

Don smiled and squeezed the hand that surely existed only in his imagination. The tired, battle-wearied eyes of the man, who was only fifty-six but had already endured a lifetime of pain, gazed at the angel standing before him. Her hair was as dark as he remembered, and her eyes as bright as the day they had kissed beneath the sycamore. Kim looked as if she hadn't aged a day.

"I'm sorry," he uttered with a trembling voice.

"You shouldn't be." She held his hand.

"I've missed you so much," he said.

"I've missed you more," she replied.

Three weeks after graduation, Don had been driving Kim home from a date when a searing ribbon of electricity sliced across the sky. It was followed by a horrific downpour, making it impossible to see. He was far from a seasoned driver, having had his license for just under a year. And the storm was so torrential that it would have given the most advanced motorist trouble. Kim screamed when the deer ran in front of the car, and Don reacted. He jerked the wheel too hard to the left and hit the telephone pole head-on. The sound of the impact resonated within him from that night forward. And the world had dissolved into the memory of that one moment.

Don looked into the chestnut-brown eyes of the eighteen-year-old girl who stood before him. "But, Kim," he said, "I watched you die."

"And now we can finally be together. You just have to let go." She smiled at him.

"But ... I can't forgive myself. What I did to you..." His face grew sullen as he turned back toward the window. The rain continued to cascade against the glass. It had become a constant companion, accompanying the landslide of guilt that consumed him. It ate away at the man he had been so many years ago, much like the cancer that now attacked his body. And he had been unable to let go of any of it. Like a bad habit, Don was addicted to his pain, to his remorse, to his own self-loathing.

"You have to be willing to change," she answered. "You've punished yourself enough."

Kim lowered her lips to Don's ear and hummed the melody once again. He felt the music as it entered his head and quickly spread throughout his body, consuming him like a drug. The sound of Kim's voice filled him and crept into his heart, causing it to burst with emotion. Don hadn't felt anything like that in years. It was wonderful. It was intoxicating. It was a miracle. And there was no longer room in his heart to hold onto anything that resembled remorse. There was only room for love ... for change.

Don gazed into Kim's chestnut-brown eyes and swung his feet off the bed. Then he took her in his arms and hugged her.

"Forever, I am yours," she sang to him.

"Eternally," he replied.

Pillars of golden sunlight flooded in through the windows of Room 116. It warmed the area where Don Reed lay. Nurse Caldwell placed her hand over his face and closed his eyes. Then she turned off the monitors and recorded the time of death: 5:56 PM, with zero chance of rain.

Four

THE DEVIL'S WELL

Gary Butler stepped carefully to the edge of the great drop-off and peered over into the dark, choppy water below. His heart somersaulted and then descended into his stomach. What little nerve he thought he might have possessed a moment ago was gone. The sight of the rock face stretching out beneath him and the massive drop made him dizzy. The waterfall cascading off the mountain to his left had etched a gorge in the side of the outcropping to create a massive churning pool at the cliff's base. Gary positioned himself at the jump point where only the bravest of the boys ever ventured. The dive was less than forty feet, but it felt like a whole lot more. The concave vector of the granite sloped inward beneath the precipice creating the illusion of a never-ending drop. Also, the ceaseless roar of the waterfall just a short arm's distance away helped befuddle the sensory perception at this altitude. Gary had been sure—today would be the day he finally made the jump. But now that he was here, standing at the edge, looking out into the ink-black abyss, he knew there was no way. It wasn't called the Devil's Well for nothing.

"Aww, I told ya he wasn't gonna do it," Timmy Birch heckled. He was a grade older than Gary and had been riding him since last year about jumping the Well. It was a rite of passage for the boys in Fairmount. For many of the girls, too. By the time they reached high school, it was expected that they all jumped the well at least once. Many had done it as early as seventh and eighth grade. Timmy Birch, Scott Clark, and Willie Thomsen had taken the plunge earlier this spring. That was during the first warm days when the black soup at the bottom of the pit was just shy of fifty degrees. The boys had come out of the water purple and damn near hypothermic. None of them expected Gary would go through with it. No sixth grader ever had.

"No way, man." Willie threw up his hands and soured his face as if he'd eaten a rotten sock. "We didn't hike all the way up here just to watch this clown chicken out," he shouted loud enough to be heard over the roar of the falls. "Get your bitch-ass up there and jump!"

The others howled and laughed at their friend's demands for a show to take place. Gary had boasted to all of them at school, saying how he was really going to do it. Today was the day, he told them. "Today, I'm going to jump the well." He'd been so convincing he had even believed it himself. That was until he looked over the edge and lost his nuts, which happened quite often. It was easy to walk around with King Kong's balls when you weren't standing on the cliff looking at just how far a drop it was. It was an entirely different story when you got right up to it. Gary walked back to where the older boys stood, feeling nervous and embarrassed.

"Let's get outta here." Scott slapped Willie on the back. "I told ya he wasn't gonna do it."

"Bullshit!" Willie spat. "This little shit dragged us all the way up here, and he's goin' in the Well if I have to throw him in myself." This statement was met with more laughter from everyone except Gary, who smiled and tried to look relaxed. He attempted to act casual as if his heart wasn't trying to jump out of his chest with every beat. But his hands were slick, and he could feel his legs trembling.

"I'm sorry, guys," he whined. "I didn't know how cold it was gonna be up here." He wrapped his arms around his chest to prove how chilly he was. It was a weak show, at that. "It'll be warmer in a week or two."

Willie threw his hands up in disgust, making a sound like all the air in his body had decided to leave at once. "Unbelievable!"

"You know, Gary." Timmy approached him. "You don't need to do this to impress anyone. No sixth grader has ever jumped the Well. I mean, it would have been pretty cool if you did. I bet the kids at school would talk about you for a real long time." Timmy was the smartest of the three and had a pretty good idea what he was doing. "But no one's gonna think you're a pussy or anything like that, at least no one who counts." He turned to his friends and exaggerated his speech. "You guys aren't gonna think Gary is a pussy, are ya?" Scott smirked and shook his head. "Guess not, probably."

Willie wasn't about to play along, not even for a minute. "To hell with that. We didn't come all this way to watch this pussy chicken out."

Timmy snickered; Willie had played his part exactly as expected. "Well, of course, some might give you a hard time. But I wouldn't worry about them." He watched the younger boy nervously shift where he stood. "You make the jump when you're good and ready. It's not for everyone. Shit, some kids never jump the Well. I won't think anything less of ya." Timmy snorted as he laughed, making Gary feel even more uneasy.

Despite the chilly breeze that raced over the crest of Mt. Hope, Gary felt the flush of frustration and embarrassment heating him up. He looked at the older boys knowing he had disappointed them. The patronizing look on Timmy Birch's face said it all. He knew all along that Gary wouldn't make the jump, and he would never let him live it down, no matter what he said to the contrary. He was going to make sure every kid in school knew that Gary had chickened out. Willie continued pacing back and forth, flailing his arms in disgust as if his entire life had been wasted due to the events of one afternoon. But it was the way Scott looked at Gary that affected him most. It was a look of pity—a look Gary knew all too well. It had been the same expression his father had made countless times in the past. It sent a very specific message: *You will never amount to shit, kid. You'll never leave your mark on this world.*

"Come on," Timmy called out over the blare of the rushing water and the growing howl of the wind that had just started to kick up. "There's always next year."

A slow boil started in the pit of Gary's chest and quickly spread to his extremities. It rushed up his neck and into his face. He could feel the sweat on his forehead even though the air had suddenly turned quite chilly. He scanned the looks of disappointment and apathy staring back at him. An image of what the rest of the school year might be like etched into his brain, clear as the present moment. It would not end here. How could it, especially after making such a show at school earlier that same day? He had even told Sarah Meyers his plans. Today, he was gonna jump the Well. He recalled the way her face lit up and the sparkle that had come to her chestnut-brown eyes with just a hint of gold around the pupils.

"Really," she gasped in amazement. "Aren't you scared?"

Her sudden interest was intoxicating. "Heck no," he had replied. "There's nothin' to it."

Her reactions prompted a far more exaggerated response than even he was prepared to process. It fueled his still-developing adolescent head with a misguided, youthful bravado. Gary had taken her interest as a prompt to elaborate on how he would be the first sixth grader to attempt such a feat. He told her how he intended to run toward the edge as fast as he could. And he told her about the giant leap he would take when his feet left the ground. Sarah listened, all the while mesmerized by his bravery and prowess.

All he could imagine now was the look on her face when she learned he had chickened out at the last second. Her smile would fade into the same disappointed look that Willie wore. Gary thought he could stand being called a chicken by the older boys and all the riding he would get. He could probably even endure the humiliation he would face from the kids in his own grade. But the idea of watching that sparkle fade from Sarah's eyes was something he couldn't handle. In the end, it had been thoughts of Sarah that prompted him toward action. Gary Butler wasn't the first, and he certainly wouldn't be the last boy to make a foolish decision just to impress a woman. At least it was one he wouldn't regret for very long.

Timmy and the other boys turned and headed toward the path leading down the mountain toward Davenport Lane. "Let's get outta here, guys." They walked off, leaving Gary alone at the top of the cliff. The sixth grader's blood began to churn, and then boil, much like the pitch-black soup at the bottom of the Well.

He watched as they walked away, hearing in his head everything they would say as soon as they had the chance. The fever reddened Gary's face until it started burning like an ember in his chest. His pounding heart consumed gallons of his fiery blood with each pronounced throb. The slow shakes that began in his legs and arms quickly escalated, and neared convulsive proportions. Gary pivoted on his heels, crouched low to gain traction, and bolted toward the drop-off at a full sprint.

Timmy, Scott, and Willie were just stepping onto the path when a high-pitched scream cut through the wind and the roar of the falls like a harpoon. They turned to see Gary rocketing toward the cliff's edge, running like a shit-house rat with its head on fire. They froze in their tracks when the small sixth grader leaped from the precipice into the air above the Well. The dumbfounded looks on all three faces were that of complete shock. What startled them most of all was what they heard Gary scream as he jumped into the air and disappeared over the ledge. Later, when questioned, all three boys would answer the same. Gary had jumped the Well and screamed, "KISS MY ASS, PUSSIES!"

The feeling of weightlessness lasted about a quarter of a second, but it was invigorating. Gary ran toward the edge as fast as he possibly could. His heart hammered in his chest. Every raw nerve in his body and every instinct told him to stop. But all he could think about was how impressed Sarah would be when she learned he had gone through with it. That he, Gary Butler, was the first and only sixth grader ever to jump the Well. The feeling of weightlessness disappeared as gravity did its thing. Suddenly, Gary was flailing toward the ink-black water below like a misguided ballistic warhead. His arms and legs beat against the air to slow his descent, but it was useless. He stopped breathing at some point as he prepared to meet the fast-approaching surface of the water.

The fall lasted only a few seconds, but from Gary's perspective, it felt a whole lot longer ... a lifetime, in fact. The satisfaction that he'd really gone through with it began to sink in. But it vanished as soon as he hit the churning surface of the dark water. An incapacitating arctic blast instantly seized him. It was cold, still in the low fifties, and the icy chill attacked his chest like a swarm of hornets as he plunged deep into the murk. His momentum continued to carry him downward, driving him deeper and deeper. The suffocating darkness enveloped him, and the thrill of the jump quickly yielded to a far more menacing sensation. As Gary was propelled further down into the abyss and the black water shrouded him more thoroughly, an overwhelming thought seized him. He wasn't alone down there.

Panic began to set in as his downward momentum slowed. He found himself God knows how far below the surface. It was black, blacker than black. It was so dark it felt as if the water were absorbing what little light dared penetrate the surface. Gary's lungs burned as he started swimming in a direction he could only hope was up. With each stroke, he forced himself to reach a little harder, to propel himself a little faster. He knew he couldn't hold his breath much longer.

Panic turned to terror while Gary kicked at the inky tar cocooning him. He felt as though cinder blocks were tied to his legs; he couldn't move them fast enough. And although he was sure his eyes were open, it was still impossible to see a thing. Then he felt it. He screamed as something brushed against his leg.

He heard his underwater voice when he cried out and sucked in a mouthful of the murk. He choked and gagged as he continued clawing toward the surface, away from whatever had brushed against him. He had been fighting his way up for what seemed like a week; he had to be close now. He coughed again and could feel himself about to take a lungful of the arctic water when the faintest shimmer of sunlight appeared less than a few feet above his head. He had made it. He was going to be alright.

Gary broke the chop of the Well and bobbed like a spastic balloon. He coughed up snot and gagged on the remainder of the water he had swallowed. Timmy, Scott, and Willie peered down over the edge at him as he splashed about on the surface. The three older boys started hooting and hollering down at him. Gary couldn't decipher the exact praises they rained on him, but he thought he had the gist of it. He gazed up to see the smile on the older children's faces and began to smile himself, momentarily forgetting about his present situation. He raised his arm out of the water and waved to them. "I did it," he called out. "I really d—"

Suddenly, Gary was yanked under the water. Something had taken hold of his leg just below the knee. Something large with an incredibly powerful grip latched onto him and dug into his flesh. Gary swallowed even more water as it dragged him down, nearly causing him to black out. He probably would have if not for the searing pain that bolted through him, setting all his nerves on fire at once. It was sharp, it was pointed, and it was strong. Whatever had grabbed Gary dug into the skin below his kneecap and into the muscles beneath. He felt it rip, followed by a sickening snap, just before it let him go. Gary fought to kick in his semi-conscious state and somehow managed to move. He broke the surface again and listed like a sea lion that had just been bitch-slapped by an Orca.

The other boys watched in horror as Gary returned to the surface. Even in the black water, they could see the color around him had changed. A deep scarlet engulfed the area where the injured boy lolled like a broken cork. He fought to hold his head up but couldn't. It continued to roll back on his neck. The look in his eyes was a mix between disorientation and unadulterated terror.

Timmy watched as Gary attempted to raise his arm. He and his friends saw Gary open his mouth and call up to them. Then something grabbed him again. The crimson-black water swallowed the boy, and he vanished into the Well. Timmy Birch had been right, after all. The kids at Fairmount would talk about Gary Butler for a very long time after that day. The only sixth grader to ever jump the Well. The last child who ever dared to try.

No remains were recovered despite a full investigation by the Fairmount police with the aid of county divers. According to the emergency responders, the Well was simply "too damn deep." The last search efforts, however, managed to discover a fissure that possibly went as far as Hell itself. It was believed to be the final resting place of the young boy.

Sarah Meyers cried for nearly a month. She never forgot the day Gary Butler told her all about the Devil's Well and how he would be the first sixth grader to jump it. For a long time, the golden flecks peppering her eyes shined a bit duller than they had in the past. But in the end, even Sarah got over it, as well as most of the town. Everyone except for Gary's mom and dad. The kid had left a mark, after all.

On the year anniversary of that tragic day, Timmy Birch, Scott Clark, and Willie Thomsen made one last trip to the Devil's Well in honor of Gary. They brought a six-pack of PBR and a can of spray paint. They shared the beers and stayed far from the drop-off until they were ready to leave. Then they took the paint and left a mark that remains there until this day. Although now it is somewhat faded. But if one were daring enough to follow the path that leads from Davenport Lane to the top of Mount Hope, it is still easy to find. An ode to Fairmount's greatest legend is scrawled on the granite outcropping that parallels the falls.

GARY BUTLER

RIP

KISS MY ASS, PUSSIES!

Five

RONALD REAGAN AND THE OH JESUS CHORD

Of all the jobs I've had in my life, the time I spent as a roadie in New York City was hands down the most exciting. It was the early nineties, and Giuliani had yet to clean up the Big Apple. Forty-Second Street was a peep show paradise. Central Park was bogged down with the homeless. And you could find just about anything you wanted at any time, day or night. It was glorious!

I was just twenty-one and still a bit green around the gills. Not half as streetwise as I thought and more than a little unprepared for the position I had in mind. But I was young, and those things didn't matter much. So, I decided to apply anyway. Studio Instrument Rentals, or S.I.R., as the logo on the big red trucks read. You can see them everywhere throughout the city and in more movies than I can count. From Tootsie to Ghostbusters, those trucks have literally been around the block. It took a bit of convincing, but I got hired and started driving those big red trucks with the trumpet decal on the side. I quickly learned the ins and outs of the five boroughs. I knew the quickest way to get to J.F.K. during rush-hour traffic. I could tell you where to find the cheapest slice of pizza, the best hotdog, or the number one falafel joint in the village. I dined at Grays Papaya, Luigi's Pizza, and The Hat, my favorite Mexican place in Alphabet City. I began to see myself as a fast-food, city-smart Renaissance Man. Not bad for a punk from Jersey.

But it wasn't the big red trucks, freedom of the road, or endless grub possibilities I found so alluring about working at S.I.R. It was the elbow-rubbing and the constant barrage of celebrity figures that made the job so damn exciting. The company has been around since the sixties and holds offices in N.Y., Nashville,

LA, and Memphis, to name a few. Anyone who's anyone in the music business utilizes their services eventually. From Prince to Barry Manilow, Vanilla Ice to Marky Mark, The Rolling Stones, Steely Dan, Elton John, and Paul McCartney—they've all walked through the doors of S.I.R. That's because they all own musical equipment. And my job was to move that equipment. I was a roadie.

I soon found myself in the most extraordinary circumstances. Most people wouldn't believe half of it if I told them everything in one sitting. I assure you, however, that every word is the truth.

S.I.R. has a long-standing contract with N.B.C. I was tasked with picking up the band gear from Saturday Night Live every weekend after the show ended. I would get off the elevator at 30 Rock as Madonna and Mike Meyers were getting on. I would find myself eating popcorn at the commissary with Chris Farley and had been there when Nirvana smashed their equipment on stage. I moved that broken equipment and carried it back to the studio in my truck. This job was my golden goose; I had found a home. I met Michael J. Fox, Steven Segal, Kathleen Turner, Rosanne Barr, Dennis Quaid (I think I dropped a name there; would you mind picking that up for me?). I watched Elvis Costello play with Sting. I did a toot with Billy Squire and kissed Melissa Manchester on New Year's Eve. But none of these extraordinary situations come close to what happened to me one day in Mid-Town Manhattan. I like to refer to it as "The Day of the Accident."

First, I must tell you that the job of a roadie is not all elbow-rubbing and name-dropping. The hours are long, and the work is back-breaking. New York City can be a fickle mistress to navigate, my friends. The service entrances and freight elevators of nearly every establishment are set up like gauntlets. There's always a passage through a bustling kitchen, the floors always coated in a thick layer of disk-herniating grease. These galleys meander through the most treacherous catacombs of unimaginable horror. They twist and turn as if blazed by alcoholic architects until they finally dump you into an even narrower passage that smells somehow worse than the previous. How they condense such a debilitatingly pungent odor into such a small area is beyond me. To this day, I can't eat at any New York Hotel, no matter how high-end it might be.

From this small passage, one gets directed to a freight elevator, which can only be run by the freight operator, who belongs to perhaps the tightest union in the city. No one is permitted to even look at the buttons on these elevators except for the operator, who is never at his post. Unfortunately, this is the only way to reach the promised land. Once you make it through the gauntlet, you've got to pay the ferryman, and by that, I mean you've got to kiss the operator's ass. So you'll wait as long as he decides to make you. This is the cross a roadie must bear.

This ordeal becomes even more problematic when pianos are involved. The men at S.I.R. are trained in the proper handling and moving of these instruments ... usually. We have delivered pianos for Billy Joel, Elton John, and the late Eddy Layton, the organist for the New York Yankees. From uprights to Baby Grands, Baldwins to Hammonds, take it from me, there isn't a light one in the lot. These bastards are heavy and cumbersome and want to fall over, even on a dry, flat surface. For the record, there are no dry, flat surfaces to be found in the back kitchens or on the sidewalks of New York City ... just in case you were wondering.

It was an early Sunday morning, and I'm sure I had a hangover of one kind or another. I was called into work that morning and not all too pleased about it. I got partnered with a guy named Jake, who worked in the U.S. on a visa. He was from Liverpool and hated when I talked about the Beatles. But Jake was a good sport and fun to joke around with. Jake was determined to shack up with an American girl and had set out to do so as soon as he arrived in the States. On his first night in town, he met Rita. She was beautiful, blonde-haired, blue-eyed, and also from England. I found it ironic.

On this particular Sunday, Jake and I arrived at work both feeling a bit dodgy and proceeded to our first destination, The Marriott Marquis, to pick up a piano. We navigated our way to the main ballroom and located our prize. We fastened the upright piano to the dolly and headed to the freight elevator. The operator, who made something like triple time for working on a Sunday, was there when we looked for him and promptly dropped us off in the garbage passage. We maneuvered down the long, narrow hallway and began making our way through the kitchen. I don't know what they were preparing in that kitchen, but more was on the floor than on the stoves. The floor was slicker than a greased pig on ice. Jake and I fought to keep our traction and maintain the upright position of our cargo. This task was nearly impossible to achieve. We somehow managed to make our way around the dishwashers, fry cooks, and bussers. Then we traversed across the grease and oil like a pair of cross-country skiers. Our work boots, which were now fully coated in a back-breaking layer of kitchen grease, made it nearly impossible to maintain our vertical status, let alone that of the piano.

Finally, we exited through the back door of the kitchen into what felt like the sweetest air I'd ever had the pleasure to breathe. I'd been closer to losing the contents of my stomach than I knew, and the refreshing city air was a Godsend. I could tell that Jake felt the same. He looked at me, a little greener around the gills than a minute before and released an exasperated sigh of relief.

That's when it happened—a momentary loss of muscular coordination. We had eased our grip on the piano for one disastrous split second, and it began rolling away from us. Instinctively, we clamored to regain our grasp and caused more harm in the process. The dolly kicked out from underneath the piano and shot into the street. The unforgettable sound of every note on a piano being struck the exact moment it crashes to the pavement is respectfully known in the industry as the 'Oh, Jesus Chord!' It can't be described any other way. The piano slammed onto its back, and the shock wave sent every pigeon in the Tri-State area in flight. As every note rang out at the very same moment, my soul screamed, "Oh, Jesus!" Although it is horrifically traumatic, it is also quite exhilarating. I recommend you try it if you ever have a twenty-thousand-dollar piano you care to destroy.

Oddly enough, that wasn't even the highlight of our day. And although a close second, the 'Oh, Jesus Chord' at the Marriot was not nearly as impressive as what was about to happen next. We loaded what remained of our lot onto the truck and tied it in extra tight. We would catch hell for trashing the instrument, but it would pass, and tomorrow would be another adventure.

I hopped in behind the wheel and proceeded to navigate my way through the early morning traffic. There were cars double-parked on both sides of the street, and it was challenging to navigate the big truck in my heightened and agitated condition. I guess I was a bit more stressed than I realized because I hadn't noticed the three black limousines in front of us until they stopped and the red flashing lights turned on.

Siren beacons began pulsing in the brake lights and on the mirrors of the limos. Then a man, dressed entirely in black and wearing mirrored sunglasses, stepped out of the vehicle closest to us. A wire ran from the lapel of his jacket to an earpiece he wore. The guy raised his hand and issued the universal sign of 'Stop right there.' I did as instructed. The guy was intimidating, and it wasn't like I could go anywhere. The limos were now double-parked on one side of the street while passenger vehicles were double-parked on the other.

I knew right away what this guy was. Maybe not precisely who he was, but I had seen movies, and he fit the stereotype to the T. There could be no doubt, the dude was secret service. What happened next made the world feel like it had shifted into slow motion. The middle vehicle's back passenger side door opened, and an older couple stepped out onto the street. I saw their faces and wrestled with acceptance for a moment. There could be no denying who it was, but I was star-struck all the same. Sure, I had been around rock stars and celebrities, but they were just average Joes compared to this.

The couple stood up in the Sunday morning sunlight and turned in our direction. I was speechless, but Jake managed to articulate what I had wanted to say. "Jesus Christ, that's fuckin Ron and Nancy."

Right before our eyes stood Ronald Reagan and the former First Lady, Nancy. They were a little older than I'd last seen them on TV, but it was absolutely them. Jake started waving, and that snapped me out of my trance. I waved to them and may have even tooted the horn once or twice. They gave us a giant grin and waved back at us. Then they quickly made their way into the building and disappeared.

"That was fuckin' Ron and Nancy," Jake repeated.

"Sure as shit was," I agreed.

My friend and I grinned at each other like a couple of teenage girls at a Taylor Swift concert. I had come about as close to American royalty as I ever would in my life. This experience was some next-level shit. I continued basking in the presidential glow as the Reagans departed from sight and left us blocking midtown traffic. Suddenly, the blaring of several horns woke me from my stupor. Also, the presence of the oppressive secret serviceman standing in front of my vehicle waving his hands gave me a start.

The man directed me to move along and pass between the double-parked limos and vehicles. He more than just urged me to do so; he commanded me to move. I felt the authority from his ominous presence and evaluated the space in which he wanted me to navigate. I don't claim to be much of a professional anything, and I'm certainly by no means a Master of Physics. I was a truck driver with a pretty good grasp of spatial perception. Still, it was apparent, at least to me, that said truck was never going to fit through said space without doing some type of said damage.

"There ain't enough room," I yelled out the window. My words appeared to anger the man, as he only pointed at me more adamantly and continued shouting for me to move the truck.

"It ain't gonna fit, mate," Jake agreed with me.

So, I related this once again to the agent directing traffic.

Finally, he gave me a look that told me he wasn't playing around, not even a little bit, and motioned once again for me to move. He was a threatening enough presence to convince me that he knew better than I. Slowly lifting my foot off the brake, I popped the truck into first and feathered the gas as I let off the clutch.

I edged between the parked vehicles and made it past the first limousine. I even started to feel comfortable that I'd make it past the rest of the cars. That's when the truck's front bumper dug into the side panel of Ronald Reagan's limo and began tearing into it like string cheese. Though it happened fast, it seemed to occur in slow motion. Be that as it may, I was helpless to stop the vehicle. I pushed through the confined space, tearing into the limo as I proceeded. I knocked the mirror from the President's car and left a gaping rip along the entire side of it.

"I knew there wasn't enough room," I think I said to myself.

I looked over at Jake, who had turned a pale shade of grey. The agent flagged me down as I emerged on the other side and asked me to step out of the truck. Another agent showed up and proceeded to take Jake in the opposite direction. At this point, I repeated what I'd told him before: There hadn't been enough room. But he didn't appear too concerned. In fact, he wasn't all that upset about the whole thing, either. Something about his demeanor told me that things like this happened more often than I could imagine.

He didn't ask for my license or insurance card, not even the registration or company ID. The only thing he asked me for, which I found surprising, was my Social Security Number. I asked the man if I would have to pay for the damage. He never answered, and I never did.

It had turned out to be an eventful day. I had destroyed a piano, had seen a real-life U.S. President, and, to top it off, trashed his limo. I had hit a true roadie trifecta and would quickly become the talk of the shop for easily the following week. But my memories of that day would last a lifetime.

Now, I can reflect on my early life and extract more than a few smiles. I never actually had a career and never lasted at a job for longer than a few years at a clip. That was never important to me. I've been married and divorced. I've owned my own home, been to several islands in the Caribbean, and also spent some time behind bars. In retrospect, I wouldn't change a thing. Sure, we all have regrets and make mistakes, but these are the building blocks that shape us. And of all the jobs I've had in my life, my time at S.I.R. is the one I remember the most. That's the job I still have dreams about when I close my eyes at night. I think that says it all.

Recently, I found myself at a job interview, trying to obtain a position for which I was clearly underqualified. I behaved courteously, spoke politely, and answered all questions to the best of my ability. I must admit, even though I was a bit out of my league, I was more than confident. You see, I always have an ace up my sleeve. I patiently wait till the point in the interview where they ask, "So, could you tell us a little bit about yourself?" That's when I tell them about the moment my front bumper made contact with the President's limo. I describe my reflection in the secret serviceman's mirrored glasses, and if there's time, I define 'The Oh Jesus Chord.' Usually, this guarantees a callback because, as it turns out, everyone loves a good story.

SOMETHING IN THE AIR

There was tension in the atmosphere as if the air itself knew something sinister was lurking on the horizon. Idris and Burke noticed the traffic on Market Street, considerably thinner than the day before, not to mention the nearly non-existent foot traffic. But that wasn't even the strangest thing. What was so unnerving was the look on the faces that drew an exaggerated birth around the men as they made their way to the bus stop. People weren't just frightened; they were scared to death, and they had every reason to be.

At first, it sounded like something out of a Stephen King novel. Certainly, the media was exaggerating the situation in China. Then the unlikely became a reality. And suddenly, it was happening. Cases had been reported in Newark, and Idris and Burke would not be going to school tomorrow. Although the school would still be open for regular students, the two men were anything but regular.

They had met at the Talbot in October after each had respectively left the prison system. The Talbot was a halfway house for those nearing the end of their sentences but still technically under the custody of the Department of Corrections. The powers that be called it re-entry, but for most of the men in the place, two hundred and seventy-seven to be exact, there wasn't a whole lot of re-entry going on. A small percentage of the residents were permitted to leave the building to work, and an even smaller number were allowed to attend school. Idris and Burke belonged to the latter. Both men had done a considerable amount of time behind the wall, as they say, and had hit it off almost instantly. They had literally become "thick as thieves," mostly because of their academic interests. Mostly.

∞

Idris had been born in Newark and then transplanted around the globe several times with the 101st airborne. He was regular Army and had joined shortly after high school. His family didn't have money, and Idris could see where his future was headed. He would more than likely end up like his brothers, a member of the UBN, 'United Blood Nation,' or, simply put, the Bloods. His oldest brother Willie had been killed outside their apartment on Spruce Street. Idris had been playing ball with Willie when a carload of Trinnies pulled up and open fired. He watched his big brother die that night, then forced himself to turn his head in the days that followed. He pretended he couldn't see the dark crimson trail that had stained the pavement so thoroughly, not even the hard Newark rains could wash them away. He avoided that stretch of asphalt like the plague, and even changed the route he walked to school. It was that summer when Idris vowed, he would never join a gang. And even if it took him the rest of his life, he would find a way out of Newark.

It hadn't taken quite that long. Although Idris hadn't been a great student, he had managed to graduate high school. And from there, he found the easiest way to be all that he could be, with the help of Uncle Sam. It was the quickest way out of Newark, so Idris latched onto the opportunity and ran with it. He found purpose and brotherhood in the ranks, and every day away from the inner city felt like a vacation. Then the war started, and Idris' platoon was sent to the Persian Gulf.

At first glance, one might think the two an unlikely pair. Idris was a street-smart black man with a military background, while Burke was none of that. Burke, or David Burker as his government-issue would have it, grew up in the suburbs of Jersey and graduated high school with high honors. He went on to NJIT to study computers and Electrical Engineering but quit after one semester when he was offered an indecent amount of money to work as a software consultant. So, he put the college education on hold and was wise to do so. Burke was the type of guy who studied physics and practiced differential equations just for the fun of it. And that caught Idris' attention almost immediately. He admired how analytical and intelligent Burke was. Moreso, it was Burke's electrical background that sealed the deal. Idris had worked as an electrician for Uncle Sam with the 101st in Bagdad, back in '92.

They had become unlikely friends, but friends nonetheless. After their initial introduction, they were inseparable and did nearly everything together. They took their first steps toward freedom together, their first breaths of fresh air, their first look at the city, and had taken their first bus ride in years. Previous transit experiences had been different for both men, with the added luxury of handcuffs, leg shackles, and full-on strip searches—nuts and butts, as they say. But the first time they stepped on the 24 after being away for so long was more than just surreal; it was eclipsing.

"I can't believe we're really doing this." Burke said, wide-eyed as his hands white-knuckled the seat in front of him. The 24 lurched ahead, making sure to hit every pothole on Frelinghuysen Avenue.

"Bro," Idris managed. "I feel like I am about to pass out." He could feel the confines of the bus tightening around his throat. A Siberian sweat broke out on his forehead and ran down his temples. He was acutely aware of the people surrounding them; they filled the seats, they packed the aisles, they even stood in the rear doorway of the coffin-tight confines of the suffocating death trap.

"Well, you look like you're handling it pretty well," Burke stated.

Idris was glad to hear he didn't look like he was about to jump out of his seat and scream *Get me the fuck out of here!* The bus came to a grinding halt at the corner of Broad and Market, and Idris nearly knocked Burke over as he scrambled for daylight. The men stepped into the crisp January air, relieved and revived. The intense sense of dread was lifted; they had been deposited in Eden. Idris wanted to kiss the pavement, then thought better.

The fresh waft of blunts being passed sauntered down Broad Street and smacked the men in the face like a warm slice of pizza. It coalesced with the sour stench of garbage mixed with despair, Nutella, and urine. Idris and Burke exchanged an awkward glance that asked, *Are we really here?* Neither man could accept the possibility.

"Let's face it," Idris yucked. "If Newark needed an enema, they would stick it at Broad and Market." It was one of the places in the city where you could get into any type of trouble you wanted. You could find anything you were looking for and catch seven different strains of herpes, all before seven a.m. But for Idris and Burke, it was paradise, a rite of passage, and the first taste of freedom they had seen in far too long. But that sense of wonder and awe was short-lived. It was replaced by a more terrifying sensation than either man had ever experienced in the prison system.

It was January, a cold, wet, and grey one at that. They made their way up Market toward the college. A freezing rain had just begun to fall. Then they heard it—the distinct sound of something barking in a most inhumane way. It grew louder and louder, echoing off the sides of the buildings and ponging off the street. Finally, the disturbance revealed itself ... and it was headed right for them. The woman charged them with wild determination. Her feet were bare; Burke wondered how she could handle the frozen concrete without even a pair of socks. Tears streamed down her face, long strands of snot hung from her chin, and she continued to bark and cry simultaneously. She was naked except for the rain-slicked plastic trash bag she used to cover her torso. She was sick ... she was obviously sick. Idris thought she might be going through withdrawals but realized there was something far worse going on with the girl. She coughed, then wheezed, and continued to bark. Instinctively, the men backed away as the woman approached and badgered them for money. Then, just as quickly as she had come, she left, running down the street coughing and barking like a sick animal. They were more than relieved when she turned the corner and disappeared. The vision of the shivering woman, however, donned in nothing but a piece of plastic, snot rockets clinging to her cold chin, stayed with them much longer.

As unnerved as they had been that day, it was nothing compared to the way they felt the afternoon of March 16th. Idris wanted to stop at the Dollar General to grab a few things: a roll of tums, a four-pack of double As, and a Kit Kat for the ride. They entered the store to find the line at the register zigzagging through the gift card aisle and extending well into the household supplies. Only the cleaning products were gone. The Lysol, the disinfectants, the Clorox, the Mr. Clean had all been scavenged and snatched up. The frightened faces of the people in line watched the men as they entered.

"What the fuck?" Idris hissed

Then they noticed that the shopping carts and the hand carriers of those in line were all filled with sanitizing products. One woman had liberated the entire supply of Clorox wipes; nearly twenty-five of the sleek containers were packed into her cart. Burke and Idris exchanged a troubled look. The place was electric; the people in the store were scared. It was in the air, dank and sour as if it were oozing from their pores. It reminded Idris of that first day on the bus. The walls of the store seemed to close in around him, the place suddenly felt claustrophobic and confined. His chest tightened, and he found it hard to breathe. They rushed out of the Dollar General and made their way to the corner of Broad and Market, possibly for the last time.

"I don't think we should go back, dude," Idris insisted, positive that returning to the halfway house was a bad idea. Still, he couldn't stop his feet as they propelled him closer to the corner and further from freedom. "I think if we go back, we'll never get out again."

"Don't get freaked out," Burke tried to assure him. "This is just a bunch of fear-mongering and sensationalized hysteria. Don't give in to it."

Idris tried to convince himself that his friend was right. The news was making a big deal out of nothing. Even if there was a problem in China, there was no way anything like that could happen here. This was America, after all. He told himself he would be back in school in a week or two.

Idris had first-hand knowledge of that gung-ho America bullshit. He had volunteered and served his country, and then his entire platoon had been hit with the gas in Anbar. He had the scars on his lungs to prove it. Sure, Uncle Sam was happy to send him to the finest Army doctors who were willing to dole out the scripts. Oxy, Morphine, and a shopping list of other meds became his daily ritual. Just enough to numb the pain, but not enough to erase the memory of his discharge. Although it had been honorable, it was still a bitter pill to swallow. They had sent him home with a 'Thank you for serving' and the promise of monthly checks. But the money had been a curse with the giant monkey he carried on his back after the war. Idris discovered the combination of opiates, idle time, and excessive disposable cash was the perfect recipe for disaster. It wasn't long before he found himself where he vowed he would never be—sitting in a trap house buying eight balls from a couple of his late brother's compadres. That's when the cops busted down the door and slapped the cuffs on him. Idris was suddenly looking at ten years for distribution. He would never forget what the judge had said the day of sentencing: "Mr. Odom, I don't care what your military record says, I see a street-level gang member in my courtroom, and I don't like gang members." It didn't matter that Idris had fought in the Gulf, and it didn't matter that he had been wounded in the line of duty. The judge might have said that he saw a gang member, but that wasn't what he meant. What the judge saw was a black man, and he didn't like black men.

∞

Idris and Burke boarded the bus and every terror-filled eye honed-in on them like lasers. The passengers studied to discern if the new arrivals were sick, if they were about to start coughing, or wheezing, or God forbid, something more inhuman, like barking. When neither showed any symptoms, the other occupants relaxed slightly. However, their gaze continued to sear into the men like contrails. The bus pulled away, leaving Broad and Market behind them. Idris wondered if he would ever see it again.

At Court Street, two men boarded and made their way to the back. Everyone watched as they stumbled down the aisle, barely lifting their feet, eyes glazed and focused on nothing, with the glisten of sweat clinging to their foreheads. Something wasn't right. The larger of the two took his seat, then started to cough. There was a mass exodus of movement as the populous pushed their way to the front exit. The man hacked and cleared his throat. Idris imagined he could see the atomized spit particles as they took flight and saturated the air. Then he heard the same noise he'd heard that January morning—the man coughed with such force it sounded as if he was barking. As he continued to do this, the faces of the passengers cartwheeled from fright to panic. When the bus pulled to the curb at its next stop, everyone, including Idris and Burke, Joyner-Kerseed for the door and rushed the street.

The wind whipped the men where they stood collecting themselves on Frelinghuysen Avenue. Their options were laid out before them. Continue to the

Talbot and accept whatever fate might throw at them, knowing that once they entered that gate, all decisions regarding their well-being would no longer be their own. Or they could run, turn the other way and never look back, which was hardly an option at all. Escaping from a halfway house or detention facility came with hefty repercussions once apprehended. And unless you could get to Costa Rica or Ecuador, you were gonna get caught. That would result in an additional five years added to the sentence, which wasn't something either man was willing to risk. So, they walked through the gate, past the metal detector, and took one last look at a grey, indifferent sky that neither knew would be the last they would see for a very long time.

The electronic deadbolt engaged behind them as the men entered the halfway house and checked in at main reception. Idris felt his options evaporate as Thorne, one of the supervisors, informed him that the place was officially on lockdown, and as of tomorrow, no one would be leaving the building. School was a done deal. The worst part was how Thorne delivered the message with a swagger and a smile.

"Hope you enjoyed yourselves 'cause you won't be going back any time soon." Thorne grinned, exposing one gold front tooth as he often did when enjoying himself. He was short and thin, had a definite Napoleon complex, and was the kind of guy who liked to shadowbox everywhere he went. He was known to wake men up at three in the morning for a surprise drug test and then stand behind them shadowboxing as they attempted to piss in the cup. He was more of a criminal than any of the inmates in the place and wasn't above bringing in contraband either. Nor was he above turning in someone after he made a few bucks on them. He would hand off the dope and then send one of the other supervisors over to bust the guy an hour later. And busting meant sending them back to prison.

Idris watched the man gloat and knew full well that he could lay the prick out with one punch. But he held it in, like always, weighed the consequences, and ate a giant spoonful of shit once again.

"Any idea when we'll be allowed back out of the building?" Burke butted in, knowing his friend was on edge.

"Are you deaf?" Thorne gooned. "We're on lockdown. The place is under quarantine." The words clapped louder than the sound of a cell door.

Idris and Burke instantly regretted their decision to come back. Now it was too late.

⁂

His name was Perry, a big guy who worked out a lot and liked to stay in shape. He had passed out at main reception an hour before the men returned from school. He had sludged his way to the front desk with a 106-degree fever, sweat pouring from him in glacial drifts. The staff member who drove Perry to the prison medical facility returned a couple hours later, not looking all that springtime fresh himself. But that didn't stop him from working the rest of the night or from walking into every dorm room and interacting with everyone in the place. And with that, he shared a little something special in the process. It was in the air, and now it was in the building.

It was a cascade. Three more men fell ill the next day and were rushed out of the building. The day after, it was seven. The following, it was twelve. After that, the staff started wearing masks and rubber gloves, but the residents were not allowed. Those directly exposed were moved into quarantine rooms while the rest were moved to another wing. It didn't matter; the effort was like rearranging deck chairs on the Titanic. Idris watched as the inmate population plummeted from two hundred and seventy-seven to one fifty and then to seventy-five. Men were dropping like flies, and so was the staff. Within two weeks, they were running on a skeleton crew as more and more staff members stopped showing up to work. That was when they started to plan.

"Dude," Idris whispered to Burke, with the television droning on in the day-room. The news was bleaker than bleak. "Shit's about to go south fast. I know you can feel it."

Burke nodded.

Channel 12 showed a mass grave that had been dug with bulldozers at Branchburg Park. The National Guard was burning the bodies.

Somehow, neither of them had taken ill. The radio spoke of Asymptomatic cases and immunity. As the rest of the inmate population appeared to be spreading, catching, and collapsing, somehow, they were not. For Idris, it felt like a cross between hitting the lottery and being a contestant on the absolute worst season of Survivor. At least they were still healthy, so far, and healthy enough to be ready for when the shit hit. And it was headed their way like a full-blown case of the runs.

"You think you could work your magic on that magnetic deadbolt?" Idris asked.

Burke didn't have to think twice about that one. He had been tinkering with electronics since he was seven and had built amplifiers and circuit boards in his basement for the fun of it.

"If you can keep them off my back for ten minutes, I can handle that door," he said with confidence.

There was no longer enough staff to juggle the work of operating the facility and transporting the sick. And the residents of the building had started to drop at an accelerated rate. That's when the men in Tyvek suits showed up. They removed the infirmed, carting the sick away to some undisclosed location, then would return the following day, sometimes hours later, to transport another group. Other than the full viral suits they wore, the most startling detail to the men's apparel was the side arms they carried, holstered and ready. Not even the cops in prison were allowed to carry guns. Clearly, these men didn't work for the Department of Corrections; Idris could recognize military anywhere. Then one day, just like most of the staff, they stopped showing up as well.

Before the phones stopped working, Idris managed to get through to his mother, who still lived at the Spruce Street apartment where he grew up.

"Idris," his mother said, her voice shrill and distracted. "I'm scared, baby. Mrs. Davis from upstairs ... they carried her out this morning. I think she was—"

"I know, Ma. Just hold on a little while. I'm coming to take care of you."

"No, baby," she cried. "Don't do anything foolish." There was a quick succession of muffled pops that could have been firecrackers, but Idris knew differently. "Oh no!" his mother screamed.

"Ma ... ma! What is it?" He waited for her to answer.

"There're soldiers in the street. My God, Idris, they're shooting … at the children!" There was another burst of weapons fire, then the phone went dead.

"Ma! Ma!" Idris tried to reconnect, but there was only static. The phones never came back on.

Not long after that, the radio and television stopped broadcasting. Shortly after that the power grid failed.

∞

"Where you muthafuckas at?" It was Thorne. The scream echoed through the building, followed by an explosion that rattled the paint from the walls. The red emergency lights revealed little of the man as he ran through the hallway with the shotgun in his hands.

"That was Thorne," Burke whispered from his position at the fire door. He and Idris worked together at the lock but been unable to break it. They had stayed up late after deciding that tonight was the night. Another deafening explosion shook the building. "Christ, he's got a fucking gun."

"Keep working," Idris urged. He stood up, removed the object from the wall, and placed it next to where they worked.

"There you are!" Thorne shouted.

"NO … no … no!" Someone screamed in the darkness.

The shotgun answered, silencing the cries. "I know you're out there; don't think you can hide, muthafucka!"

"Idris," Burke winced. "He's killin' them. Why the fuck is he killin' them?"

"Because he's sick," Idris answered. "Because he's got the gun and because he can. Now get that fuckin' lock open!" Idris took the object and squared off to cover his friend. He positioned the item behind him and took a breath. Thorne's shadow lurched in front of him, a red silhouette in the emergency lighting.

"Got you now," the crazed man shouted. Even in the dark, it was apparent how sick he was. The guy didn't have long. And by the looks of it, the lunatic was hell-bent on taking out every last inmate before he finally died himself.

"What gives you the right to play God?" Idris asked. The magnetic latch clicked behind him. "You can just let us walk out that door. You don't have to do this."

"No can do, asshole." Thorne hacked, and Idris watched the gun tremble in his hands. "No piece of shit inmate is walking out of here. My son!" he screamed. "They took my son. I couldn't even bury him. They took him, and they burned him." The man choked on the words. His breath hitched and then strangled him. "You ain't going nowhere, scumbag." Thorne raised the gun level with Idris's head and started to cough. He hacked with such violent force that it sounded like he was barking. Then he doubled over and lowered the weapon.

Idris lifted the fire extinguisher he had set behind him and threw it at the man. It collided with Thorne's chest and sent him flailing backward. It was all they needed. Burke and Idris bolted out the door and were on Frelinghuysen Avenue before Thorne could scramble to his feet.

The streetlights had gone out, and the buildings were dark. Wrecked vehicles had been left in the middle of the street; a National Guard truck had collided with a bus—it was the 24. Idris and Burke ran like their heads were on fire, in no particular direction but knowing exactly where they were headed just the same. More wrecks littered the road. Bodies carpeted the sidewalks and streets, left where they had collapsed. No one had been around to move them. The masks and scarves the population had used to protect themselves from the deadly contagion covered the pavement like mementos to mankind's final stand. The useless items had been discarded along with the hope that this virus was just another plague. It was the plague to end all others ... the final one.

The men were crossing Court Street when they first smelled it, the thick dark stench of smoke and something else. It hung in the air like a question mark. They were alerted to the rattle of gunfire from somewhere nearby. But it was impossible to tell where it had come from. And although they didn't see a soul on the abandoned street, they knew there were still people out there, some very desperate people by the sound of it. The men found themselves at the corner of Broad and Market and finally stopped to catch their breath. Idris spun around and took it in. Despite the lesions that had been left on his lungs from his time in Iraq and the presence of the smoke that filled the air, he found it easy to breathe. Surprisingly easy.

The glow of random fires flickered in the windows of several buildings. The glass panes of most of the shops had been shattered, and debris littered the road.

Random papers mixed with currency wisped across the pavement and caught at their feet. Idris looked down at the hundred-dollar bills that had been thrown away like garbage. The pizza place had burned down completely. A Fed Ex truck stuck halfway out of the McDonald's. And the Citi Bank looked as if it had exploded onto the street.

"What the hell happened?" Burke managed to say.

"It was worse than everyone thought," Idris answered. "A whole lot worse."

The wind shifted, sending a thick waft of charnel cinders across Market Street. A deep glow illuminated the distance; it looked like the Prudential Center was ablaze. Idris looked up Broad Street to where the sick woman had intercepted them. She had been wearing nothing but a plastic bag. Hard to believe only a few months had passed since that day; it felt like years. Idris jumped when Burke coughed behind him. He turned to find his friend doubled over, hacking violently and expelling such a horrendous fit it sounded as if he were barking. Idris recognized that sound. Unfortunately, so did Burke. They stared at each other, and silence fell between them.

How long? Idris wondered. Judging by how fast it had come up on Burke, he guessed not very long at all. Then it would be his turn. There was no way to avoid it. It wasn't like he could outrun the wind. There was something in the air.

Seven

THE OVERBROOK

In 1896 construction began on the Essex County Asylum for the Insane, which would later come to be known as the Overbrook. Local residents referred to the labyrinthine complex as 'The Bin'. The facility was situated on 365 remote acres high above the Peckman River. The mountain top facility was so expansive it was equipped with its own train station, power plant, farm, and fire department. Over a dozen buildings were connected by a subterranean tunnel system that spanned the property. Originally created as a rehabilitation hospital for the mentally ill, the Overbrook proved to be anything but.

During the Great Depression the Overbrook was hit with a staggering influx of homeless refugees seeking shelter. The overcrowded hospital found it impossible to feed the massive population. Then after World War II the Asylum was again filled to capacity (over 3000) with soldiers suffering from shellshock, of which the facility was ill prepared to deal with. One of the more publicized tragedies to take place at the Overbrook happened in December of 1917 when a set of the hospital's boilers broke down, resulting in a collapse of the facilities heating and lighting system. The tragic event occurred during a record cold stretch and the asylum was without power for over a month. Numerous deaths were reported. Throughout the lifespan of this house of suffering, the Bin was responsible for countless cases of neglect, abuse, starvation, escapes, and suicide. Over ten thousand patients died while under the care of the staff at the Overbrook.

Most of the complex was shut down in the late sixties and early seventies when miracle drugs were invented to help patients dealing with mental illness. The massive structure was abandoned and left to rot at the top of the mountain for decades afterwards. But the memory of the pain was left behind.

The empty husks of the old hospital buildings were never entirely empty, at least that's what the rumors would have you believe. Stories of troubled spirits that still roamed the halls of the Overbrook spread quickly throughout the neighboring counties. Escaped lunatics and wayward gangs were also reported to reside on the property. Given the dark history of the facility and the added allure of the growing urban legends, the Overbrook Asylum became a rite of passage for eager teens. All you had to do was walk through the place at night to prove your mettle, that was, if you had the guts.

By the time I heard of the Overbrook, the place was falling apart. The windows were broken, the brickwork was cracked and crumbled, and graffiti covered every inch of the decaying structure. There were gurneys and wheelchairs still left in the hallways, broken beer bottles and every kind of vandalism. One would also see discarded rubbers, and the occasionally pair of tossed panties. Files, left behind by the staff had been thrown about and littered the floor. Some of which had been collected and used as kindling to start various fires.

It had been a Friday night. George, Jim, Keith, and I decided to make the trip to the Overbrook, probably a little later in the day than we would have liked. I remember the sun being bright as we made our way up the treacherous abandoned stretch of blacktop, but it was sinking fast. Everyone knew we would be headed back down the mountain in the dark. But for some reason, none of us gave that much thought.

We crested the hill and there it was, standing before us in the distance, the Overbrook Asylum. The main building, the heart of the beast, waited like a sleeping viper ready to strike. I felt it right away ... more than just paranoia, there was a presence. An inescapable sense of anxiety gripped me; I couldn't shake the feeling that we weren't alone. Someone or something was watching us. I did my best to suppress the emotion. But looking back, I wish I had listened to my instincts. Unfortunately, foolishness and youth are synonymous.

Anyway, we had brought our own liquid courage, Bud Lite bottles to be exact. And being almost twenty-one and full of misdirected testosterone, we thought we were hot shit and didn't listen to silly things like gut instincts. We made our way through the front entrance, clowning around, and showing as much bravado as we could muster ... even if it were all just an act. We found our way to the second floor and began searching the rooms until we stumbled upon a rather large area. Something about the oversized hospital room called to us. What was so alluring about this one I have no idea. Perhaps it was the wide sitting area or the access panel in the ceiling with the missing door.

I watched as the rest of my friends entered the room one by one, then I chugged the last of my beer and pitched it down the hall. I heard it bounce once, and then twice, all hollow and clangy and waited for the glass to finally shatter. Only it never did. The empty beer bottle continued to bounce and roll down the empty hall till it came to a rest and remained silent. I didn't think anything of it, nor did I suspect that I had any reason to. So, I followed my friends and joined them inside the empty hospital room.

We stayed in there for a little while, maybe a half hour or so, smoking cigarettes and probably something else. We all had a pretty good buzz going by this point, but even that was unable to mask a far more unnerving sensation that had found its way into the room. We all felt it. An icy chill permeated the very air around us. It was accompanied by one unshakable thought ... something was very wrong.

The sun had gone down, and it was much darker than any of us were comfortable with. Fortunately, we had brought flashlights, but the weak beams did little to dispel the encroaching shadows and the feeling of impending doom. We cast the lights in every direction, praying to God that nothing would be revealed. Still, there was no ignoring it. Something was there with us, if not in the room, then very close by. There was no need to even discuss it, we all knew we had overstayed our welcome at the Overbrook. And that was more than enough to get our asses moving.

I stepped into the hallway and aimed my flashlight in the direction from which we had come. Then I looked down at my feet. My heart couldn't decide if it wanted to explode out of my chest or stop beating completely. The urgency to run gripped me like a clenched fist, but somehow, I managed to remain where I stood, staring down at the impossible.

I had been the last guy to enter the room, the only one who had a beer left. And I had thrown the empty bottle down the hall; had heard it clang but never break as it rolled out of sight into the darkness.

But ... there it was. Sitting at my feet, just to the side of the doorway, upside down with a small puddle around it. My empty beer bottle, the one I had thrown, was sitting next to the door, balanced on its one-inch mouthpiece. Surrounding it in a tight concentric ring was a small puddle of beer suds. Somehow, my bottle had found its way back to the very spot from where I had thrown it, exactly where I now stood. Someone had carefully placed it upside down.

My friends filed out of the room and stared down at the bottle centered in the beam of my flashlight. No one spoke for a what felt like a very long time, although I imagine it was only a few stagnated seconds. There was no explaining what lay before us, other than someone or something had moved the bottle while we were preoccupied inside the room. Whatever had done it hadn't made a sound. And that only meant one thing; we were not alone in the Overbrook.

The guys accused me of playing a joke on them. I wished that were the case, but the truth of the matter was, I had no idea how the bottle had gotten there. Actually, I could imagine a very terrifying scenario, but it wasn't anything I wanted to say out loud, not while we were still inside the building. We started walking, rather quickly toward the front entrance. We made our way through the dark hallways, past the abandoned rooms to the staircase in the main foyer. I know I wasn't the only one looking over his shoulder every step of the way. And I know I wasn't the only man who felt like something was watching us as we took our leave of the abandoned hospital. And although I can only speak for myself, I'm willing to bet that out of the four friends that stepped into the Overbrook Asylum that night, not a damn one of us ever stepped foot in that place again.

The Overbrook Asylum has since been torn down. But there have been countless stories told by adventurous teens who dared to walk the abandoned halls of the Bin. Stories that cannot be easily explained and are sure to set the gooseflesh rippling down the nape of your neck. I can say this about the Overbrook Asylum, there was more at play that night than the overworked imagination of a few guys who had no business being there. Something moved that bottle, and to this day, I have no idea what that something was. Homeless vagrants or some other kids messing with us, that is certainly a possibility. Ghosts ... restless spirits? Surely there is no such thing ... right? To tell you the truth, I'm not so sure about that. If there ever was a place that had every right to be haunted it was the Overbrook.

Eight

DEVLIN'S MANSE

Profound sorrow is all-encompassing; it has a way of permeating and taking on a life of its own. It thrives, like a mold, in the darkest corners of the heart. Tragedy has a memory that cannot be purged by time. Although it can be displaced for a moment, it is never entirely forgotten. There is always a residue that lingers, like a bloodstain on the carpet, or the scar left from a wound. This is not only true with people, but for houses as well. The din of sadness can never be completely hushed in dwellings that have witnessed such atrocities. Although the presence of children can pacify the pain, for a moment ... there is always a residue.

Devlin's Manse remained vacant for a lifetime. It's dark walnut floorboards, ornate twelve-foot ceilings, and elaborate cherry wood mouldings spoke of a pride in architecture long since forgotten. The three-story Victorian design, popular during the 19th century, stood sentinel over 1500 acres of real estate. Rice and tobacco were the till of the land around the time, James "Old Buck" Buchannan was taking office. It had been decades since voices graced the halls of Devlin's Manse. Longer still since the resonating echo of children's laughter had danced upon its walls. But now ... something was stirring.

"Try to find me, James," the voice of a young girl drifted from behind a second-floor closet door. She pressed her face against the cracked opening to scan the room. The dresser, the chest of drawers, and the large four-poster bed remained undisturbed. Mary listened as the sound of approaching foot falls drew near, she retreated to the back of her hide-a-way, nestled between the old coats.

"Mary, where are you?" The boy rushed into the room, dropped to the floor, and pushed the duvet aside to search beneath the bed. An army of dust bunnies was all he found. Listening, he rose to his feet and noticed the door to the closet.

He prepared to make his way toward it and was alerted by the muted sound of stifled laughter. It crept from the confines of the closet and greeted him where he stood. Quietly, he tiptoed across the floor and placed his hand on the knob. He held his breath and yanked the door open in one fluid motion.

"I've got you!" he shouted.

Mary screamed, but the look on her face was pure delight. "Oh James, you cheated!"

"No," he said. "I heard you laughing all the way downstairs."

Mary darted from the closet and took a running leap onto the bed; the thick comforter and array of goose-down pillows nearly swallowed the girl's small frame. "Don't you just love our new house?"

James followed her lead and dove headfirst after her. Rising to his feet he proceeded to jump in place. The tired old springs launched him higher with each pounce, but never came close to propelling the boy to his target of the ceiling. "What do you think?" he replied with a grin.

Mary crinkled her brow. "I think you shouldn't have your dirty shoes on the bed. That's what I think."

James took one final leap at the ceiling then fell onto his back. "Yes, Mom!" He let out a dramatic exhale.

Smiling, Mary leaned over and pecked him on the cheek. "You're it!" she cried, then leapt from the bed and darted out of the room.

"Ewww!" James wiped the kiss from his cheek. "Disgusting." He rolled from his position and took off in pursuit after her.

The room, silent once again, held onto the image like a photograph. The imprint on the bedspread remained for a moment ... if only for a moment. Then the open closet door let out a tired creak, and slowly swung shut.

The lush front lawn of Devlin's Manse sprawled for acres and reflected the care and time the new residents had invested in taking back the property from the grips of neglect. Magnolia trees adorned the grounds with a wooden swing suspended from the lower branch of one of the specimens. James pushed Mary while dappled sunlight played across her face as she arced back and forth.

"Higher," she called to the boy, who was more than happy to oblige and answered with another hearty push.

The scent of sweet magnolia blossoms filled the air. Although the trees were in full bloom, many discarded flowers littered the lawn, no doubt recent victims of the strong coastal southern breeze. Before taking flight on the swing, Mary had chosen the perfect bloom and tucked it delicately behind her right ear. The white pink of its petals danced like a flickering ember against the trailing flame of her long red hair.

"Higher, James. Higher," she called again.

"Aren't you tired yet?" he asked.

"No, but it's your turn. We can switch."

James allowed the swing's momentum to slow and then come to a halt. He grabbed the rope and helped Mary off.

"Hop on," she offered.

"That's all right," he replied, then took a seat in the shade with his back against the large tree. Mary sat next to him and lifted another blossom from the ground.

"Isn't it just perfect?" she asked, looking up at the house.

The once forgotten Manse stood before them in all its glory, revealing not even a glimmer of the years of disregard. The peeling paint, the rotting wood, all given a reprieve. Once broken windowpanes now refracted the noonday sun and suggested that the estate was healthy once again ... or perhaps, only in remission.

Mary twirled the flower within her fingertips and allowed her gaze to follow the large pillars that supported the second-floor balcony, and then up the front of the dwelling to the smaller third story windows. It happened in a flurry, one of the curtains was momentarily pushed aside and then returned to its position.

"Did you see that?" She jumped to her feet, dropping the blossom.

"See what?" James looked up puzzled.

"At the window upstairs!" she shouted. "There's someone up there. I saw it!"

"What are you talking about?" he asked. "There's no one up there."

"No, James. I saw it." Her voice rose to a shrill. "The curtain moved. I saw it!"

"Well," he said, rising to his feet. "Let's go see then. But I'm telling you. There's nobody up there." James made his way across the lawn toward the house and Mary reluctantly followed.

⌘

The stairwell to the third floor was perhaps the one place overlooked during the renovations. The wide walnut risers cantered slightly to the left as if the house had settled askew. The faded yellow wallpaper had peeled from the walls and given way to large cracks. In several places the plaster itself had fallen off, leaving only exposed lathe behind. The light switch did nothing when James tried it; the cobweb encrusted sconces remained dark. Minimal light escaped from the crack beneath the bedroom door at the top of the stairs, bathing the area in near twilight.

"I'm scared," Mary said as she crouched behind James.

"Don't be afraid. It's nothing," he reassured her. "You trust me, don't you?"

"You know I do. But I'm telling you, I saw something."

The stairs creaked and groaned as if they had not borne weight in far too long. Step by step, they made their way to the top, stealthily inching their way to the threshold. When he was within reach, James extended his hand to grasp the knob and then hesitated.

For a moment, the idea that Mary had seen something struck him as possible, and then he was sure of it. Something was lying in wait for them on the other side of the door, something that meant them grave harm.

He laughed at his foolishness, then grabbed the knob.

An icy cold shock seized his hand and froze it from the fingertips to elbow. He released his grasp at once and tucked his hand in the crook of his arm.

"What's wrong?" Mary gasped.

"It's ... it's cold." Confusion washed across his face.

He removed his hand from under his arm and examined it for a moment, it was fine. He reached for the knob again, but Mary pulled him back, nearly sending them both tumbling down the stairs.

"It's okay," he said. "It just surprised me, that's all."

His voice wavered as if he wasn't convinced, but Mary allowed him to continue and James touched the knob with his fingertips, then took it in his grip.

"Mary, the knob is freezing ... like ice." He tried to turn it to the right and then left but it would not so much as jiggle in the jamb. He let go and turned to her. "You feel it."

"I don't want to. Let's go, James. I'm scared."

"It's all right. It's just c—" But Mary had already descended the stairs and entered the hallway.

He tried the knob again, but it wouldn't budge. He pressed his shoulder against the door to find it just as cold as the knob. After a moment of futility, he gave up the attempt, and descended the stairs after her.

Evening floated in as if on gossamer wings. The sweet fragrance of Jasmine and Magnolia filled the air as the last streaks of violet gave way to even deeper shades of indigo. Fireflies rehearsed their ritualistic dance of light, as a chorus of crickets provided the soundtrack. Mary and James sat on the front porch of Devlin's Manse, soaking in the scents and sounds of summer.

"Are you mad at me?" she asked, her long nightgown hanging to her bare feet.

"Don't be silly. Why would I be mad at you?"

"I got scared and left you," she said, still shaken by the afternoon's events. "What if you..." Her voice wavered on the verge of tears.

"Hey, nothing happened, silly. I told you it would be okay." He reassured her. Although he wasn't convinced it had been entirely 'nothing,' he attempted to sound brave.

"I saw something," she repeated

"There's probably a draft up there that blew the curtains. That's why it's cold."

"James," her voice nearly drowned by a cacophony of crickets. "It's August."

After an uncomfortable pause, he leaned against her, shoulder to shoulder. "Hey, I don't know, but I'm sure there's a good reason," he waited a moment, then added, "and I'm going to find out."

"Let's just leave it alone, I don't want to get in trouble."

His dark eyes looked into her green as the first stars arrived in the August sky.

"We're gonna be fine," he replied.

"Do you promise?"

"I promise."

"Okay, but I don't want to go up there again."

"You won't have to." He reached to grasp at a firefly that was too quick, and easily slipped through his fingers.

∞

Morning sunlight, filtered through linen window treatments, cast the sitting room in a dusty mellow glow. Dapples of amber diamonds reflected off the large chandelier suspended in the center of the ceiling while Mary sat at a small table set for a tea party of three: herself, an oversized teddy bear, and her baby doll, who lay tucked within her arms. She was hardly aware of the far-off voices of the grownups as she focused her attention on her baby, doting on his every need.

"That's my boy," she said. "I love you, Christopher."

Mary pretended to feed the little one his morning bottle while teddy sat watch with a dainty cup of faux tea set on the table in front of him. The distant sound of hammers and saws lofted in from somewhere in the house but were unnoticed as Mary allowed herself to be as lost as only a child could be, forever frozen in playtime. Thoughts of yesterday's fright had been set aside as if they had never happened. Mary raised the doll to her shoulder and pretended to burp him.

"Momma loves you so much," she beamed, a smile of pure joy spread across her face.

∞

While Mary was submerged in teatime, James focused on a mission of his own. The basement of Devlin's Manse was dank and musty; a combination of scents filled the air: pickled fruit and dried meat mixed with mold, decay, and the dust of a thousand years. In the furthest corner from the stairs where James stood, sat a stack of old tables and chairs, covered in filth. A clutch of wooden boxes occupied the opposite corner and appeared to wear an equal amount of time and grime. Neither of which were the focus of his mission; what James was after lay under the stairs. He lit the candle he had taken from the kitchen cupboard and navigated his way through the dark.

Tiny creatures scurried back into their holes, and large black spiders curiously watched their new visitor. James was oblivious to his audience and to the sounds of construction from above. He made his way to the alcove beneath the stairs and halted when his foot struck something big and heavy. He directed the candlelight onto the object he had stumble upon and discovered a large chest. An ancient padlock adorned the front, holding the lid and the contents in place. He fumbled with it for a moment. It was a thick key-lock, caked in rust. On the very top of the chest set into the wood sat a rectangular piece of metal with an engraving on it. He wiped the dust away with his palm and revealed one word, the name 'JED' spelled out on the plaque. James tugged at the lock and wondered who Jed might be. He imagined one of the previous occupants who had left the chest behind. And despite his best effort he was unable to pry the lock open, which was fine, he had come to the basement in search of one key; now he would need to find two.

He raised the candle to the wall above the chest and slowly moved it to the right until the light revealed a masonry nail that had been driven into the wall. No key hung from the first nail, and he continued to search the darkness. There was no key to be found on the second nail he came across, or the third, and James's heart fluttered quick within his chest. He had been sure he would find what he was looking for. *They were down here.* He thought.

Creeping shadows suffocated the candle's reach like a wet blanket, sweat glistened on his brow despite the basement's sudden chill, and gooseflesh broke out on his arms and the nape of his neck. James found it increasingly difficult to swallow and anxiety quickly escalated into panic. A thought flashed in his head, *please don't let me find it.* He was overcome by the agonizing feeling that locating the key would be a very bad thing. He held the candle closer to the wall and revealed the fourth nail as a foggy plume of breath escaped into the icy air.

He was relieved for a fleeting moment, then a soft rustle and the sensation of movement jarred him back. James had no idea if the noise had come from across the room or right behind him. His frozen heart entered his throat and stagnated. Unable to move a muscle, he listened, then he heard it ... *thump!* It was followed by another, and then another.

James nearly screamed, then realized it was the thrum of his own pulse. Still, he waited, anticipating the repeat of the rustle, and half expecting something to seize him in the darkness. When neither happened, he wrestled the last vestige of his courage and extended the candle further into the dim. The umbra reluctantly retreated as the light fell across the stone, revealing the fifth and final nail. A single brass key reflected the flame like a lighthouse beacon. *Death lies upon these rocks.* Every nerve in the boy's body screamed for him to leave, to forget the key and abandon his search. *Whatever you do, don't touch it.* James stared at it, hypnotized by the dancing image of the candle on its shiny surface.

Last chance, boy; leave now while you still can. A voice that sounded exactly like his own, beckoned from somewhere in the dark. James let out a strangled cry, spun about on his heels and ran like a banshee up the old wooden staircase. Slamming the door behind him, he checked the lock and then made his way to the kitchen; he returned the candle to the cupboard and set off to find Mary. He made his way to the sitting room where he knew he would find her and tried his best to push all thoughts of the cold dark basement to the side. At least, that's what he should have done. Unfortunately, it was too late for that, and James remained where he was, reached out his hand, and took hold of the key.

A sharpened spike of pain penetrated his head like an ice pick; a concentrated pressure behind his eyes caused them to water and blur. The internal sound of muted jackhammers filled his ears and made him sick. *It must be the mold*, he thought, then shoved the key in his front pocket and made his way to the stairs. The fresh air from the first floor greeted him and helped clear his head slightly. James closed the door behind him and forced the experience to the back of his mind; forgotten was the fear, the sensation, and the voice. Not only this, but also forgotten, was any thought about the chest.

"Rock a bye baby, on the treetop," Mary sang to her doll. With just a hint of a tear in her eye, she pretended it was Christopher's nap time as she rocked him to sleep.

"When the wind blows, the cradle will rock." Her mind wandered to a vision of a time when she might rock her own child to sleep.

"When the bough breaks..." She held Christopher tighter, as James closed the basement door.

"The cradle will fall." Mary snuggled the doll and inhaled deeply, reminded of a smell that could only be baby, the scent of the skin, the warmth of the body.

"And down will come baby…" The tears welled up in the corners of her eyes.

"Cradle and all." The crystals in the chandelier began to chime as they lightly started to sway and strike against one another. The China cups and saucers shimmied across the table and teddy was thrown from his chair. His lifeless eyes gazed up accusingly at Mary. She drew the doll closer and shot to her feet, tipping her own chair in the process. Then the house started to shake on its foundation; the thunderous crash of heaving timbers sounded as if the place were being ripped apart. Suddenly, the China was thrown from the table and smashed against the wall. Tiny shards rained down on Mary and caught in her hair.

She screamed and pulled the baby in with a life-or-death grip. A moment later James exploded into the room, rushed to her side, and took her in his arms. The tremors continued for a moment longer, then subsided. The chandelier and its many crystals continued to pendulum, emitting a sickly-sweet calliope reverberance.

"Shh, it's alright," he tried to comfort her. "It's over now."

The room slowly settled, and the uproar was replaced by silence. Fine plaster particles, drifted in the air and gave the sunlight a faded feel. Mary continued to sob, James remained holding her, and Teddy closed his reproachful eyes.

The seismic anomaly that interrupted Mary's lullaby had been isolated to Devlin's Manse. The stairwell leading to the third floor had taken the brunt of the damage. The already cantered stairs now listed hard to port. Large fractures were evident in all the walls, and chunks of plaster littered the landings. The ceiling bowed and threatened to give way at any moment. The door to the bedroom was buckled in its frame; frigid air escaped from beneath the threshold and through the keyhole. But, this too, was forgotten.

Childhood solely has the unique and uncanny ability to distort time. The clock holds no dominion over this phase of life. It is childhood that is the master, and in command of either passing the summer in the blink of an eye or allowing a cold rainy morning to last an eternity. It freezes or it burns, it stands still, or it flies by, there is no in-between for children. In the end, however it is perceived, it is only missed when it is gone ... like childhood itself.

∞

The morning sun gave way to afternoon showers. Low lying storm clouds rolled in off the Atlantic coast and blanketed the state. Periods of thunder and lightning sporadically occupied most of the day. It blocked out much of the ambient noise within the house and the constant drumming of the overflowing gutters was both disturbing and hypnotic.

Devlin's Manse had grown dark and cold. A chill had invaded like a predator and now had a strong foothold on the estate. Mary lay in bed with a thick blanket wrapped around both her and the doll.

The pain in James's head had returned with a vengeance, the ache in his temples and behind his eyes had intensified to a throbbing roar; he found it impossible to think. The constant throng of the rain made him nauseous. He had just closed his eyes and started to drift off from his position in the large armchair, when he smelled it.

At first, the faint aroma of burning wood; the distant smokey taste of hickory touched his senses, but he barely registered it. Then, it slowly increased and intensified; it crept up and overwhelmed him.

James coughed from somewhere in the fog of dreamland as his lungs filled with choking black smoke. He finally opened his eyes and was blinded. The room was a dark grey cloud. The house was on fire. Raking in a deep lungful of toxic smoke, he violently retched and fell to the floor. He struggled and clawed his way to the bed where Mary lay.

"Mary," he croaked, his voice barely registered a whisper.

Sirens assaulted his ears as hammers sounded at his temples. Outside, the rain beat relentlessly against the windows. From somewhere came the high-pitched sound of crying.

Mary's crying. He thought for a moment. But that wasn't exactly right. The crying wasn't coming from in the room, it was coming from inside his head. It wasn't Mary's voice either, it was the tormented wail of an infant.

I'm dying. He thought, as darkness overtook him. His final reflection, *I have to save the baby.*

∞

The world was eclipsed; it floated on a shroud of shadows, deafeningly silent, glaringly dark, and sweetly bitter. It lumbered along on a dead slack tide, then was violently wrenched back by the suffocating rip. All the while, the rain continued, and Devlin's Manse retreated like a sleeping viper.

First, there was a push, then a tug, and then a shake.

"James, wake up."

James woke to find himself face down on the floor with Mary standing over him. "Wake up, wake up!" she yelled and shook him even harder.

"James, WAKE UP!"

Soupy disorientation impeded his perception. He struggled to hold onto the memory, aware for a moment of sound, and then movement; he recalled the smell of smoke, and then remembered the...

"fire" the words were barely audible.

He stirred, opened his eyes, then rolled onto his side and coughed uncontrollably.

"James." Mary tapped him on the back.

After a long while the fit passed, and the fog in his head dissipated. Alarmed and confused, he looked around and attempted to pinpoint the source of the blaze, only to find the room clear and cold. The marching band between his ears continued its assault, assisted by the oppressive sound of the rain, and the taste of burnt wood filled his mouth and sinuses.

"Fire," he gasped.

"James, what happened? Are you alright?" Mary asked, helping him to sit up.

He scanned the room again and found no sign of smoke, although he could smell it on his clothes and taste it on his lips. "The house was on fire," he said. "The room was filled with smoke."

"You must have been dreaming. I was right here, there wasn't any fire. Did you fall or something? You don't look good at all."

"I don't feel so well," he said, rubbing his head. "It was so real. The baby!"

They both turned their heads to the doll in Mary's arms.

"You better lay down. I'll make you some tea." She helped him to his feet and walked him over to the bed.

"Mary, there was smoke everywhere. I can still taste it and I heard a baby," he said as she touched her hand to his forehead.

"James, you're ice cold." She helped him onto his back and looked at the doll. "Let's go make some tea, Christopher," she cooed, then exited the room. Behind her, the cohesion of reality sloughed away, and the silent house began to stir, once again.

James moaned faintly as Mary entered the hallway. The lucidity of the vision was overpowering, and he succumbed to it completely. He dreamt of darkened tunnels and torches, catacombs and chains, ancient secrets, and pain. There was a baby; there was none. He dreamt of hidden doors, unthinkable acts of cruelty, of a world where all was red and bitter. He dreamt of secret rooms, bookshelves, stairways, old wooden chests, and keys ... above all else, he dreamt of keys.

For a moment he was struck by the gnawing sensation that something grave had been overlooked, then in a flash, it was gone. He stirred as the thick grey smoke sifted through the cracks in the floor, seeped out of the lower portion of the walls, and covered the floor in a blanket like a London fog. It surrounded the bed as if he were lying on a cloud. In his dreams, James pushed the large object to the side and ascended the staircase. Somewhere close, was the key.

Mary opened the door and made her way to the back of the large area in search of the tea. The aroma of various spices filled the stocked pantry. Sacks of rice, flour, sorghum, and pecans lined the floor. Jars of pickled beets, beans, peaches, squash, and rhubarb filled many of the shelves; others were lined with honey, preserves, tea, coffee, and spices. Mary reached for the tea then jumped back when something small scampered across her foot. She looked down to see the field mouse as it disappeared behind one of the sacks. She laughed and regained herself.

At first, she felt more than heard, the low distant rumble of a faraway train in her belly and on her skin. Then the jars on the shelf began to shake. Suddenly, the pantry door slammed shut, and Mary was plunged into an abyss of darkness. She pulled Christopher close, and the room came to life. Glass jars exploded onto the floor as they lost their purchase upon the shelves. Grain bags erupted their contents into the air. Mary was showered by the debris and pelted by shards of broken glass.

"No!" she screamed and shielded the baby.

The world was thrown sideways then turned upside down. The combination of darkness and din dissolved the last of her resolve.

"Stop it!" Tears ran down her cheeks and fell to the floor.

Every deafening crash ripped through Mary like a seizure.

Then, the pantry door swung outward, and it was over. She slowly opened her eyes to find no debris and no sign of disaster. The pantry was empty, the shelves were covered in a thick layer of dust. Spiders stared silently back at her, and the skeletal remains of several rodents littered the floor. Mary shook uncontrollably; the room was as cold as an icebox, and she could see her breath. Outside, the rain was ceaseless ... inside, the memories came flooding back.

Mary stepped out of the pantry into the kitchen to find the cabinets gone. The table and chairs had vanished; the pots, the pans, China, and flatware, as if they never were. The room looked like it had aged a hundred years. The flooring was missing in spots, pieces of the walls had fallen and much of the ceiling had given way.

Her cries hitched in her chest and Mary began to hyperventilate. Every breath shuddered in her lungs as insanity took control. Her tears fell like the rain.

"C ... Ch ... Christoph ... er ... r." She looked down to find his porcelain face had been replaced by bone, a small infant's skull wrapped in a tattered moth-eaten blanket. Empty sockets stared blindly into nothingness, a skeletal grin frozen in time.

Mary screamed and the perimeter of her vision shifted from grey to black; she fell to the floor in the middle of the old, abandoned kitchen.

As if transported from another world, a table phased into existence. It was followed by a set of chairs that faded into view. The ceiling re-materialized, along with the walls, and then the floorboards. Cabinets suddenly hung in place; pots appeared on a wood-burning stove. Everything looked as it had once been. But somewhere in time ... a baby was crying.

∾

During the near two centuries of its existence, Devlin's Manse carried the burden of far too many secrets. For the greater part, it remained silent; however, some secrets were just too hard to stifle.

In 1827, Montgomery Devlin commissioned a team of architects to design an estate that would sit upon the family's 2000 plus, Charleston acreage. After two years of scrutiny and careful revisions, construction began in the spring of '29. Tradesmen and laborers were hired for no longer than two months, at which point they were terminated and replaced by an entirely new crew. It was Devlin's intention that no single worker would know all the secrets his estate would hold.

An elaborate tunnel system was constructed around the preexisting subterranean caverns. Dark passages, blasted out of the clay and bedrock, led from the main house throughout the property. Torches and lanterns illuminated the dark halls beneath the Manse.

The house itself was a 19th Century wonder of design. Walls that pivoted on fulcrum levers revealed hidden stairwells and secret rooms, virtually invisible to the naked eye. Faux floorboards gave way to trap doors, bookshelves could be moved to expose passageways, if one knew the exact pressure point.

Montgomery wasn't exactly a southern gentleman. He was a dark brooding, covetous man, with a flair for the macabre; however, he did have the capacity for love. He loved his nephew Edward, and he loved his privacy. And although there was never any evidence to support the accusations, it was suspected by many that Montgomery's passions were dark beyond comprehension. During his time as owner of the Manse, the city of Charleston suffered a plague like no other.

Shortly after the final nail was driven into the estate, the children of the area began to disappear in scores. Boys and girls, snatched from their beds in the middle of the night, were never to be heard from again. On more than one occasion, toys and pieces of clothing had been found near the plantation, but the constable was unable to lay the blame on old Montgomery Devlin, the man was as slippery as a snake.

But the lack of evidence didn't stop everyone, the servants who worked for Devlin had seen all they needed to reach their own verdict. The walls inside the Manse were not as thick as the bedrock tunnels that lay below. And as the first shots of the civil war were being fired at Ft. Sumter, Montgomery Devlin was dying his own agonizing death. He had been poisoned, presumably by one, if not all the servants. He convulsed on his bed for two days and in the end, turned blue, and was no more.

He was mourned only by his nephew Edward, who was eleven in 1861, and Montgomery's sole heir. Edward Devlin inherited the estate, all its responsibilities, as well as a mountain of debt. Fortunately, he didn't inherit his uncle's macabre propensity. Edward was a kind-hearted young boy, an even kinder young man, and proved to be a far savvier businessman than Montgomery ever was.

The war hit the south hard, and many of the plantations were unable to survive; however, great responsibility at an early age bred great adaptability in young Edward Devlin. As reconstruction began, he saw the potential that sharecroppers held, and he capitalized. He sold off parcels of the land piece by piece and converted the rice fields into a far more profitable crop, by planting pecan trees. He was able to overcome Montgomery's vast debt and take the family name out of the red. Unfortunately, the stain of his uncle's sins would never leave the Manse. A murky puissance would forever reside on the tainted grounds of the estate.

Devlin's Manse proved to have no love for children. Edward married Charlotte in 1870, and they were soon expecting their first child. It was a difficult pregnancy, and the baby did not survive the full term. One year later, they were expecting again. Charlotte gave birth to Allison in November '73. In February, she was found dead in her crib. Edward and Charlotte were devastated, and convinced it was their fault. In a way it was, had Edward never been born a Devlin his daughter may have survived.

Reeling from Allison's death, Charlotte withdrew, and Edward immersed himself in his duties on the plantation. By 1875, most of Montgomery's secrets had been obscured and forgotten. The labyrinth was long abandoned, most of the passageways and rooms had not been used in over a decade. Charlotte did favor one hide-a-way though, the third-floor bedroom, whose staircase was secretly hidden behind a row of bookcases on the second-floor hallway. It was accessible by depressing an exact piece of moulding at the baseboard, pulling the right side outward, and revealing the stairs to the third floor. Without knowledge of the staircase and the pressure point, the passage was undetectable. Charlotte spent most of her time in the hidden room, mourning Allison in quiet reflection.

Time slowly pacified the worst of the pain, and once again Charlotte was with child. She remained in bed on the third floor during the entire pregnancy, determined not to exert any undue stress on the baby; Edward doted on her every need. In 1879, Charlotte died in childbirth; a year later Edward died of a broken heart. Their newborn son would inherit the estate; the Manse, the land, the anguish, and the secrets ... it all belonged to Jed.

Lucidity slips, there is a bright blinding light, her vision momentarily seared out of focus. White-hot fades to dull yellow and she is looking at a summer sky with the sun shining on her face. There are people gathered nearby. She feels the presence of her family but cannot make them out until he lifts the veil.

It's her wedding day. The front lawn of the estate has been set for the occasion. The guests are seated in white chairs and her parents occupy the very first row. She stands beneath a trellis decorated with roses and magnolia blossoms and thinks, *I was happy*, then leans in to be kissed, perception slips again.

She senses the feeling of being carried weightless, blissfully in motion. Images vanish, a bookcase, the stairs, a bedroom, the chimney.

For a moment she thinks, *we have to wake up*. Then, she is back on the front lawn, she is being kissed.

"I love you, Mary," he says.

She looks into his eyes, "I love you, Jed."

The roar inside her head was deafening; hammers, pickaxes, and myriad implements of torture wicked away at her equilibrium, as the odor of decay filled her sinuses. Slowly, the shroud of unconsciousness receded and gave way to the relentless pounding of the rain.

Mary opened her eyes and attempted to focus on her surroundings. The desiccated corpse of a spider lay inches from her face, long dead, and sprawled turtle-like on its back. Then she remembered falling, she had been in the kitchen. She lifted her head and gasped; the room looked ancient and forgotten, long since abandoned and bathed in a hazy miasma as if not entirely there; almost as if she were looking through a—

"My veil," she said, and lifted a hand to her face only to find nothing, then slowly her vision cleared. Mary reached for her doll and pulled it close.

"It's okay, baby. Momma's here," she said, looking him over. "Fit as a fiddle."

Mary rose to her feet and the floor shifted beneath her. Then the room brightened, a polychromatic aura flashed against every surface. Suddenly, cabinets appeared on the walls; the pots, the pans, and the wood-burning stove materialized, and the room returned to the way it had been. Prismatic light diamonded on every surface; rubies, sapphires, and opals cotillioned before her eyes. Mary buried her face against the doll to shield them both from the horrible sight.

Creeaaakk!!!

The thunderous concussion jolted her back into the moment. Mary jumped as her vision of the kitchen shifted once again; she stared in disbelief at the throng of people standing before her: workmen attacked one of the walls with steel bars and sledgehammers, a woman wearing men's clothing held a roll of papers in one hand and a ball of light in the other. Mary tried to move as two men pushed a cart toward her, but was unable, then the cart and the men passed through her as if she wasn't there.

Her stomach somersaulted and the world turned grey; Mary pulled Christopher tighter and screamed, "This isn't real!"

A blinding flash of blue-white-blue, assaulted her perception, followed by a heavy clap of thunder, and the kitchen returned to normal. The men were gone, the woman was gone, the strange light had even vanished, and for a moment, everything appeared to be calm. All except for the rain, which was relentless, but it dulled in comparison to the din of insanity.

"James!" she screamed. "We have to get out!"

Panic set Mary in motion. As she ran from the kitchen the strange light returned behind her, but she didn't dare look back. Shallow breaths raked through her lungs but provided little oxygen and one clear thought hammered into her head with certainty, *if we don't wake up, we are going to die. Oh James, please wake up.*

She sent him a mental bullet.

"WAKE UP!"

James was catapulted out of sleep and nearly thrown from the bed. He woke to find the room frigid with a thick ground fog enveloping the floor. He shivered; thick plumes of condensation escaped from his lips. "Mary. Where are you?" he screamed, scanning the room.

"Mary, we have to get out of here!" James took to his feet and ran.

He tore through the hallway, rounded the corner, and nearly passed out as his vision blurred and shifted. The walls, doorways, and bookshelves disappeared, leaving only bare studs and old insulation where they had been. He stopped and stared at a section of ancient pipe, running through an ancient chase way, fastened by ancient fittings. A man appeared at the end of the hallway who looked to be operating a drilling machine of some sort. James ran to him, but the man vanished moments before he reached him.

The house lurched and started to shake once again. The floor jumped and the walls began to crumble, plaster fell from the ceiling in large sections, and the timbers buckled then splintered all around him.

"Mary!" he screamed, just as she rounded the corner at the end of the hall.

"There's something wrong with the house, it's trying to kill us!" She grabbed his arm and turned to run. "We have to leave!"

James pulled her back to him and suddenly ... he remembered what he had forgotten. He reached into his front pocket and pulled out the key. "We need to get to the third floor. I'm not sure how I know, but I do. If we can make it to the bedroom, we will be safe."

Mary looked at him and remembered as well. "Let's go," she agreed.

A large beam moaned in distress above their heads, then crashed to the floor inches from where they stood. James took off down the hallway pulling Mary with him. Sections of plaster and splinters of wood were thrown at them like shards of shrapnel as they made their way through the gauntlet of debris. Mary shielded Christopher from the brunt of the onslaught as dust and detritus rained down on them from every angle.

Finally, they arrived where the staircase had been, only to find it replaced by a wall-sized bookcase. James fitted the tip of his shoe into a small notch in the baseboard and pressed firmly. There was a loud clunk, then he placed his hands on the right side of the case and pulled outward. The bookcase slid away easily, revealing the concealed stairwell.

"How did you...?" She looked at him

James stared back at her with eyes that had glazed over, his face was as white as death and his lips had turned a cold dark blue. "I'm not sure," he said, a foggy plume of breath escaped into the air.

The stairs tilted before them and revealed the numerous missing risers since last they saw it. The walls and the ceiling began to buckle and fold inward. Ice and frost spread out in crystal tendrils before them. Mary pulled Christopher closer, and his tiny fingers grabbed onto her dress.

Cautiously, they navigated the staircase, while Devlin's Manse did its best to stop them. An earth-moving tremor ripped through the narrow passage, raining larger sections of plaster over them. Then the floorboards under their feet began to give way as they made their ascent.

James wrapped his arm around Mary and lifted the key to the lock just as the bottom stairs splintered and were replaced by nothingness.

"Hurry, James," she cried through lips that had turned dark blue.

More stairs were pulverized behind them.

"The house doesn't want us here," he said as he slid the key into the lock.

"James," she said. "I love you. I always will."

Christopher coughed and James turned the key.

"I love you too ... both of you."

For a moment, the door was there, and then it vanished. The world exploded in a blinding blue pulse and the last of the stairs shattered beneath their feet. The past, the present, and the future, fused together into one existence ... and it was summer once again. She stood beneath a trellis of rose and magnolia blossoms on the front lawn. The sun shone down on her face through a veil of white lace. Jed lifted the veil and kissed her.

Charleston Gazette

August 7, 2023

The Historical Society of Charleston has been hard at work on the restoration of Devlin's Manse, which has lain vacant since the disappearance of the Devlin family in 1902. The plantation and the estate were declared historical landmarks, and construction began in the spring. Early Friday morning, after removing a large second-floor bookcase, workmen discovered a hidden stairwell. leading to a secret third-floor bedroom. The room was virtually obscured from the view of the exterior. When Jake Jefferies pried open the door to the room, he discovered a portal to the past and the answer to a century-old mystery. The skeletal remains of the Devlin family were found in their bed.

James Edward "Jed" Devlin, his wife Mary, and their infant son Christopher vanished in 1902. Foul-Play had been suspected, but no bodies were ever discovered. It is now believed that the family perished in their sleep. "It looks like the chimney flue was partially blocked and it's possible the family asphyxiated in their sleep," said Jefferies. The family is assumed to have died after being overcome by smoke. Medical Examiners from the Charleston Coroner's Office have positively identified the remains as that of the Devlin family.

Also, a large wooden chest belonging to James Edward Devlin, bearing the insignia J.E.D. was recovered from the basement. Along with family photos and a China tea set, workmen recovered a teddy bear and Mary Devlin's wedding dress in pristine condition. All items will be put on display at the Charleston Historical Museum. Mysterious reports of unexplained voices and the sound of a crying baby have baffled workers since renovations began. Perhaps closure to this century-old tragedy will finally allow the souls of James, Mary, and Christopher, some solace ... Rest in Peace.

Afterword

Profound sorrow is ageless and can never be completely forgotten for long. Not even the innocence of childhood can prevent the flood. To ease the pain, some houses hold onto their secrets as long as they can. But in the end ... there is always a residue.

"Try to find me, James," the voice of a young girl drifted from behind a second-floor closet door.

Nine

THE DEAD GIRL

The dead girl stood at the window, her grey features in silhouette by a despondent December moon. The frail shadow cast by her hopeless figure lay on the floor like an old, discarded blanket—a doleful reminder of a fleeting existence.

She slowly turned toward the boy on the couch. Her hair hung limp and knotted, nearly covering her face—nearly. Her skin was wan and waxen, except for her cheeks and beneath her eyes, which were sunken and sallow, a purple so dark it was almost black. Cloudy eyes fixed on the boy and glared at him accusingly.

"I'm sorry, Lizzy," he whispered.

The boy watched as she crossed the room and sat beside him. He shivered. Although she had been there for nearly two days, he still hadn't gotten comfortable with her presence; it was more than unsettling. She had appeared late Friday night, shortly after he had found her lifeless body. Now it was Sunday, and soon he would have to decide exactly how he would handle the problem in the bedroom. For now, he sat in the dark and cried.

"I'm sorry," he said again.

The dead girl stared at him in silence.

After regaining a sliver of his composure, the boy, who was twenty-two, and by all rights a man, stood up and crossed the apartment. He checked the thermostat. Bottomed out at its lowest reading, it read 50. He imagined it was probably much colder inside than that. The power had been off since he found her, and it was December, after all. A bleak, miserable December at that. He flicked the light switch, but it did nothing.

"It's probably for the best," he muttered, hoping the frigid air would help keep the body from revealing itself. At least until he was ready to deal with it. He walked to the front door and tried the knob. It held fast and would not budge. Nor would the deadbolt lock turn, no matter how hard he tried.

"I deserve this."

He had tried to leave the apartment shortly after discovering her lying there, then again when she appeared the first time. In fact, he had tried to escape no less than several hundred times since Friday night. He had become a hostage; she was holding him here.

This is what it is like to be haunted, he thought.

"I deserve this," he repeated.

He turned to find her standing threateningly close to him. Her eyes were no longer accusing. They were just sad, the broken-hearted eyes of a senseless death. She looked at him and opened her mouth. Her cold lips parted as she attempted to speak. But there was nothing.

Her clothes appeared to have lost all property of tint and tone as if cast in black and white. Dizzying shades of grey mottled together, evaporating into one another. The result was a grainy texture that was difficult to look at. The same was true for her physical self; she had lost all the essence that had bound her to this world. At times, however, she seemed completely tangible. Mark knew that if he were to try, he could reach out and take her hand. There was no translucent quality to her at all. She was in no way see-through. The gravity of her presence was profound.

Contrarily, at other times throughout the weekend, she had displayed the ability to easily pass through solid walls and doors as if they hadn't been there at all, as if they belonged to a separate reality from the one she occupied.

Her outstretched hands and beckoning grey eyes called to him like sirens. The pull of her will was virtually as powerful as the magnitude of his guilt. Wiping at the tears coursing down his face, he navigated a wide berth around her. Carefully avoiding contact, he mindlessly entered the hallway and found himself at the door to the bedroom.

After work on Friday, Mark had cashed his check and been at "The Spot" a good hour ahead of rush-hour traffic. The Spot, as it was commonly referred to, was

Straight Street and MLK Boulevard—a place where you could find just about anything if you had the cash. Lizzy and Mark had used rather heavily for the past year and a half and had chipped away toward larger habits well before that. The fact that they had met at St. Claire's Hospital on the substance abuse wing, where both had attempted detox, was a testament to their common struggle and an ill-fated omen of their impending ruin. But, since birds of a feather tended to flock, they had hooked up and had been flocking together ever since.

There is a saying: *Two Sickies don't make a Wellie.* That had been true of Lizzy and Mark. Together they had honed their skills to become efficient enablers of one another. Their combined efforts had succeeded in keeping the beast at bay, or at least the bag full ... most of the time. Putting food on the table and keeping the lights on was another story. At least they had managed to stay up to date on the rent.

Weekends had become a routine celebration for the young couple as if merely surviving another week was occasion enough. When Friday finally rolled around, it was game on. They would spend the two and a half days extremely high—actually, extremely low, snacking on Frosted Flakes and nodding out in front of the television in the bedroom.

Monday morning always arrived too soon, like a cold slap to the face. At that point, they would peel themselves from the sheets and attempt to set aside the needle for the remainder of the workweek. But the ability to maintain was a feat that had become harder and harder to pull off. Every junkie knows that maintenance never lasts long. Like a house of cards in a hurricane, it's destined to come crashing down.

Mark had scored two bricks of something called "Vapor Lock," and it had been straight fire. You had to be extra careful about what you bought these days, with all the garbage dealers used to cut their product. Fentanyl was especially one bad hombre you had to steer clear of. Junkies were dropping like flies from that shit. For that reason, Mark preferred to deal with only one connection. Trap, his main source, could be at the ready within minutes of his call. Reliability, as well as quality, were commodities severely lacking in the drug trade. Trap was usually good in both departments.

Mark and Lizzy had done everything together. They hit the needle as soon as he walked in the door. From there, it was a contest to see who would nod off first. This time, Mark figured it had been him.

He woke at 10:30 to find Lizzy fast asleep, face down in the covers.

"Wow, that was some strong-ass diesel, babe," he said. She hadn't moved. Mark had then shaken her by the leg, but Lizzy didn't so much as stir. "Babe," he called again as he took her hand. Mark recoiled at the icy touch of her fingers. Rolling her over, he noticed the ragdoll sack of flour way her body flopped in response. Her mouth was agape; her lifeless eyes stared blindly toward the ceiling. The color of her skin was wrong; it was ashen and grey, almost anemic. Lizzy had been dead for hours.

He had a vague memory of attempting to breathe life into her no longer functioning lungs and intermittent moments in which he could recall beating on her chest. Now it was all a blur. As he desperately tried to bring her back, the world began to spin out of control. The room tilted and heaved like the deck of an old wooden ship in the grips of a catastrophic storm. His actions were fruitless.

He had picked up his cell phone and dialed 911 but never hit send. There was a lot of dope in the house. He pictured himself getting arrested for her murder or, at the very least, criminal negligence. Mark panicked, dropped the phone, and cried. For hours he cried. Finally, he found himself in the living room with no recollection of having left her side. Prayer had escaped him, hope abandoned, and reality overwhelmed.

He wanted a smoke. He also thought that a couple of bags might help settle his nerves. However, both items were in the bedroom, and there was no way he was going back in there. The power had gone out as it often did when he was late with the bill. It was probably overdue, but he couldn't remember. So, he sat in the dark with his head cradled in his hands, staring at the bedroom door.

At first, his eyes blurred and watered as the shadow crossed his view—a trick of twilight taking advantage of his impaired condition. But, as he focused, he quickly realized it was neither deception nor hallucination. He watched as Lizzy passed through the bedroom door into the hallway as if she were nothing more than smoke. The dead girl walked down the hall and joined the boy on the couch.

Now standing in the hallway outside the bedroom, he was even more uncertain of his next move than ever. Lizzy once again appeared in front of him. She placed her hand on the doorknob and nodded longingly at Mark.

"I can't go back in there," he whispered. "I just can't."

Lizzy raised her arm and slowly extended a finger in his direction. She shook her head from side to side.

"I know," he said. "I'm ashamed of myself. But I don't know what to do. I can't go back in there and see you like that. I just can't do it. I'm sorry."

The dead girl hung her head as if the weight were simply too much to bear. She let her hands fall to her side.

For some time, he stood there looking at her. He had let her down, and he knew it, not only in life but in death as well. Had he been half the man he wanted to be, or a tenth of the man he imagined he could be, he would have done everything in his power to get her the help she needed, that they both needed. He should have stopped at nothing to get her clean. If he had truly had her best interests at heart, wouldn't he have done the right thing, even if the right thing was them not being together? Wouldn't he have done just that if he truly loved her? Wouldn't he have called the police right away, without fear of consequence? Could he disrespect her memory any more than by doing nothing? He thought not.

The vessel that had been Lizzy lay in a tangle of dirty sheets behind a closed bedroom door. What remained now wandered the floor of Apartment 16 as a lamentable reminder of his ruinous life.

He hadn't even realized that he had closed his eyes until he opened them again. Lizzy was no longer there. Conscious periods had become less frequent for Mark. Moments of wakefulness and intervals of restless dreams blurred into one agonizing soundtrack of desperation. He should have been severely detoxing by now. Why wasn't he hugging the bowl, sick as a dog, was beyond logic. He usually needed to hit it every few hours.

The emotional distress must have something to do with it, he reasoned.

He had also wanted a smoke, but he wasn't jonesin' as he should be. For some reason, he felt as if he didn't need one. This seemed odd but was immediately dismissed by the interruption of a heavy knock.

Thump ... Thump ... Thump

"Mark, Lizzy, it's Mr. Flores," bellowed a voice from the door. "Hello."

Thump ... Thump ... Thump

"Mark, I need to check the fire alarms. I have an inspector coming. Is anyone home?"

Mark stopped breathing and slowly turned toward the front door. Lizzy stood beside it, her eyes wide and pleading. She wanted to let Mr. Flores inside. Mark could read it on her face.

"Mark. Hello."

There was a jangle of keys from the other side of the door. Then came the scrape and click as one attempted to enter the lock.

Panic raced through Mark's heart, which beat in his chest like thunder.

Oh God, no! he thought.

Mr. Flores, the landlord, would need to check the fire alarm in the bedroom, and then he would find Lizzy's body. Mark wasn't ready to do this yet. He needed more time, time with her, time with her ghost. Mark knew that once the body was found, Lizzy would leave him. More likely, he would be the one leaving ... on his way to a jail cell. He needed just a little more time with her. They had done everything together.

The sound of metal against metal resonated as Mr. Flores tried several keys. "Ahh, these are the wrong ones."

Thump ... Thump ... Thump

"Mark, Lizzy, is anyone home?"

Lizzy stared at Mark and pointed to the door.

Mark shook his head no. "Not yet," he silently mouthed the words.

Footsteps faded down the hall as Mr. Flores turned and left. He would be back, and soon. Mark knew his time with her was nearly at an end. Or was it?

Suddenly, it became so obvious. Why he hadn't thought of it before was insane. Their time together wasn't over; in fact, it had just begun. They would be together for eternity. Mark decided he would kill himself and join her. It wasn't goodbye at all; it was a new beginning. After he was certain Mr. Flores was gone, Mark walked to the kitchen. The dead girl watched and slowly shook her head in frustration.

In life, she had been Elisabeth "Lizzy" Pulowski from Passaic, New Jersey. Tragically hip and terminally cool. Just another one of the countless souls affected by the heroin epidemic. Lizzy would never have been mistaken for a cover girl, but before she had started using, she had had her moments. On a good day, she weighed in at ninety-seven pounds. But now, at the ripe old age of twenty-two, most of her good days were sadly in the rearview.

She had made several half-hearted attempts to get clean, all unsuccessful, and met Mark during one of them. In him, she had found a kindred spirit, a brother in arms, a soul with whom to share her struggle. It had eased the burden greatly. They had instantly fallen in lust with each other, and that graduated to love almost overnight.

Suddenly, the life she had needed to escape so desperately had become bearable, almost manageable. Their love had masked the deluge of addiction. Happiness had been a band-aid over a seriously infected wound ... one that would not heal on its own. A wound that, if left untreated, would surely one day kill. Unfortunately, love has a way of hushing even the hungriest of monsters. Sadly, some monsters refuse to stay silent.

Dusty morning sunlight desperately attempted to illuminate the apartment. Stubborn shadows clung defiantly to every corner, refusing to succumb. A dull, colorless haze permeated the kitchen, invading the room like a mist. Mark entered and headed straight for the utensil drawer. The sharpest of the steak knives were in there. Surely, one was sharp enough to open a major vein or artery. *How long does it take for the human body to bleed to death?* He wondered. He imagined less than a few minutes if he hit the right one. The left side of the neck ought to do the trick. He reached for the drawer, and she was there, instantly blocking him.

"Let me do this, Lizzy," he pleaded. "I need to."

She opened her mouth to speak. Although she said nothing, Mark could easily understand the word "No" on her lips.

"We'll be able to stay together," he began to sob. "You gotta let me do this. I can't live without you."

Grey phantom tears ran down the dead girl's cheeks as she stood before him. A melancholy sadness like no other washed across her face. Why couldn't she make him understand? Why was it so impossible for him to see? Lizzy moved to the side and let him pass.

"Thank you, Lizzy. You'll see; it'll be better this way." He pulled open the kitchen drawer revealing a small collection of knives and utensils. A large, serrated blade caught his eye, one that appeared exceptionally lethal. He plunged his hand into the drawer. It easily passed through the knives and the wooden bottom of the cupboard itself. He watched as first his fingers disappeared, then his hand, and then his arm.

"What?" He pulled his hand back, and it effortlessly met no resistance.

He grabbed at the knife again and watched as spirit fingers passed through holographic blades. He could touch none of it.

He turned to Lizzy and shouted. "Why are you doing this to me? I love you!"

She turned her back to him and left the kitchen.

Mark urgently drove his hand back into the drawer in a desperate attempt for the knife. Certain that he would be able to do so since Lizzy had left the room. Once again, his hand penetrated the drawer as if it were no more tangible than smoke. He reached into the porous wood to the crook of his elbow, where the sharp stab of one of the knives caught him. He pulled his arm back from the bite and examined the wound. Dark brown blood ran down his arm all the way to his fingertips. It dried and cracked as if it had been there for far too long. Mark stared down at the place where the blade had pierced his flesh. A hypodermic hung from his arm in the exact spot he always used to shoot. The soft tissue around the vein had turned a deep shade of scarlet.

"What the hell?" he gasped as terror flooded his brain.

Suddenly, the front door burst open. Mark stood frozen, facing the two men that entered the apartment. Mr. Flores and the fire inspector immediately raised their hands to cover their mouths and noses. "Dear God, what the hell is that?" Mr. Flores gagged.

"Call the police," yelled the inspector as he used his knuckle to turn on the light switch. A careful gesture applied so as not to disturb the scene.

Mark stood in the entranceway of the kitchen as the soft light illuminated him. He raised his hands in the act of surrender and attempted to speak. He was unable to say a word.

Mr. Flores backed into the hallway and dialed 911 on his cell phone. "What should I tell them?"

"Tell them you've found a dead body in one of your apartments and to get here right away."

Flores backed up further into the hallway, doing his best to avoid the awful smell pouring out of Apartment 16. But he knew he would be smelling it for a very long time. He did as instructed and placed the call.

With over twenty years on the job, Inspector Gary Gillick was no stranger to the reek of death. In his day, he had pulled his share of bodies from the husks of burned-out tenements and crack houses. Still, it wasn't a thing you ever got used to. He walked into the apartment, shielding his face as best he could. He passed Mark, never looking at him, and walked directly to the bedroom.

Mark gasped in horror. "No," he whimpered.

His cry was heard only by Lizzy, who stood at the bedroom door with her arms outstretched for him to join her.

He went to her.

They watched as Inspector Gillick opened the door and entered the bedroom. The bodies lay amidst a tangle of sheets exactly where they had passed on Friday night. Mark and Lizzy had finally found a way to silence the monster. A serene comprehension filled him as she took him in her arms and pulled him close.

They had done everything together.

Ten

MANXIETY

The world has changed a lot in just a few short decades. Let's face it, the good old days weren't always as good as we might think. I'm not saying I had to walk uphill 'both ways in the snow' just to go to school, but our generation had to face our own unique challenges. This was especially for those of us who liked to smoke a little weed every now and then. Which wasn't me of course, I didn't like to smoke a little weed. I liked to smoke a whole lot of it, every damn day, all day, in fact. From the moment I woke up till the time I went to bed ... no exceptions. To be perfectly honest, I couldn't go a day without it. My motto was: A day without weed, is like night. Okay, it wasn't my motto, but you get the idea.

Although I started getting high when I was fifteen, I was drawn to the idea of it at a much earlier age, and I do mean drawn, in a most magnetic way. I had older aunts and uncles who introduced me to the music they like, and this in turn became the music I liked. Classic rock bands like Pink Floyd and Led Zeppelin, and the Who were like nothing I had ever heard before and I instantly fell in love with the sound. I also had the notion, even though I had never tried it, that this wonderful music and a little bit of pot would make the perfect pairing. As it turns out, my theory proved to be one hundred percent correct. I smoked a joint one afternoon during my freshman year. It was in between classes, and even though it was a pin joint of rag weed, it hit me like a freight train. I remember walking back into the school and hanging out in one of the hallways that was wall to wall windows. The sun was bright, too bright in fact. It hurt my eyes and it was nearly impossible for me to keep them open, which I found ridiculously amusing. I started giggling, and then I couldn't stop laughing no matter how hard I tried. In fact, the harder I tried, the more I cackled like a hyena. I was suddenly overcome by a warm euphoric fuzzy sensation that was absolutely wonderful. I fell in love with the way it made me feel and after that, I never looked back. Weed was everything I had expected and then some.

I soon found out that Mr. Panama Red did exactly what I thought it would. It brought out the colors and the textures I believed had been missing in the world. It made the music even more interesting, more vibrant, more complex and more enveloping. It turned sex into a mind-numbing religious experience that wrapped me in a warm blanket and hugged me on the inside. Not that I knew what sex was like without it, as I had never experienced it prior to finding old sweet leaf. You see, I was an awkward, nervous kid, who was extremely uncomfortable in his own skin. I had an inferiority complex, I never felt like I belonged anywhere, and I was dealing with some major anxiety issues. Needless to say, I hadn't fared well with the opposite sex, up until that point—then things changed. Suddenly, I was outgoing, I was funny, and I wasn't half as self-conscious as I had been without this amazing life enhancement. That nerdy freshman goofball no longer existed. He had started smoking weed, dating a junior and almost overnight, had become, a righteous dude.

I would like to get back to the whole, the world has changed a lot topic that I originally brought up. Back then, things were different for pot smokers. We were on the fringe of society and a lot of the popular kids looked down on us, or at least that was the way it was in my school. Funny thing, most of those so-called cool kids smoke weed now. In fact, everyone and their grandmother smokes weed now that it's legal or used for medical purposes. If they only knew, I was using it to cope with anxiety long before any of them knew what a blunt was. Call me a trail blazer. The most ironic thing about that is now they are smoking, and I am over it. Go figure.

But I digress, things were different for tokers, and the weed was different as well. There wasn't any of these exotic name brands or hybrid specialty weeds. There was commercial weed, which usually came from Mexico, and was full of seeds and stems. And then there was Sinsemilla, which was green and skunky and didn't have any seeds. Occasionally a batch of Thai stick or Hawaiian would show up, but that was a rarity. There was also such a thing as the drought. Usually during the summer, the weed would simply disappear, and it would become almost impossible to find any. So, we oftentimes had to take drastic measures. There were these little shops in Paterson and New York where you could put a ten-dollar bill in the tray and dime bag would pop out. During those dry times we would make the trip to these remote destinations quite often.

This wasn't the ideal method to acquire said doobage, but desperate times called for desperate measures. These shops were located deep in the hood; Spanish Harlem near the GWB, and down by the projects in P-town. It was an unnerving transaction to purchase your weed in such a fashion, but it sure as hell beat the alternative, going without.

Which brings me to where I was headed in the first place. After working in the city for a couple years I learned of another spot where I could find my daily herbal requirements. The place was called The Lion of Judah, or at least that's what the sign above the door said. It was a little shop in the East Village. There were a lot of shops just like it. They were easy to identify because they all had the same items on display in their storefront windows. A box of powdered laundry detergent, a few packs of batteries, some random groceries and possibly even a toy or two. The items were all sun faded and devoid of color as if they had been sitting there since the turn of the century. At first glance you would assume these stores had shut down years ago, that was until you rang the bell, and you were buzzed inside.

Upon entering you would find nothing within these places that remotely resembled a convenience store in any way. The Lion was cluttered from floor to ceiling with just about anything you could imagine, all thrown about in true hoarder style. Power tools, bags of clothes, wood, magazines, newspapers, tables and chairs, you name it, it was all tossed into the cramped area until there wasn't any room to walk.

Once inside you would navigate the tight path through the mountains of garbage and debris till you arrived at a plywood table near the back. There sat a man, Jamaican I'm guessing by the accent and the dreads, but I could be wrong. You would then place your money on the table, at which point he would reach into his backpack and pull out an insanely huge sack of sticky kind-bud. The man would weigh out your purchase, hand it to you and send you on your way.

This was an extremely convenient method to buy smoke, especially when I worked in the city. And it didn't matter if there was a drought or not, the Lion always had it, and it was always exceptional.

Okay, fast forward another couple of years. I am no longer working in the city, and I haven't been to the Lion in a very long time. I still smoke every day but always managed to have a readily available supply most of the time. I haven't gone a day without smoking in years and can't even remember what it was like to experience the drought. That is until one day; it's as if it were all smoked away overnight.

Anzo, my partner at the time, and I, have been working construction together for a while. We've always been able to pool our resources and find something, even during the driest of seasons. But this time is different, and despite how desperately we search, we can't find anything, anywhere. So, I get a brilliant idea, which I am often famous for. And we take a trip into the city to visit my old hook-up spot, The Lion. I hadn't been there in years and really have no idea if the place is still there. I mean, what are the chances? It's not like it was a legitimate business, and I imagine those spots come and go pretty quickly. Well, we came in through the Lincoln Tunnel and made our way downtown into the Village. And holy crap, wouldn't ya know it. There it is, The Lion, right where I had left it! The storefront is the same; I mean the same box of laundry detergent is still sitting in the exact spot it sat almost ten years ago, along with all the rest of the sun faded items. I take this as a very good sign and leave Anzo sitting in the truck, double parked on the street. I exited and made my way to the front door.

I rang the doorbell, expecting to hear the same tone I heard so many times before, only it didn't happen. I thought that maybe over the years it must have stopped working or was stuck, so I tried again … but still no luck. I gave up on the bell and gave a heavy knock. The door swung inward about two inches offering me a view of the inside of the place.

My heart jumped into my throat as I peered through the crack and focused on the table where I had made my purchases so many times before.

"Hello," I called, still unsure of what my next move was about to be. I think somewhere deep inside I knew I was about to do something stupid.

"Hello," I called again and pushed open the door a few inches more. I stepped into the store and looked around, scanning the back where the man had sat all those years ago. Everything looked just as I remembered, it was as if nothing had changed, none of it had been moved. It felt like I had traveled back in time, back to the days when I still worked in the city and would visit the Lion on a Friday afternoon.

I took another reluctant step and then I saw it. Suddenly, my heart, which had been a giant lump in my throat up until now, exploded like Mt. Vesuvius. It beat double time, triple, quadruple, and then it threatened to burst right out of my chest. My hands started shaking and sweat broke out on my forehead and ran down my back. I couldn't believe what I was looking at.

Sitting on the table, exactly where business transactions had been conducted all those years ago, sat the very same backpack I had seen many times before. Except ... this time it appeared to be far more filled than I had ever seen it in the past. In fact, this backpack was literally bursting at the seams.

I'm sure I held my breath, as I listed for the furtive sound of someone running at me full speed with an Uzi pointed at my head. And although that didn't happen, I knew it wouldn't be long before it did. My extremities were nearly inoperable, and I had to force myself to start moving. I shouted out my greeting once again, just to be certain that there was no one within the building. I quickly spun on my heels and ran back to the truck and jumped behind the wheel.

"Dude," I said, my anxiety level pegged in the red.

Anzo just looked at me as if I had gone insane or maybe seen a dead body.

"There's no one in there." I fought to catch my breath. "And there's a giant bag on the table ... I know what's in it."

I think we stared at each other for a very long time. I am sure of it, and we both knew what the other was thinking. He didn't want to tell me to go back in there and grab it, and I didn't want to bring it up myself. Still, we both knew what I was about to do. Somehow, I managed to convince myself to get out of the truck and return to the store.

"Hello," I said as I pushed open the door, not bothering to try the buzzer. There was still no answer as I stepped inside and closed it behind me. Now, more than ever I was sure I would be gunned down at any second. A gang of Jamaican men would jump out from behind one of the piles of garbage, they would charge at me with guns blazing and surely unload their arsenal into my frantic heart.

My emotions were in overdrive, my bodily functions were taxed to the limit, and my anxiety level was close to overload. Somehow, I managed to silence all of that and suppress my flight instinct. I navigated a path to the back table, with cannons thundering in my ears, fortunately it was my own pulse and not the sounds of automatic weapons. I grabbed one of the straps of the backpack and lifted. Christ, it was heavy as shit! Then I sinched it over my shoulder and made my way to the front door.

I was overcome by a familiar pungent aroma as I double timed it to the relative safety of the street. That's where they would get me. Just when I thought I had made it, they would open fire on me and take me out. But that never happened either.

I stepped outside with the massive knapsack of weed in tow and I high tailed it to the truck. I threw the bag at Anzo, got behind the wheel and was driving down the block a second later.

Adrenaline, Serotonin, Dopamine, all of it coursed through me in a flood. My head was electric, my senses were taxed, and my brain raced like a frantic baboon. We got a few blocks away and pulled over to the side of the road. I took the backpack and quickly unzipped it. I was smacked in the face by the sweetest fragrance I could have ever imagined. The fucking thing was packed with some of the largest, greenest buds I had ever seen in my life. I then took the backpack and locked it in the toolbox in the back of the truck.

Out of our minds, Anzo and I drove back to my house hooting and hollering the entire way. We were both certain we would be followed and slaughtered at any moment ... again, that never happened. I pulled into my driveway after not having a heart attack or spontaneously combusting and rushed into the garage with the package in hand. Anzo and I went straight to work and dumped the backpack out onto a large piece of cardboard. We didn't have a scale, which I really regret now as I have no idea how much we actually walked away with. I am guessing a little over two pounds of stinking, sticky green buds, some of which were nearly twelve inches long.

We divided it up into two equal portions and each took our share, because fair is fair after all. In the months that followed I recall gifting my friends with surprise ounces when the mood struck me. It was an insane experience and unfortunately one that doesn't have a moral or even a punchline. I don't exactly feel bad about stealing weed from a drug dealer, although I probably should. Not sure if that makes me a sociopath or just someone who really loved weed. I would never do anything like that now, mostly because I don't smoke grass anymore. But also because I am just not that crazy … anymore. Now, my anxiety keeps me a bit more in check and I don't give into such dangerous impulses. And since you can buy weed on any street corner in Manhattan, there would never be a need to go to such extreme measures. But it's a hell of a story, and it really happened. Think less of me if you will, but I was young and I believe we are allowed a few free passes at that age. I will take this one. Besides, like I said before, everyone loves a good story, and the great marijuana caper is certainly one for the history books.

Eleven

WITNESS

Brianna Nichols sat at her favorite bench beneath the shade of a live oak. It was hot for early June—sweltering, in fact—and the midday New Jersey sun refused to be ignored from its highest position in the sky. Even the massive boughs that canopied only did so much to take the edge off. Brie took a healthy gulp from her bottle and refilled Max's water bowl. The Yellow Lab eagerly slurped up the contents, then fixed his master with a look of appreciation.

"Who's a good boy?" Brie scratched Max in his favorite spot, right between the ears.

His big chocolate-colored eyes looked up at her as if to reply, *We've been over this a million times, lady. I'm a good boy. How many times are we gonna do this?*

They had just walked the entire length of the footpath circling the duck pond of Van Saun Park. It was a favorite spot of Max's, especially on those occasions when Brie unclipped his collar and let him chase the ducks into the water; this had been one of those occasions. He never actually caught the birds, but he loved to try, charging them at full speed, barking in his bravest voice, and sending the mallards fleeing in every direction. It was glorious, swimming for as long as Brie would allow and paddling back when she called him to return. He sometimes even got to chase a stick after playing with the ducks; this had been one of those times, as well.

They both sat enjoying the shade, Brie sipping her water from the bottle while the remainder of Max's drink drooled from the side of his chops.

"You're a good boy," Brie smiled at Max, who gave her that same inquisitive look.

What's up with this girl? Max panted.

From where they sat, Brie had a perfect view of the pond. She noticed the ducks had regained their confidence, and all was business as usual once again. Max paid them no mind. He laid his head between his paws and let out an exaggerated doggie yawn. She turned back toward the parking lot where she had parked her Cherokee nearly two hours ago. Several cars had been in the lot when they arrived; now only one other remained. A man and woman stood beside the vehicle, engaged in conversation. Brie leaned back on the bench, stretched out her arms, and released a yawn of her own. Max lifted his head to assess the situation, then laid it right back down.

"I guess we're both gonna sleep well tonight, buddy." She closed her eyes for what felt like only a couple of seconds but was soon startled by the sound of a woman shouting nearby. She and Max looked up in unison, and Brie turned toward the scene in the parking lot. The man and woman who had been talking before were now arguing. It appeared to be a lovers' quarrel, and the woman was clearly upset. She screamed at the man who stood motionless in front of her. She raised her voice even louder, but Brie still couldn't understand what she was saying. Then the man bolted toward the woman like an uncoiled spring and pulled something from his pocket. He hit her in the chest, and the sound that escaped from her was toxic. She screamed, shrill and torturous, as if she were on fire. He hit her again and again and then again. Blood spread out across the woman's shirt in a rapid frenzy, it ran down her shorts turning the world crimson then flowed onto her legs. The man hit the woman one last time, and she fell to the pavement, where she stopped moving.

Brie was breathless and unable to do anything but stare in mortified horror. She tried to convince herself she was dreaming, that she had fallen asleep on the bench and was in the grips of a nightmare triggered by the oppressive heat. But she couldn't do so for long, as Max brushed up against her and started whining. He had been roused by the woman's screams as well. Brie felt the world move in slow motion. Every detail blurred as if reality no longer existed. She watched the man open the truck of the vehicle and lift the woman's body like a rolled-up section of carpet. Then he threw her over his shoulder, tossed her into the trunk, and slammed it shut. The loud thud startled Max even more, and he let out a hefty bark, again sending the ducks into the air.

"Shhh, Max. Be quiet!" Brie reached out her hand to steady the dog. She looked back to the parking lot, hoping the man had not figured out where they were. Her blood froze. He stood at the driver's side door and stared at her for what felt like an eternity. There was nowhere to hide; Max had given away their exact location. She sat fixed to the bench as the man glared at her. It was too great a distance for Brie to make out anything about his face or identity. She prayed it was the same for him.

"Oh, my God! Oh, my God!" she gasped.

The man turned away and looked over his shoulder into the parking lot. Brie couldn't figure out what he was doing at first. Then it hit her—he was taking note of the only other vehicle in the lot, her Cherokee. And he wasn't just looking at it; he was identifying it.

"Oh, my God!" Brie said even louder. She fumbled in her pocket for her cell phone, pulled it out, and punched in 911. It was picked up on the first ring.

"911 Emergency. How can I help you?" a voice answered.

Brie looked up just as the car skidded across the gravel and fish-tailed out of the parking lot. She tried to read the license plate and take in any detail she could, but the distance was too great, and the blood was all she could think about. Shallow breaths hitched in her chest, providing little oxygen, and slowly the perimeter of her vision grew dark and threatened to close in. The phone trembled against the side of her head. And the hand that clung to it shook like a spastic jack-in-the-box. Max sensed it all and pressed his cold, wet nose against his master's thigh in a show of empathy.

"911 emergency. How can I help you?" asked the voice a second time.

Brie caught her breath and looked down into the chocolate eyes that now laser-focused on her every move. She scruffed him between the ears and finally spoke. "Y-yeah, my name is Brianna Nichols, and I-I want to report a m-murder!"

Brie told the detectives everything she could remember, which wasn't much. She figured she must have fallen asleep for at least a few minutes before the woman's screams startled her. And it had all happened so fast. One minute the couple was arguing, and the next ... there was all that blood. But the detectives kept asking her to repeat herself, which only made Brie's head spin. And the more she tried to describe what she saw, the fuzzier her memory of the incident became.

"Just one more time, Miss Nichols. I want to make sure that I'm getting this right." Detective Robinson sat across from Brie at her kitchen table, sipping his second cup of coffee. He had offered to drive her and the dog home in his vehicle after going over the entire story for nearly two hours at the park. But Brie insisted that she was alright to drive. So, Robinson and his partner followed her home to go over a few details.

Brie stared into her coffee which had long since gone cold. "I don't know what else to say that I haven't told you already." Dark circles spread out beneath her eyes.

"I know, Miss Nichols. If you could just humor me one last time. Then we'll get out of your hair."

Max sat next to Brie with his head on her lap, keeping a watchful eye on the two strangers who had entered his house. "We had just finished our walk around the duck pond."

Robinson scribbled something into his notepad. "Mmm-hmmm. Go on."

"I could see from the bench that the parking lot was nearly empty, except for one other car and the man and woman. I didn't get a good look at their faces; they were too far away. But I could tell they were fighting. Not at first. First, they were only talking."

"What can you tell us about the car, Miss Nichols?" Robinson's partner, who had remained quiet for most of the interview, finally spoke. He stood in the doorway of the kitchen, sipping his coffee. Max looked up at the tall detective and tilted his head.

"Not too much," she continued. "I guess I fell asleep for a minute or two. Then I heard the woman screaming. I didn't really focus on the car at all. I feel pretty stupid."

"Not at all," Robinson reassured her. "You're doing fine. Anything you might remember would be a huge help. Was it a truck? A minivan? Was it a compact?" He put his pad down and looked directly at Brie. He had kind eyes, light brown with a touch of green around the pupils.

"I'm not sure. It was kind of big, maybe an older model and ... black. Yeah, it was black." Brie realized she remembered a little more than she thought.

"Okay, that's good. When you say old, do you mean in-bad-shape old or vintage old?"

Robinson looked to his partner and nodded to communicate one thing: *Now we're getting somewhere.*

"It was shiny, a good paint job. I think one of those big old muscle cars," she answered.

"This is right up your alley, Pete," Robinson said to his partner, who showed slightly more interest in what the girl had to say.

"Could you tell us what type of car it was if we showed you a few pictures?" Pete Jarvis asked.

"I doubt it. It all happened so fast, and I was half asleep. Then, when he started hitting her, I didn't know what was happening. And all that blood. I just don't know." Brie's voice trembled, and she began to cry again.

Pete shrugged and rolled his eyes at Robinson: *This is going nowhere.*

"It's okay, Miss Nichols." Robinson attempted to soothe her. "You've been through a lot, and we're almost done. You said the man hit the woman. Do you know what he hit her with?"

Brie took a deep breath and struggled to steady her nerves and breathing. Max sensed his master's agitation and whined in agreement. "I don't know. I couldn't see it, but I guess it was a knife or something sharp. It had to be small because I don't think she saw it coming. He hit her with it, and then he kept hitting her until—"

Pete walked to the sink and rinsed his mug, startling Max, who jumped up barking and lifted his upper lip in a snarl. The detective backed away from the dog. "Whoa, easy boy." He raised his hands, but Max continued to bark.

Brie got up and grabbed Max by the collar. "No, Max! It's okay. Come here, boy." She led him to the back door and let him out into the yard. She returned to the kitchen, shaking her head. "I'm sorry, he's not usually like that."

"That's alright. Max had a long day, too." Robinson stood up from the table and grabbed his notepad. "I think we all have."

Max stood on his hind legs and peered through the back window at the officer. Pete retreated further until he was against the wall, as the dog hyper-focused on his every move.

"I'm sorry, Detective—" She searched for his name.

"Jarvis, Miss Nichols. Detective Jarvis," Pete answered.

"Max is usually good around strangers. I'm sorry. I'm afraid I wasn't much help."

Robinson handed her his business card. "No, you've been a big help. If you think of anything else, anything at all, don't hesitate to call me. That's my cell number on the bottom."

Brie wasn't sure, but she felt as if he smiled at her with his eyes when he mentioned his cell number. *That's a little weird*, she thought, *and talk about inappropriate*. But he was charming. She looked at the card and noticed his name.

"Michael," she said.

"It's Mike, actually." He smiled.

This time she hadn't imagined it.

"What about this guy? For Chrissake, he stared me down and then checked out my damn Jeep!" Brie's voice was shaking again. "What if he comes after me?"

Max continued to bark at the backdoor.

"This guy won't bother you, Miss Nichols. He's long gone by now. Besides, I don't think you've got anything to worry about with old Max here." Pete nodded toward the back door, looking slightly apprehensive.

"We're going to keep a black and white parked out front," Mike added. "Don't worry about a thing. We won't let anything happen to you. Just call if you think of anything or … well, if you remember anything else."

He was definitely hitting on her, which was weird, but Brie thought it kind of cute too.

Pete shot Mike a look, "Let's go. It's gonna take hours to file this."

The detectives left, and Brie walked to the backdoor and let Max inside. He bolted into the kitchen, cased the joint, and sniffed every surface. When he was confident their guests had left, he returned to Brie's side and pawed her hand to rub his favorite spot.

She complied. "Who's a good boy?"

Max chuffed.

Between the newfound silence in the kitchen and the deafening commotion of the day's events blaring in her head, Brie lost the grip she had tried to maintain. Then she started to cry for what felt like the hundredth time.

Later, Brie sat up in bed with a very good boy by her side. She replayed the horrible scene from the park in her head, trying to see if there was anything she could remember, anything she hadn't thought of earlier. She flipped Mike Robinson's card over in her hand, then placed it on the nightstand. Brie hoped she might remember even the slightest detail so she would have a reason to call him.

The first police car had arrived at the park while she was still on the phone with 911. Two more showed up minutes after that, along with Detectives Robinson and Jarvis. She told them everything she could while the officers taped off the parking lot and set up barricades. Detective Jarvis had gone to work gathering evidence samples while Detective Robinson interviewed her and tried to steady her nerves. But Max had started pacing and whining, agitated by the events, which distracted Brie, who was already having difficulty remembering exactly what had happened. She was scared to death and wanted nothing more than to get back home. The detectives agreed she could leave, provided they could finish the interview at her house.

Now that she had showered, fed Max, and taken him to the backyard to do his business, she doubted she would be able to sleep a wink. She walked from the bed to the window. The police cruiser was still parked across the street a couple of doors down. Brie smiled, relaxed a little, and got back into bed. Max lifted his head for a moment, then immediately put it back down.

"Aw, you had a rough day, didn't you, boy?"

Max didn't stir or answer; he was already chasing ducks in his doggie dream. Brie yawned, surprising herself. "Guess we both had a rough one, huh, boy?"

She laid down next to Max and passed out. Her dreams were restless and stressful. She kept seeing the man hitting the poor woman. Brie struggled to focus on his face. But she could never bring it clearly into view. The dream left her frustrated and breathless and repeated on an endless loop the entire night. She would see the man's features coming into view, and the scene would fade. Max would be chasing the ducks, or they would be sitting on the bench, looking at the lake. Then it would start all over again. From the vantage point of her dream, she approached the man and woman as they argued. Her view shifted to the right and slowly began to reveal their profiles. She strained to bring them into focus but was unable. Then her attention went to the car, where the woman leaned against the hood. The glossy black paint was almost too vibrant in the afternoon sun and hurt Brie's eyes to look directly at it. She shifted her gaze when the screaming started. Dark crimson puddles spread across the woman's clothing when the object struck her. Finally, her body fell, leaving Brie staring at the shiny grill of the car. The emblem was visible, but the veil of unconsciousness made it impossible to decipher. In her dream, she tried to make out the strange design and realized it wasn't a design at all. It was letters … two or three distinct letters.

Brie's house in Paramus always felt big after her father passed away. Now, sitting in the living room with Max at her feet, it felt humongous. Her mother had left when Brie was still in diapers. Brian Nichols had raised her as a single dad and never remarried. He remained devoted to his daughter's welfare and saw that she was well provided for. Even after his untimely death a year ago, he ensured that Brie would be taken care of in his absence. He had left the house and a sizable nest egg to his only child and sole heir. Now, as the dappled sunlight danced across the large wood floor and came to rest upon the napping Labrador at her feet, Brie was acutely aware there wasn't a single thing in the whole damn place that didn't remind her of her father. When she got up this morning, she had insisted that she was done crying; she had lied to herself.

A slamming car door stirred Max from his nap, causing him to jump and bark. Brie followed him to the front window and peered outside. The detectives had pulled up alongside the police cruiser. Mike was behind the wheel, talking to the driver of the black and white; Det. Jarvis had exited the vehicle and was walking up to her front steps. Brie answered before he could knock or ring the bell. Max continued to bark as if he were having a meltdown. The detective froze when Brie opened the door and stepped out. He checked to see that it had shut behind her.

"I'm sorry, he's usually good with people," Brie apologized.

"Good morning, Miss Nichols. We just wanted to check in and see if you've thought of anything else."

Brie followed his eyes as he looked her up and down. Realizing she was still in her pajamas, a camisole, and a pair of very short shorts, she felt self-conscious and uncomfortable.

"I was about to call you gentlemen. I think I may have remembered something, although it's probably nothing." Brie waved to Mike, who had just gotten out of the car and was walking up the sidewalk. "Give me a second to change. Why don't you let yourselves in around back, and I'll be right there."

Pete watched as she turned and entered the house, checking her out one last time.

An eight-foot vinyl fence surrounded the backyard of the Nichols residence. Mike and Pete entered through a large gate with a sturdy latch and were both taken aback by the backyard's impressive, man-cave-like setting. A huge brick paver patio extended from the house and snaked off into several footpaths. A decent-sized bar sat beneath a bamboo awning with four stools, complete with several liquor shelves, two taps, and a working sink. To the bar's right sat a stainless steel eight-burner BBQ grill. In front of that was a patio table and chair set with a large umbrella. One footpath led to a fire pit and the other one to a hammock. Mike went straight to the hammock and jumped in. Pete opened the cover of the grill to reveal a full rotisserie spit and a smoke box.

"Man, I've got to get me one of these," he said.

Mike laughed. "Not on your salary."

Pete laughed a little, knowing his partner was right; he couldn't afford anything so extravagant. "Very funny. I'll just get you to buy me one."

Mike laughed even harder. "Now that's funny."

"What's so funny?" Brie appeared on the back steps wearing something a bit less revealing.

Mike jumped up from the hammock. "Nothing, just some cop humor. We were admiring your yard. You have a very nice place."

"Thank you," she said. "My father redid the yard a few years ago. He loved it back here." She nodded to the fence. "It's a little much, I know, but he had to go with the eight-footer because Houdini was able to jump over everything else." Max barked from the kitchen as if on cue. Pete looked to see that the door was shut.

Brie took a seat at the table, and the two men joined her.

Mike pulled out his notepad, flipped through a few pages, and looked directly at Brie.

"You were saying you remembered something?" Mike smiled. He had an easy way about him that Brie found comforting.

"Well, it was something about the car. Like I said, I didn't get a good look, but I remembered when the woman fell to the ground." She paused, trying to piece it all together.

"Go on," Mike said calmly.

"Well, there was a second, right when she fell, that I could almost see something on the front of the car. You know, on the grill. She was leaning against the hood, and then he started ... you know." She paused, and the two men waited for her to start again.

"When she fell, I guess I did focus for a minute because I remember the car's grill. It had letters on it, like two or three of them."

"That's good," Mike said. "That's really good. Can you remember what letters they were exactly?" He looked at his partner, who furrowed his brow and leaned closer.

Pete spoke, "Let me make sure I got it. We're talking about an older model black car with a nice paint job and a grill with letters on it?"

He was clearly mocking her.

"Yeah," Brie said, flustered. "Pretty much."

"Could be talking about a Chevelle or a GTO," Pete said to Mike, "or even a Mustang. It's hard to tell. Possibly an early seventies make of either of those. The Mustang had the Mustang emblem. Are you sure it was letters and not an emblem?"

"Well, I'm pretty sure, but not one hundred percent positive. I think it was letters. I was really far away, though."

"So, you're not sure they were letters at all?" Pete pressed.

"I'm sorry. Like I said, it was really far away," she said, frustrated.

Mike wrote in his notepad and looked up. "Is there anything else, anything at all?" He smiled again, trying to ease her frustration. "This is very helpful."

"No, I'm sorry, that was it." She smiled back at Mike and immediately felt like an idiot, realizing she was flirting with him.

"That's all right." He pocketed the pad. "We've got quite a bit to do today. Would it be okay if one of us stopped by later with a few pictures, maybe see if you can identify what type of car it was?"

"That would be fine." She hoped it would be Mike instead of Pete who did the stopping by.

"Miss Nichols," Pete interjected. "We never found a body, and no one has been reported missing. Are you sure about what you're saying? Is it possible that you may be mistaken? You did say you were half asleep."

Heat flashed in Brie's face as her anger rose. "Yes, I'm sure!" She stared into the detective's scowl of skepticism. "He killed that girl right there in the middle of the day. He killed her. I know what I saw!" She yelled the last part.

Mike cut in. "Of course." He shot an accusing look at his partner. "Sorry, it's our job to ask these questions. We're on your side."

Brie relaxed at the sound of his voice. "Well, if you'll excuse me, detectives, I've got some things I need to take care of." She stood up, and they followed.

"Thank you very much. You've been a big help." Mike held out his hand and shook hers. "I'll see you a little later then if that's okay."

Brie noticed that he said *I'll see you a little later*, he didn't say *we*. Nor did he say *one of us*. "That would be fine," Brie answered, stifling her smile. "I'm sure you can see yourselves out then." She turned for the door.

Pete opened the gate and examined the lock for a second as only a police officer could, working the lever up and down. "Quality stuff," he said. "I've got to get me one of these."

"Dream on, pal." Mike pushed his partner along. "You got caviar taste on a hot dog budget."

"Maybe I don't come from money like the esteemed Detective Robinson, but I can still dream." Pete stuck out his chest. "Who knows, maybe I'll marry a girl with money." He pointed his thumb over his shoulder to Brie's backyard.

"Now you're just delusional, bro. You got a better chance with the dog."

The smile faded from Pete's face. "To hell with that dog. Mutt wants a piece of my ass. Never liked labs anyway."

Mike turned to his partner. They looked at each other in silence for an awkward moment, then both burst out laughing. Mike slapped Pete on the back as they left the property.

"Yeah, unfortunately, that dog is the only thing that wants a piece of your ass." They walked to the car as Brie watched from behind the curtains of her picture window.

"What do you think, Max?" she asked. "Do you like Detective Robinson?"

Max looked up at her, panting in agreement.

"Yeah, I think I like him too."

Brie Nichols had not survived independently by being naïve. Like any modern, practical, woman, she did what every girl did—she opened her laptop and Googled Detective Michael Robinson. She didn't feel the least bit embarrassed to do so.

Max was somewhere close by and never left her side for long. He had a touch of separation anxiety and needed to always be by Brie's side. She enjoyed him just as much, and since her dad's passing, she had a little separation anxiety when it came to Max, as well.

Brie read through several articles from the Bergen Record detailing various arrests and investigations that the detective had worked on in his career with the Paramus Police Department. He had quite the stellar record. Not surprising since he had graduated from the academy at the top of his class. As far as she could tell, there had never been a Mrs. Detective Robinson, and he appeared to have come from a well-to-do family. He grew up in Saddle River and attended boarding school. Then he went on to graduate from Montclair State University, where he majored in criminal justice and played football. From what Brie could tell, he still lived in Saddle River.

God, I hope he doesn't still live with his parents, she thought. That would be a definite deal-breaker. It didn't matter how much a guy had going for him; that was just too weird.

She searched the web for a while and couldn't find a single thing wrong with him, which was also weird. Usually, you could find something. Everyone had at least one skeleton in the closet. Apparently, not Michael Robinson—the guy appeared too good to be true. She clicked on a picture taken of him in his football uniform and maximized it. She smiled as Max came padding up to her. He nudged her elbow to be pet, and she obliged. "Not a bad resume at all, Max," she remarked.

Max squinted while she rubbed his favorite spot. Brie checked the time and figured she would do just a bit more snooping before calling it a day. She clicked on a recent article that showed Detectives Robinson and Jarvis standing shoulder to shoulder after arresting several persons of interest in a recent human trafficking ring. According to the report, the body of a young girl had been discovered.

Mike looked rather handsome and photogenic, while the cameras did not flatter Detective Jarvis even a little. His face was a scowl, and he seemed pissed off ... pretty much how he always looked.

Brie typed Detective Peter Jarvis into the Google toolbar and hit enter. The pages flooded the screen. There was as much information on Pete Jarvis as there had been for Mike Robinson, though none of it very flattering. He had been suspended more than once on accusations of police brutality. He had been cleared of the charges, but they were glaring blemishes on his record. There was also an older article detailing an accident in which he'd been involved. A vehicle had gone off the road on Route 23 in West Milford. Two passengers died in the accident, and Pete Jarvis, the driver, was the only one to walk away from the crash. The reporter said that Pete Jarvis was the son of Lieutenant Jarvis of the Ramsey PD, and that alcohol was not believed to have played a part in the accident.

Brie looked at Max. "I guess they don't have to fight over who gets to play *bad cop.*"

Max started to whine. It was nearly three-thirty, and they usually spent Sunday afternoon at the park. Max was a creature of habit and loved to chase the ducks. Usually, they walked there since the house was less than a mile away, but they had taken the Cherokee yesterday due to the heat. Brie figured the Jeep's AC would be needed after the long walk in the hot sun. Now it was clear that Max wanted to go see the ducks again.

"I know, boy. We can't go today, though." She had become very in tune with Max's needs over the years. "I promise I'll make it up to you."

Brie walked to the front window again, relieved to see the police cruiser parked on the opposite side of the street just a few doors down. A thought came to her, and she went to the kitchen. It was close enough to Max's dinner time and she was certain he wouldn't mind eating a little early tonight.

"Hungry, Max?" she called to him.

He jumped up so quickly from the living room floor his paws didn't catch on the hardwood when he started running; he slipped and stayed in one place like the Road Runner for several seconds. He finally gained purchase and bolted into the kitchen. Brie filled his bowl and made a pot of coffee. In the thirty seconds it took Max to inhale his kibbles, Brie grabbed a thermos from a cabinet and two sleeves of Chips Ahoy. When the pot finished brewing, she poured the coffee into the thermos, added milk and sugar, and let Max out the backdoor.

"I'll be right back, boy."

Max was already off chasing a squirrel that had the nerve to enter his yard.

Brie grabbed the coffee and cookies and left out the front. She walked across the street and approached the cruiser.

The officer rolled down the window. "Is everything alright, Miss Nichols?"

"Fine. I thought maybe you would like some coffee and cookies. I hope milk and sugar are okay, Officer..." She handed him the offering through the window.

"Ulrich." His eyes lit up as he took the thermos and cookies from Brie. "Thank you. That's very nice of you. I was getting a little hungry. This is perfect."

"Is it just you tonight?" she asked.

"Yeah, it's my turn, I guess. Don't worry about a thing. No one's getting past me." He nodded and opened the cookies.

"Well, if you need anything, just let me know. I really appreciate the extra security. It makes me feel a lot better knowing you're out here."

"Think nothing of it," Officer Ulrich said with a mouthful of Chips Ahoy. "Just doing my job, that's all."

Brie smiled and excused herself. She entered the backyard through the gate, where Max met her by jumping up and licking her face. "I missed you too, ya big mush." She let him kiss her. "Where's your ball, Max?"

Max ran to the back of the yard and retrieved a Nerf football that looked like someone's favorite snack rather than a play toy. Several large chomps of foam were missing, and the thing was riddled with teeth marks. Brie threw it far into the yard. Max honed-in on it like a Velociraptor and had it in his mouth a second after it hit the grass. He u-turned and brought the ball straight back to Brie, drenched in doggie slobber. Brie continued to throw the ball, and Max tirelessly continued to retrieve it. After half an hour, Brie sat down under the umbrella.

"Hello," Mike's voice sounded from the other side of the fence.

Max barked and ran to the gate, wagging his tail.

"It's okay," Brie called to him. "Come on in."

Mike entered, and Max greeted him the same as he had Brie, with big sloppy dog kisses on the face. "Whoa, easy guy." Mike closed the gate behind him.

"Get down, Max. That's not very polite." She pulled the dog off the detective and threw the football to the back of the yard. Max followed it. "Sorry about that. He likes you."

"He's a good dog." The detective handed her the thermos. "Officer Ulrich thanks you for the coffee."

"Oh, did he need anything else?" she asked.

"No, I told him he could take a break for a while. I wanted you to check out a couple of things I brought." He had a manila envelope tucked under his arm, which he transferred to his hand. "That is, if this is a good time for you?"

"Now is fine. I was just about to make some dinner. Have you eaten yet?"

"No, really, I wouldn't want to impose."

"Give me a break," she said. "It's only cheeseburgers. Fire up the grill while I get a few things from the kitchen, then we'll eat and check out your couple of things. I insist. If you want a beer or something else, help yourself. The bar is stocked, and there are mugs on the shelf." She turned and started for the house before he could refuse.

∞

The detective watched the young woman walk away. She was a remarkably resilient individual, and he admired that. He felt something press up against his leg and looked down to see Max offering his disgusting Nerf ball to him. He took the ball from the dog and immediately regretted it; dog slobber and dirt covered his palm. "Ughh, gross," he said and threw the ball.

Mike looked down at his pant leg to see a smeared wet spot where Max had pressed his ball. "Oh, come on." He tried to rub the grime from his pants but only managed to smear it even worse. "You gotta be kidding me." Apparently, dog slobber didn't agree with Detective Michael Robinson's impeccable demeanor.

Max returned with the ball, and Mike jumped back when the dog attempted to hand off the Nerf to him. "I'm sorry, Max," he said. "I don't do snot. Nothing personal; it's just not my thing."

Mike walked to the sink behind the bar and began scrubbing his hands under the hot water. He then went to work on his stained trouser leg. Max watched dejectedly with the Nerf ball clenched firmly in his jaw.

The man watched from his vantage point as the hotshot detective let himself into the girl's backyard. The girl had seen him and been unable to identify him, but it was only a matter of time. That prick detective had a way of helping witnesses focus on the small details they would have otherwise left forgotten.

The sun had just begun to set. In less than a half hour, he would have darkness on his side. He would wait until the time was right, let himself into the girl's house, and take care of her and the dog. He slipped his hand into his coat pocket and gripped the .38 by the handle. It felt good in his hand ... cold. In his other, he held the ice pick he had used yesterday on Gail.

He'd been planning on doing Gail for some time but hadn't expected to do it in broad daylight at the park. And certainly not where a witness could potentially identify him. Initially, he intended to work on Gail for a few more days and lure her back to his place. From there, he would get her in the basement, where he could take his time and enjoy himself. But Gail had resisted his advances and insisted he take her home. Then she started screaming and messed everything up. He thought he might be losing his touch. Maybe he had rushed it a bit with her, but he was desperate. It had been too long since he felt that power, and he craved it like a drug. He would make it up with the Nichols bitch. Now he only had to get her away from the dog, but not with the hotshot still around. Then he could take his time with her. She was going to scream; of that he was certain. He checked the street from where he hid, with the sun starting to set. His heart raced in his chest like a lunatic train; he could hardly control his excitement. It wouldn't be long now.

Brie and Mike sat at the patio table, she sipped from a cold mug of Stella, and he drank an iced tea. He politely declined the offer of a drink, and she didn't press the issue. She figured he was still on the clock and was too straight of a guy to break the rules. Either way, he didn't attempt to clarify. They were looking at the pictures he pulled out of the manila envelope. Several makes of automobiles were portrayed on the glossy 8 x 10s.

"So, this is what the SS Nova and the various Chevelle models looked like." He pointed to the SS emblem on the grill of the different cars. She leaned closer to him to get a better look. He smelled clean with a touch of cologne she couldn't identify, she thought it was a bit powdery and somewhat of a strange choice for a man, but she didn't mind.

"This is what the Mustangs look like, with the pony emblem. But you said you didn't think it was an emblem. Now that you see this, do you still think it wasn't?"

She took another sip of Stella. "Yeah, that wasn't it, definitely letters," she said. "I think so, at least."

He flipped over another picture. "This is a GTO. I've got a couple of different models here, too. This one is a little boxier than the SS Nova." He let Brie study the car for a minute, then flipped to the next picture. "And this year had a similar sty—"

"That's it!" Brie interrupted before he could finish.

"You're sure?" he asked.

"Pretty sure. As I said, it was kinda far. But if I had to put money on it, I would bet that was the one." She felt confident.

Mike pulled out his cell phone and hit a speed dial number. "That's great. It should be easy to find a match in the area. There aren't that many '71 GTOs in New Jersey. Come on, Pete, where the hell are you?" He let the phone ring for a while longer, then disconnected. "That's strange. He always picks up."

"Maybe he's busy or something."

"Pete Jarvis is never that busy. Let me try again." This time he waited till he got put through to voicemail. "Pete, where the hell are you? Look, we got a lead. You're gonna love this. This one's right up your alley, buddy. Call me back." Mike's partner was a Pontiac enthusiast, especially the old GTO models, and always bragged that he'd get one someday.

Max lifted his head off the patio and looked at the back door for a moment. Brie threw him a piece of cheeseburger from her plate, and he inhaled it.

"This is really good," Mike said as he gulped down the rest of his tea.

He watched from the darkness of the kitchen, just beyond their sight, listening. He had heard everything, and as much as he didn't want to kill Mike Robinson, he had no choice. They had identified his car; it wouldn't be long till they figured out the rest. Brianne Nichols was going to die slowly and painfully, and he would enjoy every second of it. He backed into the shadows of the kitchen and waited.

Brie stood up and began to clear the table. "Would you like some more tea or something else?" She realized she was trying too hard. For some reason, Mike hadn't made a move. It felt like he was about to when they were looking through the pictures. She was sure he had been about to kiss her, but then he backed away.

Mike grabbed his plate and glass. "Let me help you with that. I could go for a bit more tea now that you mention it."

Brie walked to the back door, and Mike followed, with Max bringing up the rear. She noticed Mike hadn't finished the last bite of his burger. "If you're not going to finish that, why don't you give it to the garbage disposal."

Mike tossed the burger into the back yard as they entered the house. Max charged after the snack as his master and the man entered, then he immediately barked to be let in.

Brie turned on the kitchen light and placed her dish in the sink. Mike followed behind her and didn't see the figure step out from behind the backdoor. The man brought the butt of the gun down on the detective's head with the full force of his strength. Brie turned around just in time to see the light go out in Mike's eyes. He hit the floor hard and lay there, motionless. A small puddle of blood started to spread outward. Then, the man slammed the door behind him. and Max immediately started barking like a demon, throwing himself at the back door repeatedly.

The man in the kitchen was tall and dressed completely in black. He wore a full face mask with a skeleton jaw covering the mouth area. "This is gonna be fun," he said.

Brie backed up from the sink, concealing her hands behind her. There was something familiar about the man in her kitchen. It was obviously the guy who killed that poor woman yesterday, but there was something else.

He stepped over Mike's body, placed the gun in his pocket, and removed a rag. Brie could smell the strong chemical odor in the air. It smelled similar to what her dad had sprayed into the snowblower engine in the winter. She knew she couldn't let the man get that rag anywhere near her and backed up another step, hitting the counter behind her. He closed in on her and lifted the rag to her face.

Mike grabbed the man by the ankle and startled him, causing the intruder to lose his balance for a second. It was all the distraction Brie needed. She raised her hand from behind her back, revealing the object she had taken from the sink, and brought her beer mug down on the intruder's head. He dropped to his knees and let go of the rag he had been holding.

Brie turned and ran through the living room to the front door. The man regained his balance, brought his foot down on Mike's head, and the detective stopped moving. Brie hit the front door and scanned the street for the police cruiser. Officer Ulrich still hadn't returned from his break. She froze for a moment, undecided about which way to run. She had seconds before the killer would burst through the door. To the left was where her nearest neighbors lived, but she feared her attacker would be on top of her before she made it that far. Brie looked back along the side of her house, where Max was going ballistic. She could hear him barking and jumping against the fence, desperate to come to her aid. She would never make it around the house in time to get to Max, either. So, she bolted off the porch and headed right to the end of the cul-de-sac just as the murderer burst out her front door.

✌

He stumbled and nearly lost his footing again. His eyes stung from the blood that ran down his forehead and flowed into them, but he could still make out Brie tearing down the street toward the dead end. There was a path through the woods that led to Van Saun Park.

Dumb bitch, he thought. *She's heading right back to the park.*

He ran after her, which wasn't an easy task with the pain in his head. The way it throbbed, he thought a piece of glass might still be stuck in his skull. But he needed to focus. He had to make sure Robinson was dead, but he couldn't risk letting the girl get away, either. His foot had come down pretty hard on the detective's head. Odds were that the guy was already done. He would just have to come back later after he caught the girl; he didn't have a choice. He followed the Nichols girl to the end of the cul-de-sac and into the woods.

✌

Max launched himself at the gate, trying to clear it. With each attempt, he got a little closer than the time before. Something had happened in the house, and the girl was in trouble. There was a smell coming from inside that raised the hair on the back of his hide. He ran to the middle of the yard and took a charging leap at the fence but missed the top by nearly a foot. Max landed hard on the sidewalk but continued barking into the night air. He ran to the middle of the yard and took another charging leap at the fence.

Brie entered the park just short of the lot. It was well-lit by several floodlights, but there were no vehicles in sight. The guy was a minute behind her at most and probably closer to only a few seconds. Running across the parking lot, she ducked under the police tape that had sectioned off the murder scene.

I can't die here, she thought to herself.

The other side of the lot transitioned to the path leading to the duck pond. Brie took off in that direction. Her lungs burned, but her adrenaline was high, and she wasn't about to stop, no matter how much her legs felt like they were about to give out.

The pond was still as Brie approached the bank. The moon was nearly full and shone down on the water like a silver dollar. It was a perfect moon for walking but terrible for hiding, almost as bright as daylight. She ran around the lake toward the bench where she had sat only yesterday.

Was it only yesterday?

God, it felt so long ago; it couldn't have been just yesterday.

A beam of light flashed across the lake, casting her long shadow across the water. Brie was running out of breath.

In through the nose, out through the mouth, she thought.

And then he hit her, tackling her from the right. They both tumbled into the water.

He was up first and grabbed her by the throat, making it impossible for her to breathe. The man dragged her deeper into the water and shoved Brie under the surface. She struggled to gain her footing but couldn't, and found it impossible to get a grip on his hands. He was far too strong and much bigger. She held her breath and tried to concentrate on not swallowing any water. She knew it was all over if she took in just one lungful of water. Brie fought to stay alive, but she was losing that fight.

The man ripped her out of the water by the throat and held her up to face him. "Do you know what trouble you put me through, bitch?" He shook her like a ragdoll.

The world turned grey as Brie began to lose consciousness. She dug deep for an ounce of strength left in her reserve.

"I'm gonna enjoy cuttin' you slow," he hissed into her face.

Brie thrust her hands up and clawed at the masked man. She tried for his eyes but only managed to snag the material. She ripped at his face, and the mask came off in her hands. Brie's eyes met his. "Oh my God," she croaked. "It's you."

The light flashed again across the surface and settled where Brie and the man stood waist-deep in the water. "Let her go, asshole," a familiar voice yelled out. "I swear to God, let go of the girl, or I'll blow your fucking head off." Detective Pete Jarvis stood on the bank.

Brie struggled to scream but was unable to warn Pete. The man with his hands around her neck, the man with his back to Detective Jarvis, was Paramus Police Officer Ulrich—the same officer assigned to watch her house, the man who had drunk her coffee and eaten her cookies.

"I said release the girl, scumbag." Pete leveled his weapon and drew a solid bead on his target.

Ulrich smiled at Brie and tossed her backward into the water. He took the .38 from his pocket, turned, and shot at Jarvis. Pete went down on his back like a brick. Brie attempted to catch her breath and stand up in the water but had difficulty doing either. Ulrich looked back at the floundering girl and knew she was as good as done.

"I'll be right back for you."

A deep cut above his eye continued to leak fresh blood down his face. He made his way out of the water toward Pete Jarvis. The detective had dropped his gun and lay cradling his wound. Ulrich's bullet had hit him in the left shoulder just below the collarbone.

Not a bad shot for on the fly, Ulrich thought. "Looks like I got the drop on you, Detective," he hissed.

Ulrich approached, gun raised, pointed at Pete's head. "You hotshots never quit." He pulled back the hammer of his revolver. "Couldn't step away from the job even for one night, could ya?"

"Ulrich?" Pete gasped in disbelief. "What the hell?" Blood flowed in a constant stream from Pete's wound.

Ulrich stood over the detective with the revolver centered on him. "Give me a break. You ain't no better. At least I have the balls to kill them outright. Everyone knows how you like to do it. You like to rough 'em up after you get the cuffs on them, knock a few teeth out, break a few ribs. We ain't that different."

"I'm nothing like you," Pete coughed.

"Yeah." Ulrich stepped closer. "I bet those kids you killed in your car don't think so. I bet they don't think too much at all. Don't judge me, you self-righteous prick."

"Fuck You!" Pete screamed defiantly.

Ulrich smiled triumphantly and steadied his weapon. A shadow flew at him from out of nowhere and clamped down on his hand. Sharp needles sank into his fist, preventing him from pulling the trigger. He screamed as the great force hit him and drove him back into the water.

Max took another running leap at the gate; he dug into the grass and jumped as high as possible. His front paws caught the very top of the gate, and his back paws scraped against the vinyl as he tried to gain purchase. He pulled and struggled, and he was over. He immediately found his human's scent and tore after her. It was easy; she had taken their usual path to the ducks. When he got to the lighted area where they sometimes left their ride, what the girl called the Cherokee, he was alerted by a thunderous bang. Then he saw the two men; one was on the ground, and the other was walking up to him. He didn't care for the one on the ground, but he didn't like the other one even more. That one wanted to hurt the girl ... his girl. Max ran at full speed and bit down on the bad man's hand like it was a Nerf Football.

Brie had just gained her footing in time to see Max charge at Officer Ulrich. Max took a running leap, flew at the cop, and seized him by the hand. She watched the gun fall into the sand. Then Max knocked the officer off his feet and went for his throat. Brie stumbled through the water to the edge of the pond where Pete lay.

Ulrich tried to stand up but Max hit him in the chest and drove him underwater. He swallowed a mouthful and choked on it, then tried to grab the beast as it bit his fingers and tore at his skin. His only chance to get away was to go for what he had in his pocket. He fished around but couldn't find anything at first. Then, finally, he found it. He pulled the ice pick from his pocket and drove it into the dog's hide. Max yelped and released the man.

Ulrich jumped out of the water and raised the pick to drive it into the beast again. The dog lay on his side in the shallow water, and Ulrich closed in on him.

"Hey, Asshole," Brie called out.

She aimed the officer's .38 and pulled the trigger. The first shot hit him in the chest. Ulrich staggered back in disbelief. He looked down at the darkening area where the bullet had entered him.

"You bitch!" he shouted, lunging at Brie.

She backed up a step and pulled the trigger again. The second bullet hit Ulrich in nearly the exact place the first one had. She pulled the trigger again. The discharge was deafening. The cop fell back into the water, bobbed like a cork for a second, then began to sink.

Pete sat up, looking on in awe. "Holy shit," he said. "Fucking Ulrich."

Brie ran to Max, who whimpered with his muzzle submerged half in the water and half out. She grabbed him and lifted him out as much as she could. He was so heavy.

Pete struggled to his feet and came to her aid. His shoulder was bleeding, but he was dealing with the pain. He bent down and lifted Max the rest of the way, then carried him back to the shore and laid him down. Pete examined the wound. The ice pick had hit Max in the hindquarters. It probably hurt like a bitch, but he was going to live.

"He's going to be okay." He smiled at Brie while ripping his shirt. He pulled off a section, bent over Max, and pressed it against the wound. He was prepared for the dog to turn and take a chunk out of his face, and Max did raise his head and let out a deep growl. But then Max looked up at Pete, licked him twice, then laid his head back down.

"Aw, Max." Brie started to cry.

"I think I might pass out here," Pete said, falling back onto the sand.

His face had turned a horrid pale, and his lips had grown dark.

Then Brie noticed that he was bleeding not only from his chest but also from his back. Ulrich's bullet had passed through him. "What should I do?" she cried.

"There's a radio in my car," he said. "Call for help." Pete passed out on the sand.

Afterword

Pete stood at the grill, doing his best to keep the steaks from burning. His left arm hung in a sling; good thing he was a righty. "I hope medium-rare is okay with everyone." He called to the group sitting around the table.

Brie got up and went to his side. "Just run mine through a warm room." She stood on her tiptoes and kissed him.

Max looked up at the two of them and wagged his tail, hoping some meat would fall to the ground. He pawed at Pete's leg and used his best begging eyes.

"Can I get you guys another drink?" Brie asked.

"I'll take another" Mike answered. His stitches were healing well, and he didn't need to wear a bandage anymore. "How about you?" Mike spoke to William, who sat beside him.

"Sure, hon," William answered.

"Two, please," Mike held up two fingers to Brie.

She had wondered why there had never been a Mrs. Robinson in Mike's life. She had also wondered why Mike hadn't tried to kiss her at the table that night. Now it made perfect sense. She initially felt a bit foolish, but she had gotten over it. There would never be a Mrs. Robinson, and Brie was definitely not Mike's type. "Two Pina Coladas coming up." She filled their glasses from a large pitcher.

The group had grown closer since that night. The three men in Brie's life had come to her rescue in one way or another. Mike had figured out the model of the vehicle, which in turn forced officer Ulrich to expose himself. Ulrich owned a 1970 GTO, and a search of his basement revealed some ghastly discoveries. Ulrich had fabricated a soundproof cell on the property that had been used on multiple occasions. Several distinct DNA signatures were identified and matched to women reported missing in the New York and North Jersey areas over the past seven years. The girl from the park was identified as Gail Marks from Plainfield. Blood samples had been taken from the park, as well as Ulrich's vehicle and were an identical match to samples collected from the girl's apartment. Her roommate claimed that Gail had been discreet about the man she'd been seeing who drove an old black hotrod-style car from either the sixties or the seventies.

Detective Peter Jarvis had been in the Home Depot checking out the prices on top-of-the-line Jenn Air gas grills and missed his partner's call. When he called back, and Mike hadn't answered, he became worried and raced to the Nichols' residence, where he expected to find him. He turned down the street and saw a man fleeing into the woods at the end of the cul-de-sac. By how the perp was dressed, Pete took the man for a burglar, at the very least. With a knowledge of the neighborhood, Detective Jarvis knew that the cul-de-sac backed up to Van Saun Park. He turned around and arrived at the park minutes later to find the assailant attacking Miss Nichols.

The bullet had passed through his shoulder cleanly, and he was expected to be back to work in no time.

Max healed faster than both detectives and was ready for Pete to drop something from the grill already. He sat at attention as the tall man struggled to flip the meat with only one working hand. Max had sensed something about the tall man and felt very jealous; call it doggie intuition. He thought that his master and this man were about to become a little closer than he was ready to allow. But some things were beyond the control of even a good boy. Besides, the tall man was very nice to her, and he dropped a lot of food when he cooked.

"Here you go, Max." Pete threw the dog a large piece of steak. Max caught it in mid-air and swallowed it whole. "I think we're all ready."

Brie met him at the grill and exchanged an intimate look with the tall detective. She took the platter from Pete and placed it on the table.

Mike looked at Pete behind the grill and nodded his approval. Pete saluted him with his two-pronged fork.

They all sat down to eat, and Brie raised her glass. "I'd like to make a toast." They all followed the gesture. She continued. "Here's to all my heroes. Here's to Mike and Pete." She touched his knee with her free hand. "And here's to Max. I love you guys."

They toasted with responses of, "Hear, hear," and "I'll drink to that."

Suddenly, Mike jumped from his seat with a start. Everyone looked in surprise as he spilled more than one of their drinks. Then they realized what had caused the commotion: Max had placed his dog-slobbered, dirt-covered Nerf ball onto Mike's perfectly pressed khaki shorts.

"Oh, come on, Max. That's disgusting!" he exclaimed.

Everyone laughed, including Mike.

Pete reached over with his good hand and scratched Max on his favorite spot. "Who's a good boy?" he asked.

Twelve

THE PARTY

Travis checked his fangs in the rearview, making sure they were straight and properly secured. He hissed into the empty cab of his Honda, practicing for his grand entrance when he would chase Darcy through the front door at Christoph's party. The bite marks on her neck would be fresh and dripping crimson, but everyone would be looking at what she was wearing—or rather, what little she would be wearing.

Darcy had donned a pair of spiderwebbed fishnet stockings, which ran down her slender thighs like warm oil. The garters holding them in place disappeared beneath a black teddy so skimpy it would have embarrassed Cardi B. The idea of dressing as a slutty vampire victim had been all Darcy's idea, too. She had insisted Travis dress as either the classic Dracula vamp or one in the vein of Lestat. She would play the part of the hapless tramp who had found herself seduced and then dominated. Travis had opted for the Lestat costume, which helped accentuate the lack of costume Darcy wore.

He checked his fangs and makeup before giving the horn a light tap. The party was already well underway; leave it to Darcy to be late as usual. It wasn't like she had all that much costume to fuss with. Travis had no idea what was taking her so long. He had started the car nearly fifteen minutes before, allowing it to warm thoroughly so his wife wouldn't freeze her underdressed tushy off. Although, he would have preferred for Darcy to run into the party with her headlights popping. That would grab everyone's attention. And once their eyes were keenly focused on his gorgeous wife's rack, he would explode through the door, hissing and bearing his fangs. It wasn't every year Halloween fell on a Saturday night, and it had been ages since it had taken place during a full moon.

It felt surreal after the previous three years of social distancing and isolation, almost like a dream. The party had been canceled last year and the year before due to the current health crisis. The first wave hit, then the second, then the Delta variant, the Omicron, Kappa, Epsilon … the list went on. Now the Sigma variant was offing nearly everyone over the age of fifty-five. Travis had lost both parents due to the Sigma strain, and they had barely been in their sixties. Many of his friends had also lost at least one parent. Most people had gotten the original shot and the boosters, but it wasn't like the government could force everyone to take booster after booster. Even those who were pro-vac were beginning to wonder if the efforts were all in vain.

Christoph had finally said "fuck it" and decided to have this year's party despite it all. None of them were getting any younger, and no one knew how many Halloweens they had left. Not these days. The past few years had been depressing enough, and without the diversion of Christoph's yearly Halloween bash, they were that much more unbearable. It was Travis's favorite time of year—not only because of the party; the feeling and the event of Halloween always brought him back to a better mental state, back to a time before the world had gone to shit.

Christoph and Travis had been friends since grade school. They had grown up in the same neighborhood, gone trick-or-treating together, and trashed the town with toilet paper and soap every October 30th. As they got older and their tastes in entertainment matured, Christoph started throwing his annual Halloween bash. It was the perfect way to take a childhood passion and parlay it into an adult-themed tradition.

The girlfriends who later became their wives helped to propel the event to the next level. There was nothing like a houseful of half-naked women to fuel the festivities. It was the one time of year when the guys got to see everybody else's wives popping out of their tops.

Travis had been nearly despondent when the first party had been canceled and close to suicidal for the second. Now staring at his awesome fangs in the rearview, he thought about how much simpler it had been back then.

He carefully tucked the half dozen eggs into the center console, barely able to contain his excitement. As soon as he got the jump on Christoph, he would unload his arsenal on the old fartknocker. Travis laughed out loud. He hadn't thought about that in a very long time; he and Christoph had a million pet slurs for one another as children, but fartknocker had been his all-time favorite. It was a personal term of endearment shared between just the two of them.

Travis was about to hit the horn again when Darcy bounced out the front door and jiggled across the lawn to the car. She hopped into the passenger seat, wide-eyed and breathless. She was amped up about the party and had gone all out. Travis followed her legs, from the spiked, black, six-inch fuck-me pumps all the way up her thighs. The netted stockings looked like spiders had carefully spun a seductive web over her smooth flesh. Her breasts heaved as she inhaled and exhaled into the cab of the Honda, making Travis consider whether they might have a little time to spare before they hit the road.

"You look incredible." He leered at her.

Darcy popped the passenger mirror down and reapplied another dab of fake blood to the bite marks on her neck. "We don't have time for that," she told him. "But just wait till I get you home."

"Are you gonna suck my blood?" Travis bore his fangs and pretended to bite her.

"Mmm-hmm, something like that."

He threw the car in reverse and backed out of the driveway. "Well, giddy up."

Traffic was light as he made his way north on Route 904, taking the Cedar Crest exit slightly faster than the recommended thirty-five. The back tires of the Civic skidded for a second on a patch of loose pavement and then bit back into the meat of the road. Darcy reached out and clutched at the dashboard as she bounced in her seat, jiggling in all the right places. Travis had to force himself to keep his eyes on the road and off her tits. The front of her teddy was so low cut that the top edges of her nipples were visible on the horizon of its lustful hem.

It had become a bit of a contest for the guys' wives to out-slut one another, but Travis was pretty sure Darcy had it in the bag. Her only competition would be from Linda, Christoph's wife, who was rumored to be dressing as Harley Quinn this year—which in itself wasn't the sluttiest of costumes, except Christoph had alluded the top part of Linda's outfit would consist of nothing but grease paint. If that was the case, then sexy vampire victim was in serious trouble. One thing was for sure, by the time the Monster Mash played, some, if not most, of the guys' wives would be damn near naked. Especially this Halloween. It would truly be a graveyard smash.

Travis turned on the radio as he followed the long stretch of dark road leading to the Clinton Barrens. Christoph had built a monster of a McMansion out on twelve acres of wooded real estate he had purchased for a song and a dance. Travis hated how far it was from the interstate and in the middle of buttfuck nowhere. Why anyone would want to live that far out in the sticks was a mystery to him, and he had often told his friend how he felt. But Christoph loved the woods. Not to mention the size of the house he had been able to build for a fraction of what his other friends had shelled out for their much smaller homes. The place was complete with a pool, jacuzzi, full bar, a movie room with actual stadium seats, five bedrooms, and four full baths. That didn't even include the man cave and massive four-car garage set in a backyard that stretched out toward the extensive wooded barrens. The only real problem, it was dark as fuck out there because the city hadn't seen any reason to put in streetlights—not for the few random idiots who had decided to build houses out that far.

Dr. Heidegger with the CDC announced FDA approval of the Sigma variant booster. The organization comes under fire from various interest groups as preparations for mass imun...

A blare of static roared through the Honda's speakers, silencing the news report. Travis hit the scan button and watched as the digital readout cycled through in a blur. White noise continued to spit and crackle like the vampiric hiss he had made not long before.

"Just as well. Who wants to hear that bullshit?" He lowered the volume and hit the preset stations. An obnoxious hiss answered him with disregard.

"What is it, honey?" Darcy asked. "Is it broken?"

"Was working fine this afternoon. I don't know what's wrong with it."

"Maybe we're out of range way out here," she offered.

Travis looked at her out of the corner of his eyes and grimaced. They had been out that way dozens of times before and had never lost reception. "I don't think so, babe." He turned on the high beams and decided not to worry about the radio. He had no idea what was wrong but figured now wasn't the time to focus on it while driving in the dark.

Dense grass and waist-high ragweed threatened to take over the pavement at every curve. The narrow two-lane road was also flanked by an army of pines keeping a sentinel watch over the lonesome tongue of blacktop. The glow of the moon, the only available light source, was nearly obscured by the giant trees. A low-lying ground fog lumbered in off the cold ground and slowly dragged itself onto the pavement around them, making it even harder for Travis to see the faded yellow line running down the center.

He drifted a bit too far to the right and immediately felt the tires leave the road surface, shuddering against the soft shoulder of gravel and ruts. He quickly compensated and pulled the wheel a bit too hard to the left. The car jumped back onto the road, causing Darcy's forehead to smack against the passenger side window.

"Fuck!" she shouted as stars lit up her field of vision. "You tryin' to kill me, asshole?"

"Christ, I'm sorry," Travis gushed as he pressed down on the brakes and brought the car to a standstill. "Are you alright, baby?" He leaned over and checked his wife's forehead in the dull cabin light of the Civic.

There was a small knot on the side of her head where she had made contact with the window, but thankfully she hadn't broken the skin.

"I am so sorry, hon. I can't see shit out here and had no idea I had drifted."

Darcy accepted his comfort and rested her head against Travis's shoulder. "Just be careful, will ya?"

She looked up into his eyes and smiled. It had been a close call, but thank God it hadn't been any worse. If the car had gone entirely off the road and barreled into the woods, there was no telling what could have happened. Darcy kissed him firmly on the lips and then pulled back.

"Let's get there," she said, "in one piece."

They laughed as Travis put the car in drive and took his foot off the brake. The engine died as if it had been turned off with a switch. There was no sputter, no cough from the motor, not even a single warning light. The car had been running one second and not the next. Travis looked at his wife and offered a half-hearted grin. He turned the key as his throat tightened. Expecting, at the very least, the soul-crushing *click, click, click* of a dead battery, Travis felt the first clench of panic when nothing happened, and the interior lights went out.

"What the fuck?" He frantically tried the ignition again.

His foot pumped the gas, and he reached for every knob, continuing to try the key. All of it was fruitless. The vehicle had been silenced. He turned to Darcy and opened his mouth to speak when he noticed a faint glow beginning to illuminate not only the cab of the civic but the stretch of pavement in front of them. It slowly grew brighter, as if a spotlight had been set to a dimmer and then directed onto the patch of road where the car had stalled.

He spun in his seat, looking out the side window. The glow illuminated the woods and the grass on that side of the street. It was a dull, greenish, almost sickly-colored light and continued to increase in magnitude by the second. The inside of the vehicle was now awash in the suffocating bath.

Darcy reached out and took his hand. Her skin was ice cold, and she was trembling. "What is it? I'm scared."

Travis clutched her hand and opened his mouth to reassure her but quickly shut it and grabbed at the wheel as the vehicle began to vibrate and then shake. The couple instinctively braced themselves between the dashboard and seats as the Honda rattled, bucked, and shimmied across the pavement. It slid sideways toward the grassy embankment, and then the passenger side tires left the road.

The light increased to such a blinding ferocity that Travis and Darcy needed to squint and shield their eyes from the glare. The cab had grown warmer, and Travis could feel the sweat running down his temples and the back of his shirt.

In a white-hot flash, the world exploded above them. The source of the light rocketed across the sky like Jupiter's balls shot from a furnace. The massive sphere of green fire passed over the car and the road, leaving a blazing trail of burning sky in its wake. The projectile's force nearly overturned the vehicle as it breached their path and continued barreling forward.

Travis and Darcy watched in horror as the object hurtled away from them, igniting the tops of the trees. They stared for what felt like an eternity, not saying a word to one another. Then, the horizon was incinerated. Whatever had been vomited out of the sky smacked into the earth several miles ahead. An encompassing greenish-white cloud devoured all, turning the night into a violent necrotic midday.

At first, it was invasive. Then the magnitude of the blast lessened. Finally, Travis could discern the gaseous cloud lifting from the ground before them. A giant green mushroom rose into the air and imploded on itself. Moments later, they were hit by the shock wave. It pounded into the car like Ron Jeremy, lifting the vehicle off the pavement and tossing it backward into the thick grass.

Darcy felt it in her stomach—that fluttery feeling she got when she went on roller coasters. A little like butterflies but not entirely, it was the sensation of being out of control yet knowing something terrible was about to happen. That's when the front wheels left the ground, and the back ones followed.

The Honda flipped once, then rolled through the air, tossed like a cornhole bag. It came down on its roof and was propelled by the momentum through the tall grasses and weeds until it finally crashed against the trunk of a large pine. Darcy had remained conscious for most of it but had blacked out when the vehicle began its death roll. She lasted longer than Travis, who had passed out almost immediately.

Cobwebs. Travis woke to find himself hanging upside down, suspended from his seatbelt, with cobwebs clouding his vision. He squinted and attempted to focus, but the blood rushing to his head fogged his thoughts and numbed his senses. Darcy hung from her own harnessed restraint, slack and lifeless like a dishrag carelessly left dangling over the kitchen faucet.

He tried to reach for her and felt a nauseating pop and then the clacking of his collarbone as the broken pieces raked against each other. He howled as the pain ripped through him, and he nearly passed out again. The agonizing jolt catapulted him from his haze and cleared the murk invading his head. With a bit more clarity and control, he noticed it wasn't cobwebs he was looking at, only the shattered, spidery veins of the Civics' broken windshield. Then he saw the cracked eggshells smashed against the dashboard and steering column, their innards dripping in long strings.

With the car resting on its roof in waist-deep grass, only the faintest glow of green pierced the damaged windows. It was a foul shade reminding Travis of sickness and decay, making him think of swamp gas or what he imagined it might look like. There was something sour about the light furtively invading the vehicle.

Travis struggled to remember. He had pulled over after almost driving off the road, and then the car had died. There was the light, and then what? His head throbbed, and the pain in his shoulder screamed bloody fucking murder. It had happened so fast, and he wasn't sure about any of it. Something had passed over the car. No, something had shredded the sky.

It had to be a meteor, he thought for a moment. But the trail it had left, the burning plume that had followed, had been green—a vile shade of green like kryptonite on meth. Nothing was that noxious a shade of green, nothing good, at least. Maybe it hadn't even been a meteor. For all Travis knew, it could have been a plane coming down. Whatever it was, it had crashed into the woods a few miles up, dangerously close to Christoph's house.

Darcy coughed and, a moment later, started to moan. Then she woke up screaming.

It took her a bit longer to clear her head and regain control of her wits than it had Travis. Somehow, she had been spared injury and was only shaken up by the incident. She removed herself from the vehicle relatively quickly. Then, proceeded to help Travis, carefully unlatching his seatbelt as he attempted to brace himself with his good arm. But gravity and his own momentum proved too much to prevent his fall entirely. He screamed and then howled again as the fractured clavicle ground against itself. Finally, with Darcy's assistance, he dragged himself out of the driver's side window.

The vision cresting the hill in the distance left the couple aghast. The glow from the mysterious projectile saturated the sky like a disease. It consumed the miles between them with an algae-tinted illumination pulsing oddly like a heart. First, it swelled, growing in intensity like a beacon crying out in pain. Then it ebbed as it slowly faded and died, only to pulse back to life a horrifying moment later.

Travis dug into his pocket with his good arm and retrieved his cell phone. He fumbled with it, depressing the button on the side, and waited for his favorite picture of Darcy to appear on the screen. It had been taken of her when they were in college. Her dimples had been more pronounced back then due to the little bit of baby fat she had worn. That was before the P90X and the Pilates. She was still a gorgeous woman, but Travis had been a fan of the little bit of extra weight she had carried; it looked good on her, especially in the trunk.

When the screen remained dark, he pressed the button once again. Still nothing. He shook it up and down, thinking he must have damaged it in the accident, but tried anyway. It was useless.

"Try yours, babe," he told her.

Darcy removed her phone from the small handbag she had rummaged out of the wreckage. She slid her finger across the screen and then looked up at Travis. "It's dead," she told him, "just like yours."

They stared at each other as they stood beside the wrecked Honda. What were the chances that both of their phones had been damaged? Darcy's had been tucked safely in her bag, and Travis had once dropped his off a ten-foot ladder. The thing hadn't so much as cracked. He looked back toward the top of the hill at the pulsing glow in the distance. Then he scanned the dead, blank screen of his phone.

"EMP," he muttered.

"What?" she asked.

"Electromagnetic Pulse. It's a wave of electromagnetic radiation that wipes out electronics. I'm willing to bet that's what happened to the car and our phones. It happens when nuclear missiles are detonated, or when..."

The green glow intensified as if aware of what the couple had been discussing.

Darcy shivered and pressed herself against Travis's good side. "What in God's name is that?"

"I have no fucking idea. But I don't think God has anything to do with it."

"It had to be a meteorite, right? I mean, if it were a nuke, we'd be dead." Darcy's voice cracked. "Jesus, it crashed almost on top of Christoph and Linda's place. Do you think they're alright?"

Travis scanned the surrounding area. The blast from the impact had flattened the grass with the force of a hurricane. Many of the trees had been knocked over, too, some even uprooted. Smoldering limbs and burning leaves lit up the wreckage of the turned-over vehicle, which was mangled, and no doubt totaled.

It was a miracle they were still alive. In the direction of the pulsing horizon, the scenery was much the same—ravaged and destroyed. It made Travis sick to think what might have happened to his friend's place, which had been far too close to the point of impact. He forced a smile and turned to his wife.

"They're okay, honey." He held her shivering body. "I don't know how I know, but they're alright."

After some time, Darcy managed to pull herself together.

"There's a sweatshirt in the backseat if you can fish it out." Travis knew she was freezing.

Darcy leaned into the wreckage and returned a moment later, holding his favorite Seton Hall sweatshirt. "What do we do now? We can't just stand here."

Travis turned in the direction of the road and began to walk. It was over ten miles back to the highway. There was no way Darcy would make the trek in her fuck-me pumps. And the idea of heading that way hadn't even crossed Travis's mind. The shockwave had tossed the Honda like a salad. There was no telling what damage it had done to his friend's house. Everyone would have been there already—Travis and Christoph's buddies from college and Darcy's girlfriends as well. At the very least, there would be a shitstorm of damage to the place. That was, if it was still standing at all. Despite what he had told his wife, Travis knew if their friends were still alive, they were in serious trouble. They were probably trapped under a mountain of debris.

"We have to get to Christoph's. They might need our help."

Darcy quickly donned the sweatshirt and followed her husband back to the road.

The knotty two-lane stretch of blacktop was littered with fallen branches and debris but had remained undamaged. The couple set out using the viridescent glow as magnetic north. Darcy removed her heels and walked barefoot, which proved far more comfortable. Travis used some of the material from his frilly pirate-like vampire shirt to bind his right arm against his chest, securing his shoulder and preventing the bones from grinding together.

With every passing mile marker, the ball of light on the horizon drew closer and more prominent. It pulsed deeply like an organism, growing brighter for a moment and then fading the next. An unnerving vibration had begun to fill

Travis's sinuses and eardrums. He observed how Darcy had started tugging at her ears, showing that she could feel it too. The vibration was toxic. It resonated within Travis's fillings and chewed at the broken bone in his shoulder.

"I don't feel so good," Darcy gasped and stopped walking. She hunched over, resting her hands on her knees, and then vomited onto the street.

Travis took a step toward her and was seized by the violent flip of his own stomach. A moment later, he joined her, spilling his dinner onto the blacktop. It happened in a whirl. One second he was looking at the dusty gravel-strewn pavement, and the next, he was on his back, looking up at the burnt olive bleed of the sky.

"Babe," Darcy's voice was distant, like a dream. She choked and then spat. "Baby, are you alright?" She scrambled over to where he lay.

His head filled with the thrumming of a virulent machine.

"I-I..." Travis tried to put will to words but was unable. He stared up at a sky that nearly choked out the moon. It was full behind the murky haze, barely permeating the dense pollution contaminating the air. He felt her touch. It helped bring him back.

Halloween, he thought.

It was Halloween, and it was a full moon. Then he remembered the ... party?

Travis sat up, placing his hands against the cold street to support himself. He turned his head to the right, then the left, and finally allowed his eyes to focus on Darcy. She stared at him in shock.

"I guess we passed out," he offered.

Darcy remained silent, gaping at him as if he had grown a second dick.

"What?" he finally asked.

She pointed at his arm.

Finally, Travis realized what had her so bugged out. He was supporting his weight with both arms. The binding he had used to secure his shoulder had come undone. Somehow, he had done this and not felt any pain. Quickly, he jerked, expecting the familiar jolt to rocket through his shoulder and arm once again. But there was none. He raised his arm and bent it, then touched the spot where his clavicle had shattered. Again, he braced himself for the excruciating pain, only to find the collarbone as solid as the road he sat on. The pain had vanished, and the fracture had miraculously mended on its own.

"What the fuck?" Darcy managed.

"I have no fucking idea," he said, rising to his feet. "But we need to keep moving." Travis continued walking to his friend's house, moving in the same direction as that horrible glow. He didn't know where to begin or what to say. Instead, he walked with a thousand thoughts overflowing the dam. The pulsing hum of the vibration drew them like a magnet, pulling the couple closer to the viridescent light and further from the relative safety of the road.

Travis had begun to lag a few paces behind his wife. The boots he had bought had obviously been the wrong size. His feet bounced around inside them, making it hard to walk. He thought about ditching them as Darcy had hers but continued to push through in his oversized boots with his full attention focused on Darcy's beautiful ass swaying ahead of him.

Of course, he would never consider saying anything to her, but now that he had a full rear view, she looked as though she had put a few pounds back on. Her cheeks were plump and jiggly like they had been in college, back when they had both been much younger. Travis wasn't sure why he hadn't noticed earlier; it wasn't as if she could have gained it back overnight. But he had been working a lot lately, and he hadn't been in the room when she changed into her teddy. Surely, he would have seen the difference then. Smiling, he shuffled along in his flopping boots, happy his wife had finally eased up on the crazy workouts.

"What the fuck?" Darcy stopped in the road.

Travis closed the distance behind her and gasped. "What the fuck?" he repeated.

They had arrived where Christoph's driveway intersected the road. The blast had mowed down the grasses and weeds along with most of the trees. Branches and boughs littered the long driveway leading to the house, which was still too far away to see from the street. The pulsing glow continued to intermittently grow and dim from the far side of the property, while the constant vibration rattled within both their heads. Darcy looked at her husband with her mouth agape; neither could believe what they saw.

A line of Jack-o'-lanterns had been positioned along the side of the driveway leading to the house. Candles had been placed inside their hollowed-out skulls, and someone had lit them. They led the way to the house like scattered breadcrumbs, their demented stares flickering in the distance as far as they could see. Many were cracked, others only partially intact. The blast had tossed them about the property, damaging most. But someone had collected their remains and replaced them along the driveway's edge. They had even taken the time to relight the candles. That meant only one thing—Christoph and the others had survived.

Darcy offered a faint-hearted smile. A wash of light from the candles fused with the green glow and etched her face, casting shadows that accentuated her dimples, making her look eerily girlish. "I guess they're alright." She didn't sound confident.

Travis took her hand and led her toward the house. "Weird, huh?" he said. "They knew we'd be on the road. They probably set them up so we could see."

It was all he could think of, but it didn't make sense. Under the circumstances, with fireballs raining from the sky, Travis was pretty sure Jack-o'-lanterns would have been the last thing he would have worried about, never mind how scattered they must have been after the blast. That must have taken some time to collect all of them. About thirty of the festive gourds led the way, all with candles secured in place and lit. Each one was more damaged than the previous. The hollowed-out zig-zag of their broken eye sockets was more than just a little disconcerting; it was jarring. Travis felt his heart hammering in his chest as they passed a half pumpkin propped against a fallen limb with its candle stuck firmly into the side of its head.

The house should have been visible by now. Travis scanned the property for the structure, expecting the darkened silhouette to jump out at any moment. They had traveled over three-quarters of the distance up the driveway and, for some reason, still couldn't see the place. Then, he noticed the debris. Shingles and shards of plywood littered the remainder of the path before them. Carefully navigating the mess, Travis led Darcy around several large two-by-twelves splintered and piled in their way. He didn't know a hell of a lot about construction, but he was pretty sure lumber that size was used to hold up the lower floors of a house. A sour knot clenched like a charley horse in the base of his nuts.

They slowly maneuvered around the rubble, only to find themselves in front of an impassible barrier of debris. Christoph's house lay in a pile of splintered timbers. It looked like it had been hit by a tornado or something worse. The mass of rubble where the foundation had been was extensive.

Darcy threw her arms around him. "No!" She began to cry. "Please, no!"

The place had been massacred. Travis held his wife as he continued to scan the property. There was no way in hell anyone could have survived it. Floorboards, plywood, roofing ... all of it had been chewed up like a stalk of celery. Whoever had been in the house would have been pulverized by the massive force. The knot he had felt in his nuts was now in his throat.

Suddenly, the noise from the vibration was pierced by a high-pitched cry. Travis quickly turned in the direction it had come from, but he was too late. It hit him in the center of his chest, knocking the air out of his lungs and causing him to double over. He clutched his knees, coughing, trying to figure out what had hit him. An answer from the edge of the property cried back. It was laughter, the sound of children.

Jesus Christ, there were kids out here, and they were still alive. He could feel Darcy's hands on his back as he slowly straightened up and examined his chest.

It was wet; he was bleeding. He looked down at the front of his shirt and saw the dark stain spreading from the wound. He began to feel lightheaded as reality sank in. He raised a hand to the area where he had been hit. Travis felt the cold soup.

Cold ... it was cold!

Another projectile sailed out of the darkness and struck him in the leg. This time, Travis saw the egg shatter against his calf. Its shells scattered and landed in the dirt.

"Son of a bitch," he wheezed.

Travis raised his hand close to his face and watched the band of yolk as it hung from his fingers in long strings. Under the strange glow of the distant illumination, it had appeared the dark reddish brown of freshly spilled blood. He extended his palm to his wife.

"Egg. See?" He was practically giddy now.

The impact from the thrown projectile had knocked the wind out of him, making Travis think he had been shot. Darcy stared at his hand for a moment, then looked up at him and giggled as if he had tickled her ass with a feather. Her eyes lit up, and her smile broadened as she chuckled like a schoolgirl. Now, Travis was positive she had put on a little weight. Darcy's dimples were more pronounced than they had been in years. The layer of baby fat that had found its way back into her features had smoothed out the small wrinkles around her eyes. Possibly, it was the strange light, or maybe Travis was still a bit turned out from the crash, but Darcy looked exactly as she had back in college.

He shook off the vibrating presence and refocused his attention. Somewhere amongst the tangle of fallen trees and debris were children. They must have been the ones who had set up the Jack-o'-lanterns. Another egg came at them from the darkness. It landed at Travis's feet, spraying more yolk and goo onto his boots.

"Come out here," he shouted. "We can help you."

He was answered by a chorus of voices echoing his words.

"Come out, come out, come out! We can help you. We can help you!" The high-pitched timbre of children's voices cut through the nauseating vibration. Boys and girls hooted and hollered back at them from the strangeness of the night.

"Stop that," Travis screamed, his temper beginning to rise. "Come out here now!"

The shrill sound of laughter penetrated the night. It was followed by the attack. An onslaught of eggs sailed through the air at the couple like Persian arrows eclipsing the sun. The splattering and crunching sound of their shells surrounded the couple at first, then some of the projectiles found their marks. One hit Travis in the shoulder; the next hit Darcy in the knee. She screamed and then laughed with delight as the barrage of chicken ovum rained down on them.

Darcy turned to her husband with zest in her eyes and grabbed him by the hand. "Let's get 'em!" she pleaded.

The couple took off running in the direction the assault had originated. Travis attempted his first leaping stride and tripped as his foot came out of his boot, snagging his pant leg. He kicked off his other boot, which suddenly felt too big as well. Then, he grabbed the waistband of his pants and refastened his belt, sinching it another loop tighter.

"When I get my hands on you"—he laughed as he struggled with his clothing—"I'm gonna kill you!"

Darcy reacted as if it were the funniest thing she had ever heard and burst into a fresh fit of giggles. She sprinted ahead of her husband into the darkness with only the venomous glow to light her way, jumping over broken timbers and hurdling fallen limbs like an athlete.

"Yeah," she shouted. "We're gonna kill you!"

She was answered by more high-pitched laughter and taunting. The children had taken flight and retreated further into the murk of the night. They yelled back at their pursuers, urging them to follow.

"Oh yeah?" one of the kids screamed. "You and whose army?"

The taunting and the thrill of the chase filled Travis with a flush of adrenalized fever. It reminded him of when he played flashlight tag as a boy—the excitement and emotion so driving and powerful that it kept the body moving well past the point of exhaustion and even dehydration. He felt the air burning in his lungs as he raced through the tangle of trees and limbs, with his wife leading the way like a gold medalist. Despite the tightness in his chest and the sensation of his muscles working harder than they should, he was driven by a euphoric intoxication filling his veins, consuming him like a narcotic.

"You're about to find out, buttface!" he howled, then suddenly broke into his own bout of laughter.

More cries of excitement and unadulterated joy saturated the air, driving him to run faster and catch up to Darcy. He watched her sail like a gazelle over a large, fallen tree trunk. With his blood pumping and his heart thrumming, Travis focused on his wife's ass as she took to the air. But the sweatshirt she had put on hung almost to the middle of her thighs, concealing the goods. For a moment, he wondered why he had been able to see it before but not now, especially with her in mid-jump. Surely, the sweatshirt would have ridden up on her as she leaped. The thought was quickly pushed aside as his pants fell to his knees and tripped him before he could reach the fallen tree. Travis quickly kicked away the bulky clothing and continued his pursuit in his boxer shorts. The frilly gothic shirt he wore now looked more like a nightgown.

"Nice PJs, dill-hole," ribbed a young boy's voice. "Is that your sister's dress?"

"No," Travis shouted back. "It's your mom's!" The sound of Darcy cackling filled Travis with a surge of bravado. "She gave it to me last night when I was doggin' her." He laughed and nearly coughed on the last word.

His reply was answered by enthusiastic laughter. Travis climbed over the fallen tree and took off after Darcy and the fleeing children.

The chase led them toward the mysterious object that had fallen from the sky. Green light continued to grow brighter with each step they took. The vibration was now more of an internal noise than one originating from someplace else. It filled their heads with its tireless warble, like a television left on while they slept or a radio playing in the background. Travis pushed his overtaxed muscles as he ascended the hill before him. He watched Darcy just as she crested the rise and then disappeared. Suddenly the pulsing glow lashed out like the flash of a strobe. It filled the sky and lit the woods around him as he raced the final steps to the top of the hill.

Travis crested the mound to find Darcy and the rest of the children gathered around the massive crater. He froze at the sight of the kids in their Halloween costumes, dressed as if they had been out trick-or-treating. One child wore a Frankenstein outfit that looked about eight sizes too big. He was barefoot and had cuffed his pants and shirtsleeves to fit better. His monster headpiece flopped awkwardly on his head like a spaghetti pot used to make Sunday dinner. The boy stood next to several other children also dressed in oversized costumes. Mr. Spock had ripped the sleeves and legs off his uniform. One of his ears had fallen off, but the other still held fast. Michael Meyers looked as if he were about ten years old and had no business being up so late. He was practically swimming in his jumpsuit, which dragged over his feet and hung from his arms. His mask was tilted far to the right as if the head inside couldn't support its mass.

Travis scanned the group, searching for his wife, then noticed the girls—all of whom were dressed outrageously mature. They wore massive amounts of makeup, with each of their costumes more alarming than the next. There was a naughty nurse whose white skirt hung to her knees. She stood next to a French maid who had resorted to tying the straps of her teddy into knots to prevent it from falling. Behind them was a sexy vampire and a girl wearing a costume Travis couldn't make out. The children all faced the giant glowing orb sitting in the middle of the crater.

"Hey, you kids," Travis called to them, "get away from that thing!"

Frankenstein turned to him with a mocking grin. "Who are you callin' kid, fartknocker?"

Travis nearly fell over. Fartknocker. There was only one person who ever used the term fartknocker.

"C-Christoph," he stammered. "Is that you?"

"Who the hell did you think it was, dickweed?" The boy was joined by a girl who had been standing behind the others.

Now Travis could see her costume; it was a Harley Quinn outfit. Her shorts were cinched around her waist with a belt that had run out of loopholes and had been tied instead. They hung baggy past her knees like a pair of capris. But the top part of her outfit caused Travis to double-take. The white and red making up Harley's shirt had been painted on. It was shocking to see a little girl shirtless with nothing but paint covering her, but the absence of breasts was even more alarming. Travis knew it was Linda beneath the paint, who had been very well endowed. But now, wearing the body of a much younger version of herself, she had not even hit puberty yet.

"Linda, is that you?"

The vibrating presence began to penetrate his joints.

"Bout time you showed up, dork." She turned toward the glowing orb. "Isn't it wonderful?"

Travis tried to steady himself as he swayed on his feet. He bent over and placed his hands on his bare knees. Frankenstein and Harley rushed to his aid and were joined by another young girl. Travis saw the baggy stockings with their spiderwebbed designs, now torn and missing the feet. The girl's little toenails were painted a fiery red but almost looked black in the pale green light.

It was Darcy's color.

Travis braced himself as he stood up. The girl standing eye-level before him wore a Seton Hall sweatshirt, now hanging well past her knees. The oversized collar fell off her shoulder, revealing the bite marks drawn onto her neck. Darcy put her arms around him and helped steady her husband.

"Are you okay, baby?" she asked, her voice several octaves higher than it had been earlier.

"Hey, dude." Christoph grabbed him by the shoulder. "You almost passed out, bro."

Linda smiled at him, her dyed pigtails bouncing on either side of her head. "Welcome to the party, kid."

"What the…" Travis spread his hands out in front of him. His wedding band was gone. It had fallen off a ring finger now half the size it had been an hour before. He rubbed his chin, finding it smoother than he could ever remember. His shirt hung past his knees, making him feel like he was wearing a dress. "How is this possible?" he managed.

"Awesome, isn't it?" Linda smirked.

Darcy looked confused but appeared to be taking it better than he was. She held his hand as he wobbled again on his unstable footing.

"You gotta see this, fartknocker," Christoph said, clapping Travis on the back, then making his way down the embankment into the crater.

"Can you walk, honey?" Darcy took him by the waist. "I'll help you."

The other children had already begun to make their way toward the glowing ball. A mess of footprints led up and down the hill. His friends had been playing in the area for some time.

Travis tried to form any of the thousand questions he desperately needed to ask but couldn't manage one. He needed to know what had happened when the meteor hit. Had they all been in the house? How had they survived? But most of all, what in God's name had suddenly caused them to grow younger?

"It's just like we always talked about." Christoph turned to him. "You know, now it can be Halloween forever. We don't have to worry about getting sick or growing old anymore."

Travis expected the radiation from the brilliant glow to incinerate them before they made it halfway down the crater, but the temperature hadn't changed a digit. They continued to traverse the loose soil as the first piece of wreckage came into focus. It was a large steel shaft nearly two inches thick and seven feet long. It had been scorched a blackish red. Another piece of the same material lay about two yards from it, half-buried in the earth. It too, had been charred to a burnt umber.

Something that looked like an engine had broken up when the object crashed, expelling its components into a thousand different pieces, littering the ground like popcorn at a carnival.

Darcy helped support him with her shoulder, and Christoph took him by his other arm. The group stopped at the base of the crater with the blazing orb in front of them. Travis could feel the vibration throughout his entire body—filling his eardrums, working through his joints, focusing on his cells. This was the cause of it. This thing had fallen from the sky and gone to work on them the second it hit the earth. The pulse and vibration worked together to rejuvenate their bodies, attacking the free radicals, curing their arthritis and afflictions, and relieving them of age.

An even larger piece of the hull stretched out, half-buried in the soil before them. Travis stood on his own, leaving his wife and best friend behind. He walked to the strange object and placed his hands on it. The burnt carbon coating wiped away with his touch, revealing the matte surface of the steel. He swept his hands to the left and the right, exposing more of the ship's outer hull. The vibration was not only in the strange ball of light but the very steel itself. The ship carrying this object was alive with the pulse. It resonated throughout his hands and forearms as he swept the dark coating from it.

At first, he thought it might be a stubborn smudge, but after several waves of his hand, Travis began to make out the writing underneath. Frantically, he uncovered more of the hidden lettering etched into the steel. Dark soot covered his palms and fingers as he discovered more of the message. The sound of a roaring jet jarred him from his task as Travis looked up to see another fiery plume of green plummeting to the earth miles away. A moment later, another seared through the distance, landing as far away as Pennsylvania. Suddenly, the sky was awash with falling plumes of green rocketing to their final destinations across the globe.

Darcy and Christoph joined him and helped uncover the lettering. They feverishly worked to reveal the message written on the strange object. There was a large T followed by a Y visible beneath the carbon. Travis uncovered a D and a C and then went to work on another part of the metal, exposing even more of the cryptic message. The group worked as the skies above were raped by the shadow fires of falling objects. Travis made another large sweep with his hands, revealing the last of the message. Then fell backward as if he had been knocked over.

The children stared at what had been revealed. Darcy rushed to where Travis sat in the dirt and threw her arms around him. He stared back at the warped piece of steel that had delivered the package. From where he sat, the sky looked like it was on fire, with a thousand other similar objects hurdling to their final resting places. He reread it, hoping he had been mistaken the first time. But it was plain to see, and there was no taking it back. The bastards had really done it. They had figured out how to take choice out of the equation.

The tangled piece of steel that had landed less than a mile from Christoph's house bore a familiar insignia with an even more familiar nation's flag beneath it. In bold letters, written like words that had been painted on a billboard, read the message: SIGMA BOOSTER: PROP. OF THE CDC. Yolk and broken shells splattered against the strange metal as the egg was hurled at them. Travis and the rest of the children broke into a fit of laughter and tore after the assailant in hot pursuit.

It was turning out to be one hell of a party.

Thirteen

THE WHEEL TURNS

Pat Sajak lowered his gaze and directed it at me with a look that only a game show host could offer. "Well, Robert," he said. "What would you like to do, spin or solve?"

I stared at the giant puzzle, and the trance slowly began to lift. How did I get here, and what do I do now, were only a few of the million thoughts that simultaneously raced through my overtaxed mind. The studio audience remained on the edge of their seats, waiting for me to do something foolish. My fellow contestants perched like leopards next to me, ready to snatch victory from my flailing grasp. My wife, somewhere in the crowd, attempted to project the answer to the puzzle into my blank consciousness. It wasn't helping.

Again, I stared at the board before me. Somehow, I had managed to guess nearly ninety percent of the letters to the phrase and had accumulated almost twelve thousand dollars. Still nothing. The words didn't make sense. The letters didn't even appear to be in English. I felt the tie I had chosen to wear tightening around my throat. My hands were sweating, and my legs started to cramp up. The studio, which felt chilly only a moment ago, was now dry, suffocating, and about as hot as the surface of the sun. Then, without thinking or even giving my brain a moment to clear, I grabbed the Wheel and spun. I braced myself and waited for the inevitable Bankrupt space to arrive and kick me in the teeth. *How did I get here?* I asked again as I watched the dreaded black space circle like a hungry vulture.

☙

It had been less than a month ago. My wife greeted me at the door when I returned from work that day. She was up to something. The smile on her face said it all. She was good for that. Karin would get these crazy ideas, to say the least. She was very spontaneous and very energetic, and that's what attracted me to her initially, even though sometimes her plans were a bit out there. This was one of those times.

"I hope you don't mind," she said and greeted me with a kiss.

I braced myself; this wasn't going to be good. "I put in an application to be on Wheel of Fortune."

That's not so bad, I thought. I knew nothing would come of it. Getting on a game show had to be about as hard as winning the lottery. I offered a smile. "That's nice. Good luck." I saw in her eyes that there was more.

"I signed you up, too."

There it was.

I guess the look on my face said all it needed to. It had been a long day, sheetrocking and spackling from seven to four was a hard way to make a living. We had just bought our first house, gutted it, and were in the process of major renovations. Even worse, we were officially out of money. The walls were bare, the electricity was half-installed, and families of crickets were finding their way into the house during the night. The lack of walls and insulation left us exposed not only to the elements but also the wildlife. "That's nice," I repeated.

I'd like to say that I had forgotten all about the gameshow thing in the days to come, but Karin wasn't the type to allow that. She was more than jazzed about the possibility, and her energy was contagious. In fact, after that, there wasn't a conversation that didn't center around the idea of one of us being on the show. There must be something to that whole Law of Attraction thing because we both received calls in less than two weeks. First, Karin received a call from a woman who worked in the contestant department for Wheel of Fortune; she had been chosen to audition. Less than an hour later, my cell phone rang.

"Hello. May I speak with Robert, please," asked the voice.

"This is Robert."

"This is Gary from Wheel. We would like you to audition for the show."

Karin and I were asked to show up at the Hilton in Fort Lee. I had been skeptical and negative, and I had been sure that this was just another of my wife's outrageous ideas that would never pan out. I had also been wrong.

The ballroom of the Hilton was packed with over fifteen hundred exuberant would-be auditioners. Karin and I sat in what felt like the exact center of the room. A panel of four sat before the crowd—three women and a man I imagined to be Gary.

What do we do? What do I do? What the hell am I doing here?

This was the kind of stuff Karin did. I was a construction worker, a regular Joe, and a bit rough around the edges. This was a place for my extroverted, energetic, bubbly better half, certainly not me.

"Here's what we're looking for," Gary said after the panel introduced themselves. "We want you to stand up and tell us a little bit about yourself, as if you were a contestant on the show." Then he sat down.

That was it? There had to be more than that. Where's the catch? I wondered.

I never claimed to be the smartest knife in the drawer, (see what I did there), but I knew it couldn't be that cut and dry, (again). As the first few rows began to stand up and proceed with their awkward introductions, I realized I was right. The look on the panelists' faces told me they were looking for something special, something that stood out. But what? I looked at Karin and thought, *Something like her.*

I didn't doubt that once my bride stood up and revealed her effervescent personality, the judges would fall for her immediately. She was infectious. The process moved quicker than I imagined, and it was our turn before I figured out what I would say. Karin stood up, said something bubbly, and I knew she had nailed it. Then it came to me. Gulp!

"My name is Robert." I smiled. "I'm a contractor, and when I met my wife, it was love at first sight. So, if anyone out there doesn't believe it can happen, take it from me; it can." I sat down and watched the faces of the female panelists and every woman in the entire place light up. Karin grabbed my hand.

Nailed it!

The audition process didn't end there. Although my gratuitous and manipulative move had secured me safe passage through the first trial, there was more to follow. Next, we had to go into New York one morning with about a hundred other applicants who had made it this far. It was time to show our skills with the Wheel as if we were playing on the show. Gary and the girls wanted to see how we worked under pressure and if we possessed whatever constituted "The right stuff."

I spun the Wheel and confidently called out the letter Q, the most uncommonly used letter in the alphabet and Wheel of Fortune's history. But this was also a strategic move, as I knew it would attract the panelists' attention.

"Exactly," Gary said. "That's how it's done. Spin the Wheel, call out the letter and be confident. Although Q isn't exactly a great choice, this is how we want you to do it."

Again, nailed it.

Some hopefuls got it, but many did not despite the example I had offered.

Karin spun the Wheel, and at the most inopportune time, someone stood in front of her as she was about to call a letter. "Ummm, Ummm," she stammered.

My heart sank. What are you doing? I felt horrible. I knew she had blown it. She knew it, too, and she would have made a great contestant. Such is life. And the Wheel turns.

Several weeks later, I was contacted by Gary and told that I'd been chosen to be a contestant during Christmas week. Karin and I flew out a day early and did a little Hollywood sightseeing. We hit the pier in Santa Monica, checked out the Sunset Strip, and had dinner at El Coyote, the very place where Sharon Tate had her last meal before meeting her untimely death at the hands of the Manson Family. Great margaritas! Despite Karin's disappointment at not making the cut herself, she was happy for me. She wished me luck with a new nightie she had bought especially for the occasion and drove me to Sony Studios the following day. I was grateful for both.

I was ushered into the contestants' green room with all the other guests. Make-up was applied, and we were given the rundown. Wheel of Fortune films an entire week's worth of shows in one day. Pat and Vanna work no more than four days a month. We were then shown the stage, a whole lot smaller than you would imagine, and asked to pick numbers out of a hat. I was to be in the first group.

I stood in the middle position, the yellow spot, number two. Pat Sajak walked out when they introduced him, looking even more intense and impressive than imaginable. There was something extra about his and Vanna's presence—a star quality that separates the nobles from the rest of us peasants. Suddenly, everything I had rehearsed in my head vanished like a mirage.

In preparation for the day, I played hangman nonstop. I bought the home version of Wheel for my PlayStation and took Gingko Biloba religiously. I was determined to nail this. Oh well, all the best-laid plans.

The first toss-up puzzle began, and I could barely think, let alone guess at what it might be. The guy to my right won the first round and then started to spin. At one point, I think I got a chance to touch the Wheel but guessed an incorrect letter, and my turn quickly passed. The same guy won again, and I felt my aspirations deflate. There was a pause for a commercial break, and the makeup lady came out to touch up what the sweat had removed from my face. I gazed at the stage setup—the giant tree, the wreaths, the ornaments. It was Christmas week, even though it was the end of November. Shows are filmed a month in advance. I think that's when I started to feel a bit better, or at least not entirely unhinged.

"Welcome back to Wheel of Fortune. I'm Pat Sajak, your host. Why don't you tell us a little about yourself, Robert?"

It was weird to have Pat Sajak talk to me like that.

"I'm from Saddle Brook, New Jersey, and I am a contractor," I told Pat, the camera, and the studio audience. "I play guitar, and I like to scuba dive." And I forgot what the hell I was about to say ... so there's that.

"Ok, Robert," Pat had a million teeth. "Here's the puzzle. The theme is, *Where are we?*"

I knew once the puzzle was solved, there would be an extra three thousand bucks for whoever guessed the answer. The puzzle was incredibly long, with nine words or more. Surely, I could guess a few of the letters correctly. I looked down at the Wheel, and it blurred before my eyes. I white-knuckle gripped it and spun. That's when the world disappeared, and I fell into a fugue state. I had the sensation of hovering above my own body, watching the events unfold.

The giant Wheel was much heavier than it looked and barely made it around a full rotation. It landed on a significant dollar value, and a voice asked for an R. It was my own, though I had no idea who had commanded it. The Wheel spun again—$500—"T, please."

"There are some Ts," Pat acknowledged.

I watched the wheel spin. It coursed past the Bankrupt space and landed on $600. "I'll take an S." Then the voice asked to buy vowels: "E. I'll take another. An A, please."

The Wheel turns.

It was a blur, a flush, a flash. A million universes coalesced into one moment and fused. I saw this happening but had no power over anything taking place. Someone was controlling my body—a power greater than me. There were voices, applause, laughter, and the sound of my pounding heart. I awoke to find myself still spinning the Wheel. I had bought every vowel needed and guessed nearly every letter on the board. A few empty spaces remained, and my eyes frantically scanned the cryptic message that wavered before me. I didn't know what it was. Why didn't I know what it was? I should know it!

"M, please."

I am thrilled to see there's an M.

"Well, Robert. What would you like to do, spin or solve?"

Damn you, Pat Sajak, for being so much larger than life. His intimidating presence was too much for me to handle, and even though I knew I had already pushed my luck beyond the acceptable threshold, I grabbed the Wheel and spun. It was too late; I see that now. I should never have spun that last time.

The Bankrupt space inched closer and closer, and I felt the pit grow in the center of my gut. How could I have been so foolish? It wasn't that I had gotten greedy. The combination of out-of-bodyness and the fact that I had no idea what the answer actually was, propelled me along that derelict path. I was neither the conductor nor the passenger; I was a bystander. The ominous black space on the Wheel clicked into place as the goliath slowed and came to a halt.

Click!

"$200." Pat looked at me as if I were the luckiest bastard to have ever been born.

"G!" My stomach spun like a thousand clowns on a carousel.

"There is a G. Well, Robert, what would you like to do, spin or solve?"

For a larger-than-life type of guy, Pat Sajak could be a snarky douche!

"I'd like to solve," my exasperated vocal cords allowed me to exclaim. I looked at the puzzle practically written out before me and read out loud. All the vowels were in place, and nearly every consonant was revealed. Surely, I couldn't bung this up!

"THE GRINCH TRIED TO STEAL CHRISTMAS FROM THIS TOWN."

"Yeah, that's it," Mr. Hollywood announced. "And for an extra $3,000, can you tell us where we are?"

I could. "WHOVILLE!" I boasted.

The dollar value beneath my name read $16,000. Had I just won sixteen thousand dollars? I had, and there was no taking it back. Even if I didn't move to the bonus round, although it looked like I would, there was no taking it back. I had won $16,000!

As the makeup people were touching us up during the next commercial break, contestant number three, a beautiful girl from Georgia, turned to me. "That was God," she told me.

I thought about that for a second. It would always be difficult to explain how I felt when I touched the Wheel. It was like I had been taken over by something, like I was under the direction of a power other than my own free will. A mix between a dream, Deja-vu, and a straight-up trance. So weird.

"That was GOD right there," she said.

I was happy to see that nice girl had walked away with ten thousand dollars. And I was moving on to the bonus round. I was led to the center of the stage, where I chatted with Pat as the crew prepared me to go up for the big money and prizes.

That was years ago, back when there were five letters you could pick to determine what your prize would be. Providing you solved the puzzle, of course. I chose L. Karin, and I had decided on L. She said because I was *Lucky at Love*. And at the time, I was. But times change.

My free letters were R, S, T, L, N, and E. It was my turn to guess three consonants and one vowel. I guessed—M, F, and D for my consonants and A for my vowel.

"Well, the topic is, A Phrase," Pat said. "And I'm afraid you're not gonna get too much help here." At least I had made it this far. I prepared for the worst, knowing how complex the phrases could be, especially when you got no help from the letters. This was what was shown.

__   __A D   A   __ __ N __ __

I saw the emptiness of the puzzle, and my brain went into overdrive. Deductive reasoning skills that I had no idea I possessed began to fire off neurotransmitters that had not worked in years. I saw the blank first letter and knew it was not the letter A. Therefore, it had to be the letter I. My mind read I __ A D. Clearly, that had to be I HAD. There was no other option the way I saw it. I HAD A, I scanned the final word, and it jumped out at me. An N in the direct center, with the words I HAD A before it. There was nothing else it could be.

"I HAD A HUNCH!" I shouted.

"Yeah, that's it." Pat was just as impressed as I was.

And the crowd went wild! Karin was jumping in her seat, literally bursting at the seams.

"So, let's see what you've won." He opened the envelope marked with an L and showed it to me. It read, *Christmas Stocking.*

Suddenly a giant stocking, taller than I and larger than Pat's humongous game show personality, found its way to the stage. Then Pat began to open packages. He pulled the lid off the first one, revealing what looked like a pair of skis. Charlie O'Donnell's voice boomed over the sound system.

"Head to the mountain with your new Arbor snowboards. With these custom-designed Arbor snowboards, you'll look stylish on the slopes this year."

For the record, I hate the snow. I hate the cold, and I hate skiing. I was about to be seriously disappointed when I found out that I'd won a ski trip.

Pat opened another gift. It was impossible to tell what it was.

"Yakima Racks," Charlie boasted. "Carry your Arbor snowboards in your new Yakima rack system." The racks were the big bulky type that fastened to the top of a vehicle. This was getting interesting, and I realized that it could go either way.

Pat fumbled with a package much smaller than the others and the last one. He opened the lid and held up precisely what I was hoping for.

I watched the keys catch the light as they dangled from his fingertip. A glint in his eye said, "You did it," or maybe, "I can't believe you pulled that out of your ass." It was impossible to tell which.

"Carry your Yakima racks on your new Chevy Tahoe. The fully loaded Chevy Tahoe comes complete with heated leather seats, a state-of-the-art sound system, and four-wheel drive. Your total cash and prizes come to fifty-seven thousand nine hundred dollars.

I remember grabbing Pat and hugging him. I know that Karin rushed to the stage and gave us both a giant hug as well. Pat was more interested in her than he was in me at that point, but I didn't mind. I was introduced to Vanna, who shook my hand as if I might have leprosy. She was more than stand-offish, but that didn't bother me either. I was somewhere between cloud nine and walking on sunshine. It sounds a bit cliché, but what can I say? It was a surreal moment.

With my winnings, I finished the repairs on my house. There was even enough left to take my mother and sister on a cruise. Karin and I had always wanted to do that for them, and we finally had the means to do so. I drove that Tahoe with pride and a comfortable heated tushy for years and years after that. I've told this story many times since then, and every time I do, I'm reminded of how I felt when the sensation first overtook me. It was one of those rare moments when all the stars aligned, and everything clicked. I'm not sure exactly how many of those moments we get in a lifetime—one, maybe two. I'm sure some people experience them more than others, and some never experience them at all. I think it worked out so well because, when it happened—when I first felt the presence enter me, or whatever you might call it, when it first took control, and I took my hands off the Wheel (literally)—I didn't fight it. Now that I'm older and have had the chance to look back on that day countless times, hopefully through the eyes of a slightly wiser man, I'm fairly certain that's the only reason things turned out as miraculously as they did. Because when divine intervention, fate, or karma intercedes, the last thing you want to do is get in its way. If I learned anything from that experience, it's that the universe knows what it's doing. So, sit back and try to enjoy the ride ... As the Wheel Turns.

Fourteen

THE WIDOWER

David Reese woke up at four forty-five a.m., panicked and gasping for breath. He had dreamt about Penny again last night. This time, he could almost remember what it had been about ... almost. But now, in the cold, still morning hours as he struggled to recall, he failed to summon its specifics.

Nearly every night since Penny's passing, he had been visited with one lucid vision after the next, all leaving him temporarily paralyzed. Inescapable claustrophobia would grip him in the throes of his slumber, directing him like a mechanical toy until finished with him. David would then be expelled from the dream and rocketed into agitated wakefulness. He would always find himself as he did now, fighting to breathe, heart racing to keep up with the adrenaline it was being force-fed, thinking about Penelope.

Even now, he was sure he could smell the faintest whisps of her perfume as it too vanished with the dream. David reached for his phone with the memory fading even further from his grasp. He struggled to focus on the blurry screen, and his thick fingers fumbled with the tiny buttons as he attempted to check the time.

Damn!

He didn't need to be up for another hour and a half, but there was no sense in trying to go back to sleep. That sure as hell wasn't happening. To say the world had been turned upside down since Penny had died was simply not enough. It had been steamrolled, gutted, thrown down a flight of stairs, and then shit on.

That was the thing about cancer—it really knew how to fuck with you.

In the end, it had taken her so quickly ... so goddamn quickly.

He waited for the hazy fog of cobwebs to clear from his head. "Why, Penn?" he asked the silence. "Why?"

He lay there a moment longer, wondering how his heart could show such insolence and continue beating without her—every blood vessel, every nerve, all still functioning as if nothing had ever happened. He listened to the breath filling his lungs. Every exhale he knew would not be his last was only one more to endure the loss. *How could this body still live*, he wondered?

"Dammit, Penn"

The large master bedroom was cold and unfurnished. A king-sized mattress and box spring had been tucked into the far corner of the room, and the only other objects were the suitcases from which David had been living for God only knew how long. The paint peeled from the walls, cracks ran through the plaster, and the floorboards were buckled and bowed. He placed his bare feet against the ancient walnut and stood. It was difficult to tell if the creaking he heard came from the flooring or his own tired bones. A chill raced up through his feet and into his lower extremities; he was sure he could feel the frozen dirt of the crawl space below.

David pushed aside the large tarp that was his bedroom door and walked into the disaster that was the rest of the house. Plastic sheets hung in a maze-like fashion to section off the safe areas. He navigated a path to the bathroom to relieve himself.

It was the only room in the entire house completely intact. Penelope had renovated it all herself before she had gotten sick. It probably should have brought David a little peace to have it. But looking at the vanity she had installed and the bright porcelain fixtures she had picked out only made his heart hurt more. The teal-colored bath linens she had bought were still placed in the seashell towel bars she had hung. The perfect-edged lines of deep cerulean etched against the ceiling's pure white cut like ice on a razor's edge. The work she had done was exceptional.

He stood in the cold bathroom, staring at his face in the mirror. His skin hung loose and had assumed an overall ashen look. Dark circles bled beneath his eyes, making him look as if he were closer to fifty-five than thirty-three. He turned off the light and closed the door.

The old Victorian had been their dream home. But it had needed a lot of work, and that was Penny's thing—she was the handywoman. It had been her dream to buy the place. She was the talented one. David didn't know anything about construction and had never swung a hammer in his life. He was an accountant for New York Life, great with numbers and finance but not handy in the least. In fact, David had a hard time folding a paper bag. The couple had bought the place and gotten a pretty good deal on it, too. Penny had known what they were getting into and had assured her husband they would be fine.

"I'll take care of everything," she had said. "I can do the work little by little. I'll start with the bathroom and then move on to the kitchen. If we come up with some extra cash, we can hire a couple of laborers to help out." She had been bubbling when she told him. Her bright eyes lit up the room when she explained the details of the renovation process. "We can fix the bedroom later and set the mattress up on the floor. It'll be like camping out. Won't that be fun?"

David had been unsure. But being around Penny was infectious. He wanted his wife to be happy, and it was clear the house and this massive project would do it. So, they bought the place in July and immediately went about gutting the old plaster in most of the living areas, even part of the floor in the large family room situated off the kitchen. The old walnut had rotted through to the sub-flooring. There was no saving it. It was more work than even Penny had anticipated, but it hadn't seemed to phase her all that much. It wasn't long after that she had taken ill.

The doctors had said it was in her pancreas. It was very aggressive and resilient against treatment. Penn had started her first round of chemo, which zapped her reserve even more. Less than a month after her diagnosis, David Reese held his wife's hand and told her he loved her for the last time. She had lost so much weight, and her skin had grown paper-thin. Cancer had literally sucked the life out of her. Penny Reese passed away on September 26.

David walked through the husked-out shadows of a house haunted by the memory of his wife. He entered the pale light of the kitchen and froze. The plywood used to block off the entrance to the family room had been knocked down again. The wooden sheets lay on the floor, and the screws used to fasten them pointed up into the air, just waiting for him to come along and step on them.

"Sons of bitches!" he shouted as he turned on a halogen lamp set up on a workbench.

The room was suddenly filled with unforgiving illumination. David could feel his skin cooking from the canned heat. He scanned the kitchen to survey the damage. The coffee maker beside the lamp hadn't been tampered with, and the Yeti cooler on the floor beneath the bench appeared untouched. Still...

"Fucking raccoons!" he spat.

The sneaky critters had been getting into the house repeatedly. It didn't matter what he did. He had first used nails to secure the plywood to the studs surrounding the frame. Then, when the little bastards knocked that down, he had resorted to using screws. He had even set spackle buckets in front of the plywood, but they still found a way to knock it down.

"Must be a damn raccoon army coming through here."

They had to be making one hell of a racket, too, surely loud enough that he would have heard them. But he hadn't—not even a peep. It was more than odd. The little vermin were coming up through the missing floorboards in the family room, declaring an all-out siege upon the plywood entranceway, then tearing through the house in the middle of the night. All the while, David was oblivious. He had slept through it all and hadn't heard so much as a mouse fart.

That's the thing about depression, he thought. *It really knew how to fuck with you.*

He wrestled the plywood back into place and tried his best to secure it, telling himself he had probably missed the studs fastening it the last time. Then he made a pot of coffee and attempted to visualize his day—just another nine hours behind the desk punching numbers. Most men would have gone insane years ago. But David was looking forward to it. At least it would get him out of the cold, empty, Penny-less house.

David's cubicle looked like every other cubicle on the seventh floor of the NYL building. In fact, it looked exactly like the ones on the eighth, ninth, and all the other floors. Everything was neat and linear and grey ... so very, very grey. He sat at his desk, absorbed in his work. It was the only time he didn't dwell upon his loss.

"Hey, buddy."

David nearly jumped out of his chair from the sudden voice behind him. Gill Herbert patted him on the back.

"Great work on the Devlin account. You really came through in the clutch." Gill was one of the senior partners, and although not exactly David's boss per se, he held a higher position with the firm.

David tensed when Gill touched him.

"Whoa, easy, buddy." Gill sat on the edge of the desk and leaned in. "I just wanted to see how you were doing, Dave. How are you making out?"

So, there it was. David thought he just might make it through an entire morning without someone stopping by to ask him how he was doing, without someone asking him if he was okay or looking at him with that same expression Gill wore now. It was the look of sour pity.

Christ, he thought. *How do you think I'm making out? Just this morning, I wondered how my heart had the balls to continue beating, and then I considered gouging my eyes out with my toothbrush for at least a full minute.*

David looked up and smiled. "I'm good." He nodded. "Really. Thanks for asking, though."

"You know," Gill continued, "if you feel you need to take a little more time off, you certainly could. You'd be well within your right to do so."

This wasn't making him feel any better. He had missed plenty of days when Penny had gotten sick. Then he'd missed even more when she had died so suddenly. David was positive that the last thing he needed was more idle time on his hands. What was he supposed to do, sit around a gutted-out house all day? Right now, he needed to bury his nose into the work and try to push through. Eventually, he would have to decide what he was doing with the house. He had considered that selling it "as-is" was probably the best option. But he wasn't quite ready for that yet. When the time came, and he was ready, he might have to take some time off.

"I appreciate that, Gill, but I'm alright." He smiled again and even managed to crease his eyes. He had heard that a smile didn't look genuine unless the person's eyes were creased.

Gill studied his features for a second and then returned the smile.

"Well, if you're sure." He patted David on the shoulder again, then brushed at something on his jacket. "I didn't know you had a dog. What kind did you get?" Gill held out more than a few thick black hairs.

"Huh?" David looked at what Gill was holding. The hairs were dark black and looked relatively coarse. "Sons of bitches," he said for the second time that morning.

He knew where the hair had come from—the goddamn raccoons. They had gotten into the house and even rummaged through his clothes. But that meant they had been in the bedroom while David was sleeping. Was it possible he could have slept through such a thing? Maybe if they were quiet enough, but he doubted it. The truth was, he didn't know all that much about raccoons. They could be stealthy like furry little ninjas or reckless and obnoxious like buffalo in heat. David had no idea how he'd slept through it all, so he thought it best not to say anything about it to Gill.

"Oh, yeah," he said. "I mean, no ... my neighbor stopped by with his dog. Thing must have brushed up against my suit. Thanks for pointing that out."

"No problem, mi amigo. But you might want to take a lint roller to the back. Looks like you got an awful lot of it there."

"Thanks, I will." David was glad when Gill stood up and moved on to another cubicle. He then removed his jacket and examined it. What he found was shocking. How could he not have noticed it sooner? The back of his coat looked as if an animal had used it for a bed. Thick black hairs were littered across the fabric nearly everywhere. David plucked at them and studied the strange fiber in the light. It felt almost like wire, too thick and coarse to belong to any raccoon. He wasn't sure, but he doubted if it was animal fur at all. It wasn't soft and bendable as he imagined their pelts to be. Instead, it was rigid and firm, like the bristle of a brush.

It even looks too durable to be a whisker, he thought.

He would have to do a much better job of securing the plywood if he was ever going to be able to sleep in that house again. He doubted that would happen, not now. Still, he intended to barricade the crap out of the family room entrance as soon as he got home. More than anything, he needed one good night's sleep, one free from nightly visitors and one not affected by the nightmares. There were so many loose ends left in his life and so many things that needed to be done, but David Reese was just so damn tired. Exhausted, really. It was more than physical; he could feel it in his soul.

That was it—David's soul was weary.

∞

After work, he stopped at La Arana for a quick bite and a couple of shots of Don Julio. He figured the tequila might settle his nerves and give him the edge he needed to do the work awaiting him. The place had been a favorite of Penny's before…

It occurred to David that he was always coming back to that same thought. *We used to come here before… Penny liked to do this before…* Now life was divided into two distinct categories: before and after.

After was the hard part. *After* was where all the dirty work was done—from making arrangements and settling affairs to surviving. Somehow, he was supposed to survive. And that had turned out to be the trickiest one of all.

The waitress, a young girl with dark hair and even darker eyes, placed his order of Enchiladas Suizas on the table in front of him and retreated. David stared down at the colorful plate, suddenly overcome with fear. His chest tightened, and his heart began to race at the sight of the strange pattern on the food. An impending sense of unshakable dread seized him within its grip.

His attention focused on how the sour cream crisscrossed over the cocooned enchiladas. The array of thin white lines set against the darker backdrop of red and green was eerily familiar. It struck David as something he had seen before, perhaps recently. He fought against the irrational urge to run from the table and tried to tell himself that it was nothing. He was overtired—that was all. Still, the longer he stared at the web-like design on his plate, the quicker his heart began to race and the more confident he became that there was something more to it.

David grabbed his fork and quickly went to work on the Mexican dish by spreading the sour cream into an unrecognizable pattern. Soon, the image on his plate reminded him of nothing at all, certainly nothing threatening. He managed a few bites but couldn't thoroughly shake the feeling of dread. So he focused on the Don Julio instead and decided it was time to head back home.

The house was cold and darker than dark. David turned on as many of the work lights as possible, which lit up the place like the face of the sun and helped to heat it similarly. He winced and pinched his nose at the sour odor that hit him as he entered the kitchen.

It reeks to high hell, he thought.

The pungent smell possessed a deep, dank quality like foul dirt. The plywood remained intact where David had left it, and there were no signs of forced entry. He approached the boarded-up entrance to the family room, and the stink grew increasingly unbearable.

"What in the hell is *that*?" he asked the empty room.

The smell was oppressive and so much more than the foul stench of sour earth. There was a prevailing odor of decay he could taste in the air. David imagined one of his intruders had likely found its final resting place in the family room, where it had begun to rot. At least that was one less bastard trying to get into the house in the middle of the night. However, there would be no living with the stink currently dominating the residence. He was going to have to do something about it.

David changed out of his suit into a pair of jeans and a sweatshirt. Then he donned his work boots, which had never seen all that much work, and found a set of Penny's old gloves. Next, he fumbled with the cordless screw gun and removed the plywood barricade.

It rushed at him like a train from the darkness. He gagged when the insulting stench of rot bitch-slapped him across the face.

Something is definitely dead in here, he thought, *but where?*

Using one of the halogen lights, he maneuvered it into the entranceway to better look into the darkness. The bare walls were exactly as he last saw them, and the floor joists also appeared intact. There was no sign of any animal carcass as far as he could see, at least not from where he stood in the entranceway. Of course, it wasn't going to be that easy. The animal was obviously caught under the floor beams; it was somewhere in the crawlspace beneath. David poked his head further into the family room and immediately recoiled as if a snake had bitten him. The smell was far more aggressive in the cold room and too intense. Returning to the area below the workbench where Penny had kept a hoard of her essential construction goods, he removed one of the dust masks from a package. Then he went to the bathroom, retrieved a bottle of Obsession for men, and sprayed the inside of the mask.

David carefully stepped into the family room with a large crowbar in one hand, a flashlight in the other, and his scented mask fitted securely over his mouth and nose. Even with the protection, he could detect the toxic stench over the cologne. He suffered through it and proceeded into the room.

Each step was a balancing act as he placed one foot onto a floor beam and the other onto the next. The joists were spaced twelve inches equally apart, just enough to allow most of David's body to pass through if he were to fall. His knees and elbows, and probably his head, would not be quite as lucky. Undoubtedly, one, if not all of them, would contact the unforgiving wood if he fell. He tried his best to make sure that didn't happen. The four shots of Julio weren't helping his balance, but they assisted with his courage.

The beam of the flashlight illuminated the dark earth below. Shadows jumped out and shrank back with each wave of his hand. David scanned the best he could for any sign of what might be the cause of the funk. He balanced and stepped, one beam at a time, into the center of the room while continuing to survey the ground below. The stink was now heavier than ever, and David knew he must be close. He studied the ground intently and noticed the dirt had been displaced. Something had been at work in the crawlspace. It was impossible to tell what had made them, but there were tracks in the loose soil beneath him. He bent over slightly and focused the light on the ground. That was when his right foot lost contact with the floor joist.

David came down hard, his right leg plummeting into the darkness. He fell across the length of timber where he had stood. First, his balls slammed against the beam, then his chin followed. The air was knocked out of him as his nuts were forced up into his throat. David dropped the flashlight and crowbar when his face met the wood.

He lay there, trying to catch his breath. The throbbing in his groin had its own heartbeat and felt hot, like a soldering gun working on his private parts. The pain continued to intensify, drowning out the sting he felt in his chin and mouth. He had a vague sense that he tasted blood but was still too rattled to realize where it was coming from or what had happened to him. Finally, after ten minutes or more, the stars and alarms blinding his senses began to fade, and the world slowly crept back into view.

He found himself sprawled across two beams with his arms, legs, and face dangling into the darkness below. He stared down at what looked like a massive hole dug into the earth.

The flashlight and crowbar had come to rest at the entrance of a large burrow. The dirt had been flung into a pile near the mouth of the opening. It was riddled with scores of indentations that David assumed must be tracks of some type. However, they weren't like any animal print he had ever seen. Instead, they looked as if someone had repeatedly taken a stick or poker and jammed it into the ground. The tracks were deep, too, as if whatever had made them possessed a bit of weight.

"What the hell?" he managed to utter as he slowly righted himself and stared further into the large opening.

Then he saw it.

About two feet inside the tunnel, there fell a shadow. Whatever it was, it was motionless. He waited a moment while his eyes adjusted to the darkness to see if the object would stir. Then the shadow became a bit clearer and the shape a bit more recognizable.

"Sons of bitches," he gasped.

He had found the source of the decay. Something had died all right, and it lay only a few feet inside its burrow. He looked at the flashlight and then at the crowbar. It was only about a three-foot drop into the crawl space. David weighed his options and thought better of it. He had already taken one spill that night and wasn't about to risk another. Besides, he didn't know if his little dead friend had any buddies still alive in there.

He got back to his feet with his nuts still singing a battle hymn and made his way to the dining room where Penny kept her tools. He returned with a large plastic garbage bag and a long rake with sharp steel teeth at the business end. David then made his way even more carefully to the center of the room and straddled the two beams where he had fallen. The flashlight showed into the dark tunnel where the animal had died. He lowered himself onto the joists with his legs hanging over into the crawlspace. The cologne he had used was now diluted by another scent accompanied by a coppery taste. He ran his tongue over his lips and felt the area he had bit down on when he landed. It was swollen and sore and had bled some.

With as much care and caution as he could muster, David extended the rake into the freshly dug hole in his crawlspace and reached for the large shadow within. He was unable to grab the carcass, as he remained a good foot or two shy of it. He repositioned himself on the beams almost exactly where he had fallen. David then extended the rake into the hole once again and clawed for the body. He could just see the dark shadow beyond the reach of the light.

It has to be a raccoon, he thought. *It looks too big to be anything else.*

He thrust the rake into the darkness and forced it down toward the dirt.

Bingo! He felt the teeth sink into the animal's remains.

David began to pull at the carcass, which appeared stuck for a moment. Then it freed itself from whatever it had been snagged on and easily slid toward him. He grasped at the rake and dragged the body out of the hole toward the beam of light.

A scream escaped David's lips when the carcass was revealed. It belonged to an animal, most likely a raccoon, but its condition was something for which David had been wholly unprepared. The animal had been tightly wrapped in what looked like a cocoon of some sort. He could just make out the creature's muzzle beneath the woven threads that encapsulated its body. The raccoon's eyes were fixed open, staring up at David as if terrified. A snarl had been eternally frozen on the creature's face, as the thread-like fibers wove throughout the animal's mouth.

The vision of the Enchiladas Suizas that had nearly brought on a nervous breakdown reappeared. The crisscross of threads surrounding the cocooned body of the animal was the same pattern that had panicked David in the restaurant. He had seen that horrific sight somewhere before. The enchiladas had triggered a repressed memory. He suddenly knew where he had seen such a horror.

In his dreams.

"Dear God," David gasped. The smell was more overpowering than before, but he hardly noticed it. All he could smell was his own fear.

It happened so fast that David was almost pulled off balance and into the crawl-space. The raccoon was suddenly ripped back into the hole with such force that the rake was yanked out of David's grip. Both the animal and the tool disappeared into the shadows of the burrow. Something had dragged the tasty morsel back into its lair. The violent movement preceded the most unearthly noise David had ever heard—a cross between a hiss and gargle. But there was something more to it.

It almost sounded like a voice.

He recoiled and shot to his feet so quickly he nearly missed the beams and practically ended up falling in the crawlspace. Then, without looking where he was going, he tore off his mask, sprinted across the floor joists and bolted toward the safety of the kitchen. He didn't know if it was actually all that safe, but it was a hell of a lot better than where he had stood only a few seconds before. As David was reaching the entranceway, the sound came again from the family room, only this time it was louder and much closer.

His mind raced as he tried to comprehend what was happening, but there was no understanding to be found.

Something is in that fucking hole, his head screamed. *Something big is in that hole!*

Then he heard the scraping, the sound of resistance against the wood. Whatever lived down there was now pulling itself up through the floor joists.

David could picture himself running full speed to the front door. He could visualize himself exiting the house, tearing down the street without so much as stopping for his car keys, and never looking back. To hell with the house and to hell with whatever monstrosity resided in the crawlspace.

He could clearly see everything as if it had already occurred. But none of it happened. Instead, David paused. He didn't even know what compelled him to stop—curiosity maybe, unwarranted bravery brought on by the tequila ... perhaps, sheer stupidity ... most definitely. For whatever reason, as David reached the kitchen with only a dozen or more strides to safety, he turned back in the direction the sound had come from and froze.

It pulled itself up from the crawlspace; its thick body compressed to a most unnatural distorted shape as its long, black, hideous legs positioned themselves upon the wooden beams. The sound of dry paper rasping against leathery flesh assaulted David's ears as the beast maneuvered into full view and looked at him. The coarse black hair Gill had found on David's jacket covered the creature. It grew from its legs, far too many to even count. It thatched from its head and midsection in long, sick bristles. The hind section was obscured from view, but David knew, if he were to see it, it too would be covered in the same scratchy fibers.

Paralysis seized David like a stroke. The panic and terror rocketing through his organs threw him near the brink of unconsciousness. The ability to move had escaped him, taken over by something too powerful to resist. He was helpless and incapacitated. All he could do was watch as the creature moved closer to him.

Then it spoke: "Daaaaviiiiiiiddd!"

The horrible hiss that emanated from the beast curdled in David's ears and ate what little sanity he had left. His bladder let go as the giant spider moved closer into view.

"Daaavviiiiiddddd," it hissed again with distinct familiarity.

Although altered by the creature's alien vocal cords and the earth in which it dwelled, the voice was still recognizable. He knew that voice ... and he knew it well.

Then he saw it.

The creature quickly rushed to within three feet of where David stood trembling and frozen. Its eyes! They focused on him and held him fast within their gaze. He was still able to think and knew everything that was happening to him. He was able to feel every ounce of the crippling fear and could hear his heart struggling to beat out of his chest. And he could see the eyes; they were green. Jesus Christ, they were green! They were Penny's.

David stared coldly into his dead wife's eyes. A long string of drool ran from his opened mouth and hung from his chin, all while the thick black legs of the abomination inched ever closer to where he stood. The distinctly green eyes of the creature were unmistakably Penny's, and as it drew within inches from him, the beast's face slowly began to distort and change.

First, it wavered as if in flux, and then it blurred unrecognizably in front of him. Suddenly, he was staring at Penelope Reese. The massive spider that lumbered before him wore the face of the woman he had loved. Somehow, the beast and his wife were one and the same.

"Daaaaavviiiiidddd," she hissed once again as she reached out with her giant appendages and touched her husband's face.

In that touch, something was exchanged. An impossible knowledge suddenly filled David, and a sense of understanding washed over him. This was the source of Penny's cancer. The creature had come to visit her almost immediately after they had moved into the house. It had started as soon as they had ripped up the flooring in the family room. It had been living there for a very long time.

The beast had come in the night and had fed on her, just as it was now feeding on David. It had taken all that had made her who she was and had left only a husk behind. It had consumed her essence, leaving only a shell. But here she was, standing right in front of him. David reached out toward the monstrosity wearing his wife's face and embraced it.

"Daaavviiiiidddd," his spider/wife hissed again, rearing back on its hind legs to expose a vicious set of dripping fangs.

The venom smelled as foul as the earth from which the beast had emerged, but to David's senses, it was the scent of Penny's perfume. It was warm, welcoming, and dreamily intoxicating. He moaned as the creature ransacked and manipulated his consciousness.

David pulled what he believed to be his wife closer to him. It had been so long, and he was so tired. Yet, even in his ravaged state, he was aware that soon it would all be over.

"Oh, Penn," he moaned.

"Daaavvviiiiddd," the thing replied as it landed on him and drove him to the ground. The stomach-churning sound as the creature feasted on David was nearly drowned out by the sound of his strangled cries. The noises that escaped from his lips were not exactly the cries of a man in pain. Nor were they precisely the anguished wails of sorrow. The sound that David expressed as the beast drained him was much closer to that of relief. That was the thing about death—it really knew how to fuck with you.

Fifteen

THE LAST WALTZ

Nancy Lomax attempted to soak in the impossible promised freedom of the Gulf of Mexico. She had always wanted to come but never been allowed. Her bare feet dug into the sand with the gentle surf lapping at her toes, never judging or raising a finger against her. She wiped another tear that had no business rolling down her cheek. Salty as the sea and twice as bitter. She never imagined she could enjoy a scene such as this or realize such a moment.

A sun as big as a clenched fist rolled above a bruised ocean onto a cloudless backdrop of black and blue. She had been driving all night and finally made it to Tampa to witness the sunrise. Beth lived in Florida; she hadn't seen her in years, one of the many things she had not been allowed to do. As darkness slowly acquiesced to daylight and the memory of Murfreesboro faded even slower, Nancy pulled the meaningless scrap of metal from her finger and threw it into the sea. She didn't hesitate to look at it one last time. *What's done is done.* She remembered feeling as if she would never be free, would never learn to fly, would never feel the sun on her skin. The surprisingly guiltless feel of the Tampa sun was as liberating as a confession. She looked at the crimson stain that bled under the fingernails of her right hand. *What comes from the sea shall return.* She dipped her fingers into the brine and washed it away.

The events of last night had permanently seared into her memory. Broken glass littered the floor along with the remnants of the hamburger helper she had made. How long ago had it been, four hours? Five? Only one? Nancy was unsure if time had sped up or stopped completely.

"Oh my God! Oh my God!" she chanted as she ran from the living room to the bedroom with her favorite bra in one hand and a wooden spoon in the other. The siren of a five-alarm fire screamed from somewhere deep inside her skull. Her heart fought to keep up with the adrenaline that coursed through her in a frenzy. It had happened so fast, but didn't it always? Now all she could think to do was escape. She ran in a dizzied circle from one room to the next, trying her best to avoid the mess in the kitchen at all costs. But she couldn't avoid it for long; she would have to pass through on her way out the front door.

"Oh, my God!" She mumbled again.

What was that? Was something burning?

Nancy couldn't remember if she had turned the burner off before leaving the kitchen.

How could she have? She hadn't even had time to think.

Then she smelled it again, stronger this time. Definitely smoke. Nancy ran to the kitchen and stopped in her tracks before her feet hit the linoleum. She swallowed hard as the urge to gag nearly crippled her. Far too many stenches assaulted her at once. Burning carbon from the canned corn she had left sizzling on the stove sent a charred cloud into the air that attempted to mask the other odors. It mixed with the greasy tang of the hamburger helper that had congealed on the floor. The slow acrid spread of a scarlet sauce had infused with the strewn noodles, meat, and near-empty bottle of Jim Beam that Donald had launched at her. The sight turned her stomach.

Did I make sauce? She thought. *Donald hates Ragu.*

Under it all, a deeper, darker, far more desperate stench.

Nancy almost slipped in the aftermath on her way to the stove. She carefully stepped over the heaping mass and turned off the burner. Then she bent over and picked up the object from the kitchen floor. Back in the bedroom, she clawed a few more items into her tattered bag and wrestled it shut. Before leaving, her eyes came to rest on the chair in the corner. Donald's jacket slumped over, slack and lifeless. She dug into the pocket where he kept his wallet and removed the sacred item. Her hands shook uncontrollably, and her head swam. The steady *thud ... thud ... thud* that continued to tighten in her throat was all she could hear. It sent a nauseating pulse to the growing bruise on her cheek; she could feel her right eye beginning to swell shut. Without thinking about where she was going, she grabbed the bag and headed back to the kitchen.

Get out! Get out! Her internal mantra changed as the walls of thirteen Piedmont closed in on her at an alarming pace. Nancy Lomax was practically sprinting as she exited the front door, and she had broken into a full-out run before she reached the old Ford in the driveway.

Great white bodies eclipsed against the blue. Rising and dipping and meandering on the stream. Nancy watched as the large gulls rode the currents of air, suspended in a wave of perpetual motion.

It was a dance, she thought, as if they had rehearsed.

There was no design, but it was beautiful. She watched as the two creatures worked the canvas in tandem. Their bodies nearly collided in mid-air only to turn at the last second and soar independently in opposite directions.

That's how it should be, she thought, making her way back to the car.

She left the parking lot and the beach behind her and pointed the vehicle south. She'd been driving south nearly the entire time since leaving Tennessee with only a slight easterly drift as she moved through the night, mostly on autopilot, caught somewhere between *what have I done* and *what do I do now*? Two clear thoughts permeated the din of insanity and threatened to send her over the edge. The first had been Beth—dear, sweet Beth—her only sister and best friend. Beth would know what to do; she would help. The other thought spiraled in a double helix with the first, and that was south, keep heading south. Beth lived in Tampa; Tampa was south. Keep heading south.

Less than twelve hours ago, Nancy stood at the stove nervously watching the clock. The little hand was on the six, and the big hand was about to smack the twelve like a welterweight. Donald would be home in less than fifteen minutes, and supper wasn't even close to ready. Her stomach tightened, and her back cramped at the base of her spine. What was taking so long? It was only hamburger helper and canned corn. Not like she was making a steak. Lord knew they couldn't afford that. It was no wonder that Donald was upset lately. For some reason, she was always running late, dropping things, or just plain messing up.

"What's wrong with you, girl?" Nancy asked herself. It was as if she wanted to aggravate the man. "You best wake up, Nancy Lomax." *At least the rent was paid, and the lights were on,* she tried to console herself. *There are lots of folks worse off than us.*

Donald was under a lot of pressure at work; it was only natural for him to get a little testy from time to time. Lord knew her constant clumsiness hadn't helped matters. And now supper would be late.

The slamming of the truck door echoed off the walls of the small kitchen, rattling the cabinet that held the tiny teacups Beth had sent her for Christmas. Nancy's heart jumped into her throat.

"Oh, God!"

She knew what that slam meant. Funny how she could predict an evening by the sound of two objects colliding. Her eyes darted from the frying pan to the clock to the half-opened utensil drawer. She stared for perhaps a moment too long at the contents within. Nancy braced herself as the front door burst inward.

The speed limit on I-75 was just that, 75, and Nancy was eating up every bit of it. Despite pressing the accelerator almost to the floor, she barely kept up with the flow of traffic, and it wasn't even seven a.m. She pushed a bit harder and watched the odometer as it crept to 80 mph. It was exhilarating and terrifying at the same time. An indifferent sun blazed to her left and had already begun to sear the pavement that stretched before her like a million unfulfilled promises. The Gulf of Mexico spooned the right side of the highway. Mangroves and seafoam-kissed beaches washed past her in a blur. At this speed, it was hard to tell if she was running toward something or still just running away.

She raced past the first sign that said *Sunshine Skyway Bridge 2 Miles Ahead* and could already see the ominous structure as it revealed itself in the distance. It grew larger and larger as she ate up the blacktop and continued south. Nancy stared at the giant steel cables suspending the massive bridge above Tampa Bay. Even from this far, she could imagine each individual thread to be almost a foot in diameter. They draped across and snaked themselves throughout the expanse, looking like a cross between a spider's web and a prison cell. Captivated by the site of the monstrosity, entranced by the refracted sunlight through its maniacal webbing, Nancy lost all thought of how fast she had been traveling. She didn't see the half-concealed Florida Highway patrol car as she sailed by doing 85 mph. She was even less attentive when it rocketed toward her with the cherries blazing. Nancy was catapulted back into reality when the trooper hit the siren. Her hands slicked instantly, and her heart jumped into her throat.

"Oh, my God," she moaned for perhaps the hundredth time. "Oh, my God!"

"I'm sorry, baby. I didn't mean it. I am so sorry," Donald stood over her in the kitchen. Nancy clutched her cheek and shrank away as he approached. It had happened so fast—one second, they were arguing about the electric bill, and the next, *wham!* Stars filled her field of vision, and the next thing she knew, she was on the kitchen floor. She hadn't seen it coming and had never imagined Donald was capable of such a thing. Where the hell did that come from? Fresh tears coursed down her already swelling cheek and indignantly fell on her blouse. That was the first time he had hit her, less than a year after they got married.

Her breath hitched in her chest as she tried to speak, but she gagged on the words. "Y-you ... h-hit me!"

Donald knelt beside her and placed his hands on her knees. "I'm so sorry, baby. It was a reaction. I didn't think you were that close. I was just kind of..." His face was calm and had lost the deep-red shade and distorted shape it wore only a moment ago. "You kinda walked into it, you know. I was only reacting and threw my hands up in disgust. You really wouldn't let it go, and, well, I was just so mad."

Nancy cowered as he reached out to touch her, not knowing what to expect. She had never in a million years imagined that Donald might actually hit her. He had shown his temper more and more lately, but Christ, he had really hit her.

"Here, let me see. There, that's not so bad, barely a mark." He checked Nancy's face as she trembled. He stood up and went to the freezer to retrieve a bag of frozen peas. "Let me fix that, baby," he said, touching the bag to the swelling.

"I can't believe you hit me," Nancy whispered. Her breaths hitched as she reluctantly accepted Donald's comfort.

"I'm sorry, baby," he kissed her forehead. "It will never happen again."

"You hit me," she cried.

"I said it was an accident." His face returned to its original darker shade. "Now get up off the floor and help me clean this fucking mess!"

∞

Nancy sat white-knuckling the steering wheel in the far-right breakdown lane of I-75. She turned off the ignition and watched as the trooper opened the door to his patrol car and made his way toward her. Time crawled as he meandered the twenty paces. Nancy wiped her sweat-slicked hands on her blouse and then checked herself in the rearview. The concealer she had applied hours ago was still holding up, and the extra-large sunglasses that had become a staple in her day-to-day covered most of her face. No sign of the angry bruise that lay beneath them. Well worth the $5.99 she had spent at the Walmart. She wiped her hands again. The thundering inside her seemed to meld with the concussion of the tractor-trailers as they soared past. Nancy could feel them sucking the air out of the claustrophobic confines of the old Taurus and found it difficult to breathe and even harder to think. Tiny dark spots spread across her field of vision and threatened to extinguish her light completely.

Don't pass out, don't pass out, she urged herself.

"License, registration, and insurance," the voice came from somewhere far away.

The darkening splotches swam closer and closer together. The feeling that she had been submerged underwater was overwhelming. Nancy was sure that she was about to pass out. She bit down on her bottom lip, and bright stars lit the darkening splotches like a solar flare. Nancy was propelled from her daze to find an extremely large Florida State Trooper looming before her.

"License, registration, and insurance," he repeated a bit more aggressively.

"Of course, Officer," she answered, trying not to show the panic boiling below the surface. "Of course."

The officer continued to stare.

He knows. The thought thundered in her head. *He knows!*

Nancy forced a smile that was offered to pacify but was wasted. The hulking figure perched over her, silently waited for her to produce the documents. She leaned over and popped open the glove box. Expecting to find her paperwork stacked in an orderly fashion as she always kept it, the compartment's actual state started her; it was anything but orderly. The contents appeared as if they had been ransacked by a derelict fool, which was undoubtedly the case. A cold sweat broke across Nancy's forehead and raced to the back of her skull. Donald had no doubt torn the place apart, looking for something he had obviously not found.

You son of a bitch! she cursed as her eyes focused on the plastic baggy tucked into the back corner of the box. The white powder within was visible to her, and it was apparent what it was. Surely, it would be just as evident to the trooper, who was almost close enough to be inside the car with her.

You Son of a Bitch! Nancy hissed under her breath as she moved a few papers as carefully as possible to conceal the baggy. She had known that Donald was still using, it had been obvious, but the bastard had denied it to the hilt. He had swayed her once again, so Nancy had dropped it. That was Donald for ya—the Master Manipulator, Mr. Smooth Talker, the King of Swords. She thought her days of getting screwed by him were over; at least, that's what she had been telling herself the entire ride south. But here she was, pulled over by the FHP with a pile of Mr. Slick's drugs in her glove box. *You're still fuckin me, aren't ya, Donnie Boy?*

The giant cop shifted impatiently as Nancy rooted around for her documents. She tried to act composed but knew she was doing a terrible job of it. Fortunately, Donald hadn't discarded any of her paperwork when he tore through her glove box, trying to find his stash. With more than a bit of difficulty, she found what she was looking for, removed the items, and quickly closed the glove box.

"Here you go, Officer." She handed him her credentials.

The cop took them and stood there. He didn't bother to look at the paperwork; he continued to stare at Nancy. The pulse that hammered in her temples grew so intense she could feel the skin on the sides of her face expanding with each throb. Surely the cop would notice that. Certainly, he knew she was hiding something. There was no way in hell that he hadn't seen Donald's cocaine when she opened the glove box. He was going to search the car; Nancy was sure of it. He was going to find the coke, and then he would look even more thoroughly. Then, Nancy remembered...

Why did you bring it with you? she asked herself.

It seemed like the thing to do at the time. She remembered stepping over the mess in the kitchen, turning off the burner, and then picking it up off the floor. She had wrapped it in a towel and thrown it in her bag. It wasn't as if she could leave it; her fingerprints were all over the damn thing ... then there was the blood.

"Wait right here," the cop said. "I'll be right back."

Oh my, God!

Nancy knew that soon it would all be over. In a way, she welcomed it. She couldn't keep this up. She was already tired of running.

∞

"Ladies and Gentlemen," the DJ announced. "Please give a big hand for the first time as man and wife, Mr. and Mrs. Donald Lomax."

Nancy and Donald had been waiting for their cue in the tight hallway of the VFW. They exchanged another eager kiss that brought a flush to both their faces. Then they put on their most proper smiles, pushed through the double doors, and were met with a roar of delight from their friends and families. Donald double-stepped and nearly tripped over his own shoes as they made their way to the center of the dance floor. The rental tux had been a bit restricting and the shoes somewhat tight, not to mention the flask of Jack Daniels the groomsmen had passed around in the parking lot before the ceremony. Nancy had thought it was cute how nervous Donald had been and how he had needed a few drinks to settle him down. Adorable!

The VFW was the only place they could afford, and since Donald's father had served and was the chapter president, the price was just right—nada. The music started playing; the Ed Sheeran song had been impossible to avoid for over a year now and had become their own. Donald took Nancy in his arms and began to sway with her in time to the beat. One, two, three. One, two, three. The crowd erupted as he reached around and grabbed her ass. She blushed even harder when he kissed her and slid a bourbon-soaked tongue into her mouth in front of her mother, father, and the entire family. Nancy came out of the kiss and Ed continued to croon. She was swooning; it was the happiest day of her life. Donald spun her around again; this time, Nancy's eyes met her sister's. Beth glared at her from across the room. For some reason, Beth had it out for Donald from the moment they met, and she'd been dead set against the wedding. She told Nancy so. She had even refused to join the wedding party. But Nancy finally convinced her through days and days of pleading.

"It's my wedding, and I love him," she cried. "How can I enjoy my special day without my sister by my side?"

Beth had given in reluctantly. But there was something about Donald that she knew was wrong. For some reason, Nancy was unable or just unwilling to see it.

Donald reached down and grabbed Nancy's ass with both hands, a little too hard this time. She jumped with a start, and her eyes grew wide. Donald smiled and winked, which melted her heart. The couple kissed again as Ed continued to schmaltz away. Beth watched with a sour knot growing in the pit of her stomach.

Nancy was so caught up in the thrill of marrying her high school sweetheart that all she could focus on was the dance. One, two, three. One, two, three. She counted in her head.

How old-fashioned, she thought, *to have picked a waltz for our wedding song.*

With Nancy's credentials in hand, the jumbo-sized Florida trooper walked back to his car even slower than he had approached. Tears welled in the corners of her eyes as she followed his movements in the rearview. He entered his vehicle and disappeared behind the glare of the sun. The first thought that came to mind was to put the Taurus in drive and punch it.

That's what I should do, she told herself. *I should make a run for it!*

She stared at the looming fortress of the Sunshine Skyway Bridge spread out before her. The ominous structure looked less like a spider's web now that she was closer to it. The equally spaced cables could be compared to nothing other than prison bars. The last turn-off exit was a mile behind her. If she was going to make a run for it, she would have to cross the bridge. Even with a head start, there was no way she could outrun the eight cylinders under the hood of the FHP. Running wasn't an option.

It felt like she had been sitting in the vehicle for at least an hour. Her heart continued to pound out of control in her chest, and her pulse still throbbed in her temples. Nancy's eyes darted from the glove box that held the coke to the bag on the floor that held something worse. Finally, she looked out the passenger window at the bay. The gentle surf lapped at the narrow stretch of sand less than fifteen feet from the side of the road. She could make it to the water in about a second and a half. Then what? She didn't know. Maybe she could swim as far as she could until, finally, her strength gave out. She could slip beneath the surface, easy peasy, lemon squeezy.

Who are you kidding? she asked herself.

She wasn't capable of suicide. Though, up until twelve hours ago, she hadn't been capable of many things. She had sure surprised the shit out of Donald. Then a familiar flicker of movement caught her eye.

They sailed and dipped in a symbiotic flow of give and take. Their great white bodies carouseled upon an effortless canvas without resistance. Nancy gasped when she saw them. The two gulls danced in perfect time with one another as if they had rehearsed every step. They crested the invisible mountains of air, nearly touching wingtips, rising and falling in tandem. The forgotten melody crept up from nowhere and invaded her memory. One, two, three. One, two, three.

"Oh my God," Nancy gasped in the front seat.

It was impossible to contain. The tears coursed freely. She hadn't thought of that day in years. She'd had no reason to. Donald had shown his true self, and that blocked out the memory of the good times. A shadow had been cast over all of it.

"God damn you, Donald," she said, choking on the words.

She tried to focus through the salty sting. They had followed her. She didn't know how she knew, but she did. The gulls that now waltzed above the bay were the same ones she had watched this morning at the beach. Somehow, she knew. Nancy remembered learning that some birds mated for life. She didn't know if it was true for seagulls, but she liked the idea of it.

"Till death do us part," she whispered.

That's how it should be, how it was meant to be. Nancy decided that as soon as the officer returned, she would turn herself in. She would confess.

❧

Nancy Walsh sat on the bleachers with Amy Whipple, Sue Gaston, and several other cheerleaders. They watched as the Springfield High School football team practiced their famous Hail Mary pass. It had won them the championship last year. And it looked pretty good for them this year, as well.

"I think he likes you," Amy said as she elbowed Nancy. "What're ya gonna say if he asks?"

"I have no idea what you're talking about," Nancy smirked.

She watched intently as the team broke formation and executed the play. The quarterback sent the ball flying up the field into the hands of the running back. A huge smile spread out across her face.

"Oh, stop it. Everyone knows he likes you. Donald Lomax is like the hottest guy in class and Captain of the football team. He's perfect."

"Yeah, he is pretty perfect." Nancy blushed. "But I don't know. I guess … I mean … I might go out with him."

"What?" Sue exclaimed. "You'd be a fool not to. He's totally hot, and every girl wants him."

"I guess," Nancy smirked. "I hadn't really thought about it."

"Well, you better start thinking about it." Amy nudged her friend again. "Cause he's coming this way.

"Hi, Nancy." Donald Lomax walked up, helmet in hand and shoulder pads extending to the sky. Nancy held her breath and tried her best not to choke. "I was wondering if you were busy Saturday night?" he asked. "Mike Singer's folks are going out of town, and we're gonna get a keg."

"Oh," Nancy coyed. "I don't know. Neither of us is old enough to drink." She played with him.

"Oh, come on," Donald flirted back. "A couple beers never hurt anyone."

One, two, three. One two, three. Nancy remembered the dance. She had been so happy. The song cut through the shadows and played once again. The lyrics echoed in her head and brought back all the memories she had forced into the shadows.

The tears were unstoppable when the officer finally returned. "Ma'am is everything alright?" he asked.

"N-no." Nancy prepared herself. "M-m-my." She couldn't get the words out, although she knew what she needed to say. She wanted to confess, and for the officer to finally put the handcuffs on her. Then ... it would all be over. "Offic-cerrrrr," she cried. "I ki—"

"Here," he said, forcing her credentials through the open window. "You gotta slow it down, or you're gonna kill someone, and probably yourself as well. I don't usually give warnings, so think of it as your lucky day." He dropped the documents into Nancy's hand and doubled timed it back to his cruiser. He sped off south on I-75, leaving Nancy Lomax crying in the breakdown lane. The gulls soared above her, and soon she was hypnotized by them once again. One, two, three. One, two, three.

∞

Nancy eased the Taurus into the driveway and turned off the engine. She sat for a moment, trying to collect herself, as if she could. What would she say? How? It had been years since she had seen Beth. Would her sister even welcome her after all that had happened? As she got out of the car, the front door opened, and Beth stepped into the morning sunlight. The sisters stood frozen, staring at each other for what felt like a wonderfully long time. Again, the tears released in an unfettered flow.

Their eyes met with an exchange of knowledge, and Nancy knew she didn't need to say a thing. Still, she felt compelled.

"Beth," she stammered. "I need..."

Beth rushed to her sister and swept her into her arms. "It doesn't matter. Whatever it is. We'll deal with it together."

Beth led Nancy through the front door and into the coolness of the small house. They were greeted by the arctic blast from the central air conditioning system. An immediate chill raced throughout Nancy's body, and she lost control. Her hands, legs, and chest trembled as if she were seizing. Although the living room was dim from the half-drawn shades and curtain sheers, the contents and furnishings were easily recognizable. Nancy noticed the portraits right away. Graduation photos of her and Beth hung on either side of a family portrait taken when Nancy was seven and Beth was only five. It had been Easter, and the Walsh family had gone to a professional photography studio to have their family portrait taken. Nancy's father and mother sat with a daughter on each of their laps. Their smiles were genuine and enormous. She remembered that day, feeling so grown up in her big girl dress and helping braid Beth's hair. She hadn't seen the picture in years and had no idea what had even become of it. So long ago. So innocent. So young.

What happened to that little girl? What went wrong? Nancy wondered.

Her thoughts were drawn back to thirteen Piedmont Avenue and the mess that would eventually be found on the kitchen floor. Not so innocent anymore.

What happened to that little girl? What went wrong? Nancy wondered again.

Somewhere above the tiny house, suspended on a ripple of breath, a symbiotic dance of perfection continued to unfold. How it should be. How it was meant to be.

One, two, three. One, two, three.

Sixteen

Scream in the Dark: An Excerpt from The Ojanox

Sally Ann Richards had been up half the night setting cold compresses and monitoring the twins' fevers. The kids had the flu. Erin was running at a steady 102, which had her concerned, but at one point, Ben's temperature had shot to nearly 104. She set him in a cool bath and given him an adult aspirin which managed to bring the fever down slightly. But the poor things were miserable. It took Sally Ann everything in her power to get them to eat even a few tablespoons of Lipton Soup. Erin usually loved the Ring-o-Noodles, but tonight, they hadn't eaten half a bowl between them.

The twins continued to toss and turn throughout the night. They had sweat through their pajamas and soaked their bedsheets. Sally Ann changed their clothes and watched over them till they both finally fell asleep around three-thirty. Then she retreated to the living room, worrying as only a mother could, and began to nod off herself. Her husband, Dennis, was in their bedroom, and managed to sleep through the night undisturbed. Sally Ann had let him; he was currently working nights at the plant, and by the time he dragged himself home every morning, he was exhausted. Saturday into Sunday was his only night off, and she knew if she woke him, he would have been fit to be tied and taken it out on her. She did everything she could to not aggravate Dennis these days. He never actually hit her, but there were times he had come close and given her a firm shove. Once, he grabbed her arm so hard the bruises had lasted for two weeks. *It wasn't his fault,* Sally told herself. Dennis was trying so hard to keep the bills paid and food on the table, plus he had a lot of responsibilities at the plant since the layoff. They were lucky he still had a job; nearly half the men at Faber Manufacturing were standing on the unemployment line. Dennis had a right to get a little angry every now and then. Times were tough, and the gas shortage had everyone on edge. Also, Dennis was livid at the idea of an actor running for president.

"I'd vote for Walter Matthau before I voted for Ronald Reagan. Whoever heard of an actor as president? What's next, Sammy Davis Jr. as Secretary of State?" He screamed one day over the breakfast table.

Sally Ann listened and agreed to Dennis's rants. What did she know about politics anyway? She didn't care much about that stuff. She'd liked Kennedy, but that was because she thought he was handsome. These days she was happy Dennis was still working and she had time to take care of the twins and the house. Besides, Dennis liked things a certain way, and she liked it when he was happy. It was a whole lot better than when he was not.

Last night had been rough, but she had finally gotten the twins' fevers down slightly. Hopefully, she could catch a few winks herself before Dennis woke up. She had an hour or so before he would be looking for his coffee and bacon, just enough time for a little cat nap.

Seconds after she closed her eyes, Sally Ann woke to the faint sound of Erin calling for her. The child's voice was whisper thin. At first, she thought she was dreaming, and her daughter was speaking to her from far away. She opened her eyes to find the girl standing nearly on top of her. Erin held out something in her hand to show her mother.

"Mommy," her voice was barely a breath; she sounded as if she had something in her mouth. "My tooth fell out."

She had to be dreaming, both kids had lost the last of their baby teeth over a year ago. The girl spoke again, finally waking her mother.

"Let me see." Sally felt the heat billowing from her. "Oh my God!"

One of Erin's top incisors lay in her hand. The root was red, and there was blood on her palm. Sally opened Erin's mouth to examine her; there was a large gap where her tooth had been.

"Erin, what on earth happened?" Sally cried.

"I don't know, Mommy, I felt it in my mouth." Erin swayed on her feet, and Sally steadied her.

"Dear God, baby, you're on fire."

"I don't feel good, Mommy." Erin shook for a short second and then bent over and vomited onto the floor. Sally watched in horror as Erin retched. What came out of the child smelled like death. The little bit of soup she had eaten was expelled in a deluge of dark red blood. She coughed, and a second tooth flew from her mouth and landed in the mess. Sally screamed for Dennis, with little concern as to what kind of mood he woke up in. She scooped up Erin, who immediately began to shake in her arms. "Dennis, wake up!" she screamed again.

Erin began heaving and violently flailing in her arms as Dennis rushed from the bedroom in his boxer shorts.

"What the hell's going on out here? I'm trying to—" He stopped when he saw the state of the living room and his daughter convulsing. He grabbed Erin from Sally and nearly slipped in the vomit. "What happened?"

Before Sally had time to answer, Ben started screaming as if his fingernails were being ripped out with needle-nose pliers. Dennis stared at his wife with disbelief and panic in his eyes. "Sally," he pleaded. "What the hell is going on?"

Author's Notes

**The Boy in the Center of the
Road**
Originally published Jan '21, The Dark Moon Digest: Issue 46

It's only fitting that this story finds itself at the beginning of the collection. I may have disguised it in a fictional style narrative, but this is true account of a very traumatic point in my life. You see, I am the boy in the center of the road. When I was ten, I was hit by a car while riding my bicycle. One second, I was tearing up Jackson Ave. and the next I was laying in the middle of the street, all messed up. I broke my femur, cracked several vertebrae, and fractured my skull. The nightmares and visions that plagued me in the days and weeks that followed are ones I will never forget. The overpowering momentum of the dream, and the sensation of the cord being pulled from within my head have stayed with me even after all these years. And to this day, I am often jarred from my sleep by a crippling sound that is much too familiar. You see, they never completely left me ... the rats that is. I can still hear them gnawing on the soft tissue inside my head, it sounds like wet Styrofoam.

Recalculating
Originally released summer '22, Godless.com

Although this story is a work of fiction, it was inspired by true events. While I was in the county jail, I worked in the kitchen with a guy who had been arrested for grand theft auto. This fellow had stolen a car in the city, and being unfamiliar with the area, he had no idea how to get onto the highway. He decided to use the vehicle's nav system for directions to aid in his escape. Well, either this guy was just the unluckiest car thief alive, or there were other forces working against him that day. The nav system continued to lead the poor bastard in circles around the city for several hours. All the while it kept changing course and repeating ... recalculating. The car eventually ran out of gas in front of a parked police car, and the would-be thief was apprehended. I guess that's what you get for not knowing how to read a map.

5:56 PM

Originally published Sept. '21, The Green Shoes Sanctuary Magazine

Remorse and regret are two very real demons that I have squared off against at various points in my life. I'm sure that can be said for nearly everyone, unless of course you walk on water and shit sunshine. Really, these are the beasts that will literally eat you alive, one bite at a time. You either deal with them or they will deal with you. My own battles with addiction, depression and anxiety have offered me a wealth of knowledge on the subjects. Thankfully, I found a ladder out of my rock bottom abyss. 5:56 PM is one of those therapeutic stories I wrote to help me work through that struggle. Written while I was in prison, this story offered a message that I needed to hear. Change is possible, and wherever there is change, there is also hope.

The Devil's Well

Originally published Summer '22, Godless.com

The real Devil's Well exists in Hawley Pennsylvania. I went there shortly after I graduated high school with my girlfriend and a few buddies. The drop off and the waterfall are exactly as I described them. And the feeling of weightlessness that lasts for a fraction of a second before gravity kicks in and pulls you down is a very real thing. The icy water in the Well stays cold all summer long, as it is spring fed, and it is as black as Indian Ink. It took me nearly an hour to build up the nerve to jump the Well, something I did only once. My downward momentum plunged me deeper and deeper below the surface until I found myself alone in the void. I kicked to propel myself upward, and then it hit me. It brushed against my leg, and I heard myself scream underwater. I'm sure it was a weed, or maybe a fish, or some other benign object. I'm sure of it ... almost.

Ronald Reagan and the Oh Jesus Chord
Originally published May/June '21, The Writers and Readers' Magazine UK issue: 16

This story reads like a memoir because it is. I didn't even bother to change Jake's name. I think he will probably be okay with that, at least that's what I'm hoping. The Oh Jesus chord is an industry term for the sound made when one drops a piano, well it was at the time. It has been years since I worked in the entertainment business, but I think that is a tag that has probably stuck. There were a lot of crazy things that happened to me during those days at S.I.R. The day I hit Ronnie's limo stands out as the culmination of all those combined memories and experiences. It certainly trumps all the rock stars and actors I met and was even more memorable than kissing Melissa Manchester. I am willing to bet that I didn't leave a lasting impression on her either.

Something in the Air
Originally published May '21, The Green Shoe Sanctuary Magazine

Toward the end of my prison sentence, I was transferred to a halfway house and offered the chance to attend college. I experienced my first breaths of freedom at the corner of Broad and Market in the heart of Newark NJ. I road the 24 to get there, I walked the chilly streets with my buddy, and we were stopped dead in our tracks when a woman wearing only a garbage bag intercepted us. Again, this story is true up to a certain point where it deviates and drifts into the land of fiction. However, for those of us who lived through it, there was nothing more frightening than the reality of it. Not many are aware of how hard the prison and re entry systems were hit during the pandemic, especially during the first months when information was nil. It was a nightmare, and I imagine there were more than a few guys who considered running like Idris and Burke. I'm not sure which character I identified most with while writing this story. Who am I kidding ... it was Idris of course.

The Overbrook

To set the record straight: Yes, this all happened exactly as it is written. Maybe the adjectives and the metaphors were added to increase the tension and set the mood, but this was absolutely the scariest thing that ever happened to me. You can check out what the Overbrook looked like online and read the countless occurrences written by other visitors. The history of the place is dark and as I said in the story, if there is one place that deserved to be haunted, it was the Overbrook. What I didn't say in the story was that after the hospital was shut down there were a few movies and televisions shows filmed there. Ghost Hunters did an episode there, and parts of the movie version of Choke, the novel written by Chuck Palahniuk was also filmed at the Overbrook. Looking back now, I would probably still jump at the chance to go inside a place like that. However, I would only do it in broad daylight.

Devlin's Manse
From These Lingering Shadows 10/8/22

This is the first short story I ever wrote, and one that will always remain dear to me. It was originally jotted down on a yellow legal pad early into my prison sentence. I had started taking college classes and always knew I wanted to become a writer. However, my previous lifestyle and habits had kept me from rising to the challenge. But prison offers you a valuable commodity, and that is time. This is the product of what I did with that time; I wrote Devlin's Manse, and although it needed a lot of work, I thought it wasn't half bad. This story has been redrafted and reworked more than anything else I have ever written and was originally told in the present tense. Truth be told, I liked this story so much that I knew I had to find a home for it, even if I had to create that home myself. So, when the idea came about for an anthology, I knew exactly what the theme should be: Gothic Horror. And that is how These Lingering Shadows came about, and Devlin's Manse finally found a home.

The Dead Girl

Originally published August '21, Green Shoes Sanctuary Summer Writing Prompt Contest 3rd place

As a recovering addict, I am constantly reminded every time I turn on the news that my story could have ended much differently. Many of the people I used with are no longer around and never got the second chance that I did. The story of Mark and Lizzy is inspired by a struggle I remember all too well. I recall the desperation and isolation I felt during my darkest days. It didn't end well for the characters in this story, and there is more fact than fiction in that narrative. The possible outcomes we face as addicts are limited to say the least. But it doesn't have to be that way. There is help out there if you are willing to accept it. If you or someone you know is struggling with addiction, please contact Narcotics Anonymous at 800-407-7195 or

Find

Narcotics Anonymous Meetings

Manxiety

Honestly, what can I say about this one other than, yeah, it really happened.

Witness

I wanted to write a story from a dog's perspective but once I got started with the Witness, I found myself moving off in a different direction. I often wonder what our doggie friends think about themselves and what they might think of us. I know there is some serious contemplation going on in my own pooch's head by the inquisitive looks he gives me. This could just be me giving the little guy a bit too much credit. Still, dogs are quite complicated when you really think about it. I mean, on one hand they have no problem eating goose poop at the park, but the second we try to give them a pill hidden in a piece of fillet mignon, they snub their noses and turn into Gordon Ramsey.

The Party
Originally published Feb '22, Drawn & Quartered

This is definitely a reactionary story to the current health crisis going on when I wrote it. It is in no way a stand on how I feel about anything ... at all. I wanted to write a story in the style of a Twilight Zone episode, and I hope that I did that. I am a fan of the twist and love to hit the reader when they least expect it. I have a buddy who calls it the 'Manx Moment' which I absolutely love. I wrote this story in hope to place it in an anthology at a former publishing house I was signed with. Unfortunately, or fortunately, that never happened, and I was able to release it myself. I thought it worthy of joining the ranks in this collection, and hope you found it as entertaining to read, as I did to write it.

The Wheel Turns

Originally published July/Aug. '21, The Writers and Readers' Magazine Issue: 17

This is another memoir that illustrates a very lucky moment in my life. It happened in Nov. and Dec. of 1999 and if one were so inclined to search the internet, they just might find the episode that aired on Dec. 20th during Christmas week. Of course, then you would find out my real name and see what I looked like when I was just a lad. It's crazy how Pat and Vanna have hardly aged since that day, while I on the other hand... Well, let's just say, I probably lived a harder life than they did. Since being a contestant on the show I've met a few other people who have had the same experience. So that tells me it isn't impossible for an everyday Joe to get lucky every now and then. My advice to anyone who might find themselves in similar shoes, do practice before you head out to California. And when fate, or destiny, or whatever you want to call it, steps in to take hold of the wheel ... get the hell out of its way.

The Widower
Originally published Jan '22, Piece by Piece

There are parts of this story that were inspired from the early days of my marriage and the experiences we had with the first house we bought. It was a fixer upper to say the least and we ended up having to gut nearly the entire place. All of the drywall had to come down, and even a section of the floor in the family room, where there was a funky old crawlspace. My wife and I ended up living in one of the bedrooms out of a couple suitcases with the mattress set up on the floor. The only room in the house that remained intact was the bathroom, which had recently been remodeled. Even the part about the hundreds of crickets finding their way inside was something we lived through. That's where my imagination took over and this was the result. Ultimately, I was hoping to illustrate the living manifestation of depression and sorrow. Something I hope I have accomplished. Whether I did or not is something I will have to leave up to the reader. I know that both emotions are quite tangible and certainly have the ability to take on a life of their own. Maybe not as literally as they do in this story, but then again ... who knows?

The Last Waltz

I wanted to try a few things with this story. The first being the use of symbolism and metaphor, as I wanted that to be representative of violence and abuse. A black and blue sky, a sun as big as a clenched fist ... you get the idea. The next thing I wanted to try was writing a story that moved backward in time, so the flashbacks start where the story begins and work backward to the point where Nancy and Donald first met. I thought that might be a better way to show the progression of domestic abuse, and how the victim is always blindsided. "He was always such a nice guy." I love how Nancy is the one washing her hands in the Gulf of Mexico in the opening paragraph. She is literally washing her hands of her scumbag husband. I should also mention that the story came first, and then it became the name of my publishing company. Both were inspired by the album The Last Waltz by The Band.

Acknowledgments

I'd like to thank my Higher Power for another day, clean and sober.

About the Author

Daemon Manx is an American speculative-horror author. He is a member of the Horror Writers Association (HWA) and has been featured in magazines in both the U.S. and the U.K. He has recently been nominated for a Splatterpunk award for his debut, Abigail in the best short story category. In 2021 he received a HAG award for his story The Dead Girl.

In 1991, Daemon was involved in a motor vehicle accident with Ronald Reagan's motorcade, when he crashed into the former president's limousine on a New York City Street shortly after Ron and Nancy stepped out of the vehicle. No one was injured, except for maybe the pride of the secret service agent who was directing traffic.

Daemon recently opened Last Waltz Publishing, an indie horror label focused on undiscovered voices and elevating new authors. He lives with his sister, author Danielle Manx and their narcoleptic cat, Sydney where they patiently prepare for the apocalypse. There is a good chance they will runout of coffee far too soon.

www.daemonmanx.com

www.lastwaltzpublishing.com

Also By Daemon Manx

Abigail
Piece by Piece
Drawn & Quartered with Diana Olney
Hacked in Two with James G. Carlson
These Lingering Shadows: An Anthology
Arcranium with Mark Towse

Coming soon: The Ojanox Series
Book I: Scream in the Dark
Book II: Ashes to Ashes
Book III: All Fall Down
Book IV: Fire on the Mountain

LAST WALTZ PUBLISHING

Visit our website for a list of titles and authors

FOLLOW DAEMON MANX

Abigail Chapter 1: The Daemon Manx Newsletter